NOTHING STAYS BURIED

By
L. Concepcion

Legend

Italics- Words written in italics are meant for either inner thoughts or when the wolf and their human host converse with one another.

Bold- Words written in bold are for telepathic communication between wolves or humans.

Characters and Their Wolves

Kristofer – Zeus (wolf)
Iris – Nora (wolf)
Atlas – Leo (wolf)
Cassius – Wolfie (wolf)
Alex – Peyton (wolf)
Mavis – Ivar (wolf)
Demetrius –Alcide (wolf)
Hugo – Czar (wolf)
Scott – Elu (wolf)

Lore

Wolves and humans' souls are treated as two separate entities that co-exist within one body. While it is rare for a human to remember their past lives, it may still occur under special circumstances. The wolf souls, however, can reincarnate and still remember everything as they transfer from one human host to the another after the death of their host.

While the wolves have a long history within the mythical world, they weren't always around, and only came to be after a greedy shaman desired more power.

Now, due to unknown reasons, the wolves were exposed, and humans know of their existence. This revelation adds a new level of threat to their species since humans have now taken to killing them for sport.

First Edition October 2024
ISBN: 979-8-9907520-1-6

Chapter 1

Kristofer

IS THIS WHAT I HAVE BEEN reduced to? The night is quiet and cold, even colder than most, I'd dare say, but I enjoy the weather like this. It's in these quiet moments that I can gather my thoughts and truly organize my feelings. Although I didn't always seek solitude in the comfort of the cold weather, it is a direct result of learning how to compartmentalize after my father died. A feeling I wish to never experience again. But I guess it's better than falling apart knowing my mother needs me to be strong. If not for me then at least for the pack. Coping with my father's death is still the hardest thing I ever done, even as an Alpha. Yet, the time to cry in mourning is shorter for me than it is for most.

As a leader, I must hold it together for everyone and show them that even in a time of grief, I can still be strong for them. I can mourn because it is only normal to do so, but I must quickly recover as well. Hide the unshed tears and lock them away for a rainy day. So, I have a library of sorts in my mind where I sort out my thoughts into books and shelve them in their respective genres. Now and then, when I am alone and the rain hits the windowpane, I find that book and open it to its bookmarked page, so I can pick up my emotions where I last left off.

I pull out my favorite gray sweater and zip it up using the worn-out, faded zipper that tends to snag on the stressed fabric. The material is worn down by the wrist from excessive use and a couple of small holes grace the lining of the sweater which I am sure is due to the ancient washer we have. Our washing machine has been known to destroy a shirt or two.

A small stitch comes undone on the hem of the left sleeve and unwinds a bit more as I tug the cuff. I yank on the thread to break it off but because of its character, it's the most comfortable sweater I own and like me, it is coming undone.

I have had it for years now and it simply has personality and holds memories that I am not ready to let go of. The only time I can wear it is during this time of year, when the temperature drops to where the bite from the chilly wind is enough to add on an extra layer of clothing. Even with winter upon us, as a breed of werewolves, we don't need much to keep us warm. Well, at least for most of us, that seems to be the case.

Normally, wolves have warmer bodies than humans, and when we shift, our thick fur keeps us toasty against the cold. Yet, as we evolve and interbreed with humans, some wolves are born without the ability to regulate their bodies to the same degree that most can. But even with the ability to keep warm, now and then an extra layer is needed—like tonight. And while I have a lot of muscle, I still need my trusty sweater.

Content with my attire, I step out of my room into the silence of the lived-in walls I call home. The house is empty at the moment, and yet, I feel suffocated within it. With every step I take, the walls cave in on me and it hurries my steps. I distract my mind, reminding myself where everyone is. Alex is hanging out with Demetrius doing some training, Cassius is with his new mate, Atlas, and my mother is…well…she is out. That's everyone that lives in the house, though I do suspect that sometime soon Cassius will move in with his mate as the new Luna. And Alex will move out the second he finds his mate. It's almost like I would end up getting the empty nest feeling even though they are not my children. But might as well be, considering that I look over them as the Alpha of the pack.

My mind slips back to the idea of my mother and the fact that she is now dating Martha. I try to shake off the uncomfortable feeling that never seems to roll off my shoulders at the thought, but it's pointless. As grown as I am, I just can't seem to let go of the idea or rather what it represents which is my father being officially gone and out of her memory and our lives.

I step outside into the clear night with an inhale of the calm breeze in hopes that it will settle my wandering mind. As if on autopilot, my feet take me around back to the old swing I built as a kid in the backyard. Just looking at it, the tension previously building in my shoulder dissipates. The swing aged well for something built on a whim and withstanding the weather of time. The long sun-bleached ropes are still intact and sturdy while the wooden plank, although not the original, sits strong with little stress on the grains of the wood.

My father helped me put it together on a random Saturday morning and every memory of us filters through my fingers as I run my calloused hands over the aged, lacquered wood. The cold pricks at my skin from the ice that settled between the cracks, sending chills through my bones. It reminds me of the day we had to replace it, because Cassius and I both stood on it at the same time trying to prove the quality of my handy work. That day the seat broke in half and Cassius twisted his ankle. My father taught me a lesson in the form of running laps around the property that I remember well to this day. My muscles gave out in a burn I'll never forget. Yet, it is my favorite place to be when I want to think or be alone.

Out of all the things that have come and gone in my life, this swing is the only thing that remains the same. The constant to the forever revolving door that is my life. It's become my haven of sorts. While I did also try to go to my mother with my thoughts, I realized it isn't fair to burden her with her new kindling romance or rather rekindling. And honestly, it's okay. The guilt I would feel if I sabotaged their relationship is far worse than the fog clouding me.

I can't wrap my mind around her and Martha being an item. To no fault of their own. How can I explain that it's simply hard seeing someone other than my father by her side, without making her feel bad about it?

I rest my weight on the old slab as it screams from the weight it hasn't held in a long time. Either that or I have put on a few pounds, and it is testing the limits of the rope's strength. The half breath in my throat holds as the final creak releases from the wood and I can safely relax into the seat. I look up at the stars admiring the clear sky, twinkling as if in morse code, revealing the events of its past. The child in me hides behind the tears at the thought of my late father. There is so much that he is missing out on.

With wet eyes blurring my vision, I trace in the air the constellations above me with my finger. I have them all memorized after doing the same thing for so long. Spotting the constellations at this point comes easy to me.

With another deep breath I blink away the threatening tears on the brink of escape and focus again on the stars. I search for my father's favorite in futile effort because it only appears in the summer. I always liked pointing out the Lupus constellation to him because my father would then tell me stories of the great wolf. It is the first one he showed me as a kid and now I believe the stories he told me were of the Shaman.

Nothing Stays Buried

The late November wind blows hard against me, rocking the swing in place as I spot the stars directly above me, Orion's belt. Always the easiest one to distinguish among the others.

An owl hoots in the distance, pulling my attention to the left of the trees surrounding me. The moon hangs above them almost complete in its phase. In two nights, it will be a full moon, and it thrills me to no end knowing it is almost time for our monthly run. I want to feel the escape. I want to let go and let my wolf, Zeus, take over. Running with my pack and bonding with them freely is a feeling like no other. It'll give me the clarity I need during this confusing time. Not that I couldn't just shift now as I am, but it's a different feeling during a full moon.

Shifting under the powers of the moon means relinquishing control to the goddess. And the confusion in my heart is not only about my mother but…Iris. Something that I need the guidance of the moon goddess to help me understand. With my eyes closed in thought, I take one last deep breath and exhale slowly the exhaust my mind is drowning in. Using the weight of my body, I begin to swing, letting my feet dangle and kick the higher I go.

Another gust of wind aids my momentum and sends a slight chill down the small patch of bare skin exposed between my lifted shirt and my pants. It is a clear reminder that next week is thanksgiving and we are inching closer to Christmas. Both our packs, Alpha Atlas' and mine, want to have dinner together but I don't know if I am ready to be around my mate now that she clearly and blatantly rejects me.

I know I should have said something when we first met but I let the shock of it all get the best of me. Not only did the situation she was in shock me, but I was also shocked that my mate lived so close to me, and I never knew. Now too much time is filling the space between us, and I am left wondering if I should end the bond. How can I live thirty years and finally find my mate, only to have her run from me? It was just my luck to find and lose my partner at the same time.

I suck my teeth at the thought. I should have said something. Iris might have reacted differently... or maybe not, I don't know, but it hurts, nevertheless. It sucks being rejected to my face without being given a chance. Now, as it is, I will never get the opportunity to try and love her because she is opposed to having love exist in the first place. At least that's how it seems.

The fear with how her brows wear scrunched up and the tears-stained cheeks haunt my thoughts every time I think of her. Her quivering lips and heaving chest made her seem like she was simply waiting for her inevitable end. No one should ever have to experience that kind of feeling. She went through an ordeal I cannot fathom, but the bond certainly helps with healing, right? I am sure that if I have the opportunity, I can help her work through her trauma.

A tear finally breaks free from me and slowly rolls down my stubble and down my neck. I hate that I feel this way because honestly, even listening to myself

I know I sound like a prick. I am putting my own broken heart before her traumatic experience.

Another gust of wind kicks up and this time it slices through my sweater, allowing me to feel the bite of the cold a bit harsher.

If only the cold could numb me just enough to think with my head and not my aching heart. I just don't want to hurt like this anymore. The fact the I never allowed myself to grieve my father's death properly is now taking its toll. For so long, the responsibilities of the pack did well to push his memory aside but watching my mother find love while my own ends before it starts is digging up wounds that I forgot I had. I know if I give up Iris, then this pain wouldn't last long, but I want a fighting chance. I just need to convince her to give me and us a chance. If not, the bond will eventually die and although that thought terrifies me, it is what it is.

"UGH!"

I kick the air causing my swing to twist a little. The creaking of the swing echoes into the night scaring off a few squirrels in the process. The thing about a mate bond is that it only really gives you a suggestion as to who could be your perfect match. It's like a spiritual cupid if you will. It amplifies the ability to see the redeeming qualities of both parties and to cut down the time it would normally take on your own. I guess it was made that way to help preserve the species. The faster we find love the faster we want to reproduce.

The mate bond doesn't force you to love either, it just makes it easier to do so. Of course, if you truly don't like the person for whatever reason, then a mutual rejection between both parties would erase the bond completely. Unfortunately, if only one person rejects it, then it becomes agonizing until the bond fades on its own or the other gives in. But I won't give Iris that satisfaction unless she gives me a reason to let her go.

"I wish I could see you", I whisper into the wind almost expecting it to grant me my wish.

I can still smell Iris. Her scent is like warm brownies freshly baked out of the oven and roasted marshmallows. It's captivating. Who knew I would develop a serious sweet tooth after meeting her. I groan at the pang in my chest. Iris is beautiful with curves that accentuate her small waist and thighs that are strong enough to crack my head if I dare put my face between them. Her adorable messy hair she keeps in a top bun and the almost too small worn-out clothes she wore when I last saw her, stirs something inside me.

The shorts are a treat to see her in because it gives me a perfect view of her deliciously rounded bottom. At least one conversation would have been nice with her, my mind momentarily laments again, and I shift uncomfortably in my seat with how tight my briefs are becoming at the image I conjured up.

If I must pick a feature, I'd say her hazel eyes are probably the most heavenly of them all. I couldn't look away from them the moment they caught me. They suck me right in and I don't mind it at all. My wolf, Zeus, whines inside as my thoughts reel like a movie at a drive through. Zeus wants to see her again and meet her wolf. **Trust me Zeus, I want to see her too**. I remind him.

The swing comes to a full stop. The wind, now gentle and wispy, picks up a few leaves and whisks them away before me in a small twirl. I smile at how carefree it all seems and wish I could be as such. Carefree without all this confusion in my heart. Uncomplicated. Unphased. Instead, witnessing the whimsical nature only makes my heart heavier than before.

Tires rolling on gravel reach my ears followed by doors slamming shut and giggles. Martha and my mother are back from their date, and it sours my mood further. I guess it's good they arrive now to break up my thoughts because I was depressing myself regardless. What I thought will be a moment of clearing my mind on the swing, ends up being a session of self-deprecation and pity. This needs to stop because it is only doing more harm than good. For the first time, the swing failed to tame this old man.

I hop off the swing and drag my feet around to the front of the house only to find my mother's tongue down Martha's throat. My mother's hands are cupping Martha face as she slides her arms around my mother's waist and pulls her in close to her body. I truly do not know how to feel whenever I see the intimacy between the two. They are moving too fast despite how natural it seems for them.

I barely find out about her and my father's escapades with Atlas' parents and here she is flaunting it…. everywhere…all the time. For all to see. It may have been a while for her but it's fresh for me. I clench my fist, anger cracking at my knuckles. I don't want to watch them necking but I won't dare say anything either. Stomping right by them, I slam the front door behind me as I make my way into the house. The seesaw of emotions weighing on either side of me between Iris and my mother teeters violently. My chest tightens. How can my mother not care about father's memory? I know my mother said that they were all together at one point, but things have changed.

Everything I remember, all I know, is her and my dad. Just them. No one else. No third or fourth person. Now, I am to accept that it was four of them this whole time. It's one thing to hear my mom talk about it but to see it, to see her with Martha so eager and intimate, shakes me. It's now real and it feels like a betrayal to my father's memory. I continue stomping up to my room not caring how loud I am in the process and throw myself in bed.

Tantrum much? Zeus echoes in my mind.

Shut up! I mentally retaliate. I know how I am acting or mentally sound, but I don't care.

***

Tossing in my bed, I wipe the sweat from my brow. The sheets tangle around my legs as I continue to find a new position because everything is uncomfortable. I feel like someone knocked down all the books from my mental library and I must carefully pick each one up and put them back where they belong. All I want is Iris and fuck everything else. For once, I want my chance at a happy ending too. Even though I thought I was fine without it and bragged to Cassius about remaining alone, I realize that I simply did not want to admit the truth. But I want it. And I want her.

I punch my pillow over and over to fluff it. Angry, frustrated with me, sad, confused, and... lonely. Everything I am feeling, I direct it at my poor pillow, "When is it my turn to be happy?" I whisper into the quiet of my room before I drift to sleep.

*****

The morning sun shining into the room is melting the top half of my face. With the window being directly behind my bed, the open curtains allow the sun to shower me in warmth. During the summer it is especially annoying if I forget to turn on the air conditioner. I end up cooking myself with the morning sun. The sounds of people talking and laughing downstairs carry into my room and chases away the silence.

My chest vibrates in a deep growl matching the eye roll I learned from the little wolf that visits now and then with her parents. I stretch in my bed and try to release the tightness in my muscles along with the sleep that is lingering in my body. For the first time, my bed feels uncomfortable, but I can't stay in this slump hiding in my covers like a moody teenager that didn't get his way. Although, I'd much rather do that right now than face people.

My heavy feet touch the cold wooden floor and stand firm as I will my body to go to the bathroom. The reflection in the mirror mocks me with a face that is haggard. The wrinkles on my face are more prominent along with the dryness of my lips and the dull complexion that complement the dark circles. I stick out my tongue at the unrecognizable version of me and undress for my shower. The water starts cold at first and my toes lift away from the tub as the water pools towards my feet. Little by little the steam begins to build as the water heats up.

With one foot first, I step into the running water and allow my skin to adjust to the temperature before I submerge my body completely. Each drop washes away my sleep which sits crusted on my eyes lids and embedded in my bones. It is exactly what I need to change my mood and recharge my mind.

Lathering up, I scrub myself with my blue loofah and work through every inch of my skin. From my head to my toes, I work every inch of me, finding every nook and cranny of my aching body. I melt and relax just a bit more with each scrub and rinse away the residual of last night.

Drying off with the gray towel I recently bought, I do a little shimmy with it on my back before tying it off around my waist. Droplets of water make a trail as I leave the bathroom and walk over to my closet with my wet hair. The walk-in is a neatly lined on the right, with my shirts on the bottom row, and suits at the top. To my left I have wooden shelves with my jeans, sweats, and shorts folded neatly on one row while the other shelves have a few of my dress shoes, sneakers, and work boots. Towards the back of the closet, I have a cabinet that encloses my neatly folded ties and arranged accessories.

For today, I want to keep my attire casual and pull out a light gray short-sleeve tee and a light pair of jeans. I roll up the hem of the sleeves a little and throw on a black belt. The shirt remains partially tucked in front and I finish off the look with black combat boots.

I make my way downstairs and of course, Martha and my mother are chatting away and eating sandwiches. *I guess she slept over,* I think to myself and sigh at how much my thoughts are annoying me.

"Good afternoon, son."

"Good mor-afternoon, mom...Martha," I furrow my brows but add Martha's name to my greeting to avoid the glare I will no doubt receive if I ignore Martha's presence.

I mumble to myself how tired I already am without looking at them but instead looking at the clock on the wall as it ticks onto the hour and confirms, it is indeed the afternoon. Guess I slept longer than I intended to and there is much to do for the day. Although, I can't say much of it will get done if I don't clear my mind. One of them says something to me but the question barely filters into my ears, and I grunt in response.

Tantrums again? Zeus snickers at me from the back of my mind.

Mind your business, I snap but Zeus laughs, infuriating me even more.

"Have you spoken to Iris yet?" Just the sound of her name is enough to take the edge off my building mood, but I grunt again in response to the voice that said it. "What did she say?" Martha insists. I slam the fridge shut causing both to jump in their seat. The contents of the refrigerator rattle and I am sure something inside fell.

"She ran away!" I shout, truly not intending to. I leave the kitchen and grab my keys from the tray by the door. I will find my breakfast elsewhere because being home is not it. My anger once again rears its ugly head, and I am the only one to blame. My emotions are nowhere near being under control and the last thing I want is to let it out on anyone. I see easily I am allowing myself to be triggered, and I hate it.

The only thing I can do is remove myself from the situation and drive away. I look in the rear-view mirror as I slam my door closed, spotting my mom by the house entrance. The pain in my chest grows tighter at the sight of my mother crying and Martha hugging her from behind. It not that I said anything insulting but I also never lash out like that toward my mother. I throw the vehicle into drive and watch as they grow smaller behind me. There's no doubt that I want to be happy for my mom, I do, but I need to get myself straight before I can see her with someone else that isn't my father.

It's selfish, I realize that, but I can't help how I feel. It is what it is and this whole thing with Iris just has me on edge. Both situations are playing off each other and I feel like I will fall no matter which side tips over. If I hadn't met Iris yet, then maybe my mom's situation wouldn't be as tough to deal with but when is life ever that easy?

Moments later I pull into a diner and order the breakfast special with a large coffee. Emphasis on large. The diner is small and near the outskirts of town. Its food is better than most and the place is family owned. The vibes are always welcoming, and it is what drew me in since day one. The furniture is old, and the leather seats are cracking from age. The tabletops are a bit newer, and the floors were recently redone, but it still doesn't take away from the feel the place gives off. Even with the few remodeled touches, the history is still well-established. The hanging pictures of family, past celebrity signatures, and the old clock that stopped working ages ago add to the homey vibes that you can feel in your soul. It is like visiting grandma's house on a Sunday morning.

"Coming right up, big guy," Jodi taps my shoulder with her notepad and walks away after I rattled off my usual order. She is one of the more mature ladies who work the morning shift. She is the sister of the owner's son's wife. The eldest son now runs the place since his father is too old to work. Being in his late eighties, the owner only comes around to hang out by the bar from time to time. Unfortunately, his arthritis ended up becoming too painful for him to keep up with the demands of the diner.

Off, Jodi goes humming the same tune that seems to stay resident in her mind. The longest earworm if I ever heard one. I hum the same tune to myself with a smile. After hearing the tune so much, I learned her song and made a habit of sitting at the same table. It is another one of my safe havens when I want to get away from it all. Because of this, Jodi has watched me grow up and knows just about everything short of me not being human. I doubt she would mind and sometimes I think she knows but I wouldn't dare be the first to say it out loud unless I had to.

My food arrives and Jodi sits across from me locking her wrinkled fingers together, "so what's troubling you son." I look at her and ponder for a bit. I can't tell her about mate bonds, so, I guess my mother, it is.

"My mom is dating again, and I can't accept it. Even though

dad died a while ago; I still can't accept someone else with my mother. It almost feels like she is betraying his memory. The woman is a good person and treats my mom well but...." I stuff food into my mouth before I end up saying too much and out myself as a wolf.

"Is she happy?" Jodi simply asks.

I stop chewing and look her in the eye. The answer is there, and she knows but still waits for me to respond, "Yes, it seems so."

"Listen son, I understand how you feel but you need to see it from her perspective. She is probably lonely. She won't have many years left compared to you. I remember clearly when you first came here after your father passed away. I remember how distraught and alone you felt. Imagine your mother. She was hurting because she lost her husband and the father of her children. She isn't betraying your father's memory. I'm sure he would want her happy after all this time, especially if the lady is treating her right. Wouldn't you want a warm bed after being cold for so long?" Jodi's name is called out by one of the cooks to pick up an order for another table.

Jodi gets up and offers me a smile before tending to her other tables. She is right. Who wouldn't want a warm bed. Look at me now, for example. I have been alone for thirty years basically and after one sniff of Iris, she is all I crave. I can't imagine how it is for my mother who has already had Martha in her arms only to lose her and find her again. They aren't even mates and yet they love each other as if they were. Jodi returns to her seat.

"Listen to me Kristofer. You are a good kid, but you are also a grown man and the head of the household. Think long and hard about why you are reacting like this and truly ask yourself if it is your mother, you are angry about, or something else. There is something you are not telling me and that's okay but do not give Cecile the cold shoulder out of selfishness. You hear me?" Jodi lifts her brow waiting for a response while pointing her finger at me.

"Yes, ma'am." I reply.

"Good, now eat up." Jodi stands up again and gives my shoulder a squeeze imbuing comfort and a warning to do better.

It is true that mom grieved long enough and deserves to be happy. I need to accept that aside from being my mother she is her own person. Maybe I'm just projecting my own anger on her since I can't be with Iris. Seeing her happiness while I can't have my own could very well be the trigger. Yet knowing the truth of my feelings doesn't make it easier to control. This just makes me feel more like a prick.

My plate is practically clean as I mindlessly eat while lost in my thoughts. Finishing my breakfast with the last gulp of coffee, I leave a tip for Jodi tucked under the mug. She waves goodbye and I return her warm smile. She must think I am such a mama's boy, but her deductive skills are impressive. Back into the truck, I sit to let the vehicle warm up before I make my way back home.

Chapter 2
Kristofer

THE LAST TWO DAYS blur into one another in a swirl of nothingness. With my mood residing in a numb state, I only remember starting my arm tattooed but nothing before or after that. I am just grateful that the artist never found out that I didn't eat before starting the session. At least, I don't think I did. My arm hums in slight tingles from the vibration of the machine against my skin. The initial pain from the tattoo is now a dull series of pricks against my skin. This is something I've been meaning to do for a while but never found the chance to finish what I started.

I've always wanted a sleeve to compliment my chest piece. Thankfully as a wolf, I don't have to suffer the long healing process that humans usually do. Two days are all I need for my tattoos to fully heal, and my artist is the only one I go to because he is the only one in town that I revealed my true nature to. That also means, if anyone from town comes at me, he would be the one that I would be questioning first. I admire the tribal and moon on my arm that he intricately designed.

It complements the portrait of my father's wolf on my chest very well.

The artist wraps up my arm just in time for tonight as it is the full moon. The excitement of being able to pull back and hide fills me up inside. Just the idea of being able to relinquish myself to my wolf, Zeus, and sit back as he runs freely. Running from everything his heart desires. To run and be free, if even for a moment, to help me with my problems is something I never take for granted. Just like the swing, I use that time to try to clear my thoughts, rid my anger, and find peace.

Enough peace to finally be able to talk to my mom and ask for forgiveness for how rude I have been. I need to feel my roots and bond with the earth. Realign myself with the goddess because I know more than anyone that I have been off kilter. I reconnect with my spiritual ancestors so they can guide me and my ease aching heart.

The air is buzzing with magic in the pack house as the time for the shift approaches. Everyone fidgets in place waiting for the sunset so the moon can rise high enough to initiate the shift. I wrap a towel around my naked waist and walk through the people crowding the house wrapped in their towel of choice. Usually, we don't worry about seeing each other naked since transforming is instant, but with the full moon, it's a bit different. We aren't transforming at will. We are letting the moon do it for us. And the time that it takes us to transform is different every time as well. But the real reason we cover ourselves has more to do with an individual who couldn't follow rules.

A very long time ago, when I was a child, we had a pervert who kept making passes at the women. He was a young rouge my father had picked up and initiated into our pack. No one knew how bad it had been until he was finally caught. None of the women said anything because they were too scared of what he would do if they did. It wasn't until the husband of one of the women, found out and killed the abuser on the spot out of pure rage.

Of course, killing should never be the answer and the husband was handed to the council where he was later imprisoned to serve his sentence. Due to the nature of the conviction, his sentence was lighter than normal. If I remember correctly, he should be out on parole in the next year. Since then, my dad opted to have everyone covered to minimize wandering eyes, reduce temptation, and until everyone felt comfortable again. Even though I trust everyone to behave after that ordeal, covering up kind of just stuck. No one wants to revert to how it was, and I am okay with that if it gives everyone peace of mind.

"Everyone, we have a half hour before the sun fully sets. Let's all step into the backyard and wait for the moon to bless us. We have been through a lot these past few months and we are finally getting back to a comfortable norm. Please enjoy the refreshments and food at the end of the run. Once you can shift back, feel free to return as a pair. No one returns home alone." The crowd erupts in cheerful howls.

The buddy system is another net of safety I implemented to keep everyone safe. The way hunter activity is increasing, it is best to never be found alone.

The sun is setting low to the horizon and the conversations among the pack are down to a dull whisper. My skin fills with goosebumps as time goes on and the moon reaches its peak. The air is changing as the magic that triggers our transformation lingers. The pack falls silent in wait. My wolf claws inside me anxiously waiting. Zeus wants to run already. He needs to feel the moonlight on his fur and the charge that comes with it.

Finally, after moments of staring at the moon, it rises just enough, and I release the first howl of the night. The moon's energy fills me whole, and I am immediately pushed aside by my wolf taking over. My body aches as my bones crack and reform. Dark fur sprouts from my skin in patches until it covers me completely as my fingers fuse together turning into paws. I drop on all fours and shake my body to fluff myself out. My face fractures and realigns into a snout while my canines drop into place. My spine elongates and a tail grows out wagging freely. With another shake of my fur Zeus is in full form.

ZEUS

Looking around, one by one, everyone is shifting. They howl signifying the completion of their shift and ready to speed off. I mind-link with everyone's wolf to stay safe and enjoy before we go into the woods. I take the lead running through the trees and jumping rocks. My paws hit the ground in hard thuds cracking branches as I go. It's liberating, to feel the cold air gently on my fur.

Flutters course through my body and I can only assume it is the goddess filling me with her power as I howl in delight. I wouldn't trade this feeling for the world. It's the only time I feel the strong connection between me and Mother Earth. This is the one time, I, as a wolf, get this much time to myself. I am fully in control and not just a passenger. All of us wolves are merely passengers in the humans we reside in.

Before, when times weren't as organized as it is now, we were constantly fighting and killing. We were used for vengeance and malice no matter how big or small the matter was. Back then we had to prove our worth as Alphas, protect our lands and children from other supernatural, and claim our place in the world. By doing so, we wolves shifted more often but we weren't free. We were slaves to the aggression, anger, and death our humans commanded. With times evolving as they have, we spend more time as mere companions to our human kin, and I rather have it this way.

My ears twitch at distant rustling filtering my way. I come to a complete halt prompting everyone around me to stop as well. I sniff the air and listen. And there it is.

Hunters, I tell Kristofer.

Get everyone back to the house. We can't shift back yet so we need to hide. It's not safe, Kristofer replies, and he is right.

We need to double back. I mind-link with the other wolves and we head back towards the house but not before chaos ensues.

A bullet whizzes by me barely missing my ear. I dodge to the left and run zigzagging as I go in the hopes that I won't get hit. We are only an hour into our run and have another hour or so before we can freely shift back. It is times like this where it is unfortunate that once the moon triggers our shift, we are subject to wait for the moon to release us.

I'm going to link with Wolfie and see if they are alright, I tell Kristofer who is oddly calm.

Okay, Kristofer replies.

Wolfie, are you guys alright? I link to Wolfie, Cassius' inner wolf in hopes that everyone there caught on to the hunters and are safe.

Zeus! We sniffed out some hunters, but we are safely in our basement. Wolfie, replies.

Good, we are currently under fire but making our way home. Stay hidden until you shift back.

Most of the pack makes it back to the house but with having so many in wolf form, fitting inside the house will prove to be difficult. I stay the furthest behind making sure the wolves are safe and take count of the ones I see the best I can.

A yip of distress echoes in the woods, and I dash because it is one, I know all too well. Blood pumps in my ears and I wait, listening for another yip. *Blood!* My heart pounds against my chest with the way the metallic scent grips my senses. The thought that a hunter is attacking my family is fueling a different kind of beast within me. Another yip redirects my run, and I halt when I confirm who it is. One of my younger male wolves, Peyton, is caught in a trap. I panic as my claws dig into the dirt. I can't shift yet to help him out. My Beta, Demetrius' wolf, Alcide, comes over to help me keep watch over him.

Then quiet. Nothing moves nor makes a sound. The stillness settles in the air with an unease that is more alarming than the flying bullets from before. They are playing a dangerous mind game with us. Trying to lull us into a false sense of safety. No branches cracking beneath moving feet, no stench of dry blood. If they were close, I would be able to smell them, but I don't. It's eerily still and we have another thirty minutes to go. The scenarios conjuring up in my mind taunt me as we wait for something to happen.

Why is it so quiet? What are they waiting for? I ask myself, trying to scan every inch of the woods as far as I can see. *I don't like this Kris,* I whisper in my mind and slow my breathing trying to listen to my surroundings, but nothing.

I think you should try sniffing deeply. Check if their scent is simply not there or weakening, Kristofer suggests to me.

It is a good idea and that's why he makes such a great Alpha. His ability to think clearly in these situations is why our pack does so well. I exhale nice and slow before slowly inhaling through my nose as deep as I can. The air fills my lungs with my surroundings. The fresh scent of trees, the other wolves in my pack, the blood from Peyton, all catch within me one by one and then, there. The very faint smell of dried mixed blood. The signature scent of the hunters.

You're right, it's weakening, I confirm to Kristofer and continue looking around feeling a bit more relaxed. Fifteen more minutes to go or at least, it should be. This is the slowest time has ever crawled. I need to remain calm and protect Peyton, Alex's wolf, since he is knocked out cold. Most likely from the pain of his injured leg.

The air begins to change again. It's almost time. I can feel Kristofer stirring in the back of my mind ready to spring into action. Although he is calm, I can tell he has been waiting to do something to ensure everyone's safety. There it is the change.

My bones break and realign themselves into human shapes and sizes. I shed my fur into nothingness and continue to morph. I honestly hate this part. The pain is never something you get used to. Almost fully upright, I finally take human form and shift back to

Kristofer. I return my control and quietly watch as his companion once again.

Kristofer

I pry open the trap that is caught on Peyton and remove his leg just in time for him and Alcide to shift back into Alex and Demetrius. Had he shifted while still trapped, it could have cost him losing a limb. I think the goddess that is not the case and wait for my Beta. Demetrius gives a good stretch and carries Alex in his arms while he tries to call out to him. Alex doesn't move and panic sets into my Beta in the form of a run. He is practically sprinting towards the house while I pull the bear trap from the ground and turn to run home as well when a shot rings through my ears.

"Fuck", I yell clutching my thigh. Pain radiates in hot pulses from my exposed skin. I failed to notice that one hunter is still lingering close by and most likely keeping watch. "Son of a bitch hid upwind."

My Beta stops but I motion for him to keep going. He is already too far ahead and needs to get Alex to the pack doctor to take care of anything that may be in his wound. The pain continues to pulse through my leg, but I brace myself and start running as best I could. My six-foot-three frame makes the pain shoot through my body as my weight falls on the wound with each step.

No other shot is heard and either I have gone deaf, they left, or they are waiting. *Was this a warning? Are they toying with us?* I shake the thought. For now, I need to focus on getting home safe and checking that everyone else made it back okay. My lips quiver as my chest struggles to inflate as I trudge my way home. I'm struggling and slowing down the further I go and now I wonder if the bullet is laced. If it is, then all I did is speed up its effects by running. Fortunately, I can feel it went straight through as blood drips in front and behind my thigh but enough of whatever is on the bullet is already in my system.

Everything before me blurs as I make it home. I drop onto the back porch and turn on my back desperately trying to fill my lungs, but I can't. I scratch my chest to stop the burning sensation, but I simply can't breathe. My breaths are short and rapid and the world around me in shrinking into a pinhole. I barely make out my Beta and his swinging dick just above my head as he squats to pick me up before I finally embrace total darkness. *Why is that the last thing I see?*

Chapter 3
Iris

TONIGHT IS FINALLY THE full moon. I have spent the last few days trying to wrap my head around the fact that I found my mate. It is both the most exhilarating and scariest feeling. Out of all times to find my mate, why did it have to be now and not when I first turned 18 like most others? It would have made the discovery a joyous occasion and not one filled with embarrassment and guilt.

While I know there isn't any bad intention from Kristofer, and for a moment, everything seemed brighter and full of roses, that's where it ends. All those memories of what I went through came flooding back when Kristofer touched me.

My mate's gentle fingers turned into Rick's disgusting whiskey smell and groping hands. The way he manhandled me and tied me up all exposed, brought bile to my throat. All of it rushed through me and Kristofer, the innocent man that he is, no longer felt warm and inviting. It made my stomach churn and the guilt inside me that I am projecting this onto my mate, made my skin crawl.

It isn't fair to him but my instinct to run away is strong the second I feel threatened. The fear that Rick managed to instill in me in such a short amount of time, is now an everlasting prison. I let go of my bottom lip not realizing how hard I am biting into it and pop in my earbuds on to put on some music to wait for the full moon. I need to calm down and let my feelings pass. Letting everything that happened to me roll over like a wave finding its current, is all I can do to not break down.

I told Luna Cassius that I am not going to wait with everyone else for the moon rise. Seeing naked bodies and questioning gazes my way is too much to handle now. Instead, I am going to wait in my room and then join everyone once I shift. I don't want to feel vulnerable again. Luna understood and gave me my space, but my stupid brother badgered me until Cassius convinced him to leave me be. Atlas insisting that I stay with everyone put me back on edge with my anxiety through the roof. Goddess, bless my brother-in-law.

My eyes follow the shadows of the ceiling from the setting sun as they dance within the last of the daylight. The stain glass on my window twinkles a prism of colors that overtakes my walls. The gleeful colors explode over the white canvas my room offers and drown out the darkness that I feel inside. It's why I added the stain glass to my window. It is the only thing that can heal the dark passenger inside my mind and remind me of the person I can be and the person that I used to be.

I flip over on my stomach and look out the window just in time to see the sun finish setting and the colors on my walls chase after the bit of light that leaves my room.

Removing the ear buds, I put them away and ready myself. *Guess it's almost time.* I undress and snuggle under my blanket and my mind drifts to my mate again. The hurt in his face when I ran away fills my heart. Even now some of his sadness is washing over me as I lay here. He yearns for me and every day I struggle to ignore it. I would be lying if I said I wasn't affected by it but I'm not ready to accept it either. I don't want intimacy right now.

The thought of a man's fingers sliding across my skin and scraping the length of me makes me shutter. Even the thought of a man's breath burning my skin under its assault makes me want to scream. Mentally, I'm not ready to accept anyone but myself and even though my heart wants to know what it is like to have a mate, I'm scared.

My eyes close as a feeling grabs hold of me. The air is changing, and I can finally let go. I stand up and open my window taking a breath of fresh air, waiting for the moon to take over and bless me with her love. Light shines on to my skin and the shift takes hold. My light brown fur emerges as I land on all fours. My hands and feet morph into paws and my wolf form, Nora, emerges.

Nothing Stays Buried

Nora

I nudge the partially closed door with my snout and run through the house. My weight thumps loudly against the old wooden floorboards while I scurry down the hall and the stairs. Atlas is going to kill Iris in the morning when he sees the scratches on the floor. I'll have to make sure to tell Leo to convince Atlas to be nice. Jumping down the last few steps, I make my way outside and regroup with the others.

I howl alongside Atlas' wolf, Leo. It's great to be this free and surrounded by the ones we love. To give my human, Iris, the chance to sit back and breathe for a bit is a great feeling. She deserved the chance to hide away without others prying as to why since this is the one time that everyone must change. We wait for the rest of the pack to finish shifting before we begin our run. In unison, we all race into the tree line and chase the riverside.

We follow the flowing water and howl in delight at one another. The grass tickles my paws with its gentle blades while the wind hugs my fur in gentle strokes. It's liberating. The sound of the rushing water in my ears, the smell of the pine trees through my snout, and the crisp night air flood my senses in a way that invigorates my soul. Cassius' wolf, Wolfie, pushes me aside playfully and it triggers us to race each other until I trip and tumble. Wolfie's laughter booms into my head while he jumps around mocking me. Wolfie is just as much a clown as his human host.

Rolling in the dirt, I inhale a deep breath. The control I feel, the clarity in my mind, everything that it is to be a wolf comes alive. I love my human, but nothing compares to having my soul take physical shape and experiencing the world around me.

I promise to take you on runs more, Iris whispers in my mind.

Thank you, you always treat me so well, I reply, and she does.

Iris doesn't have to and yet she includes me in all her decisions. Iris never forgets that I am a part of her and when she takes me on runs, she always gives me full control. Unlike the other reincarnations, I had as host. They only ever used me to fight or didn't use me at all, but Iris makes me feel very much alive.

I've never told her that I can remember every life I've lived but this one is the best by far. Which is why I hurt for her deeply. She needs time away from questioning eyes. Time to herself to hide and lick her wounds. Wolfie stops jumping around and gets into a fighting stance.

Luna Wolfie, what's going on? I ask.

Something is wrong here; I can sense people approaching. Maybe hunters? Wolfie speeds off toward Leo. **Go home and hide. Take as many with you as possible.**

Okay, I reply and dash off to the wolves in front of me who have noticed the hunters as well.

I take off, mind-linking as many wolves as possible as I run. It is only an hour in, and we can't freely shift back. Thankfully I left the door open to the house when I left making entering the home easy. Most of the wolves run inside the house while others go to find some that straggled off.

We reach the closed basement door and with my paw, I push aside the rug in front of it. With all my weight I pounce onto one of the planks closest to the wall and it gives way to reveal it is hollow underneath. Atlas has a countermeasure for times like these. It is something he did during a close call a while back.

He made sure to put in a secret way to open a separate hatch in the wall next to the basement door. By making the plank lift, I press the button that is revealed. The hatch opens and we all go down the slide that leads into the basement. One by one, the wolves descend, and I make sure everyone is accounted for. All that is left is my brother, Luna, and our Beta Mavis.

Through three small windows near the ceiling of the basement, enough moonlight filters into the room keeping our shifted bodies in a comfortable state. Had the room been completely dark, our shift would have felt uncomfortable and strained. We need to bathe in constant moonlight to safely maintain this state. Once Wolfie, Leo, and Ivar slide down, I push one of the bricks in the wall next to the light switch and the hatch upstairs closes. It is seriously ingenious, and I must thank Atlas for it. This is the first time we had to use it and it worked perfectly.

Iris stirs inside me. As much as she doesn't want to admit it, she is worried about Kristofer. But as that thought enters my mind, pain surges through my body. *Iris, I think Kristofer is hurt.* She doesn't respond but I can hear the silent whimpers. She is crying and too afraid to say anything.

Wolfie! Kristofer is injured. I link with Luna instead.

Wolfie shoots a look at me and nods in understanding before he lowers his head as if trying to link with someone, most likely Kristofer. It amazes me how he can communicate with everyone. Ever since he became the Shaman wolf, Shoneah, he can freely link with any wolf no matter which pack they are from. While the rest of us would need to blood link with anyone outside of our pack unless they are our mate. At that point, once you mate with someone, your ability to communicate then extends to each other's packs.

I can't reach him, Wolfie calls back out then lowers his head again.

What if he is dead? What if my one chance to have my wolf mate was taken from me by hunters? The room darkness and I can only assume the moon is no longer at its peak. Everyone shifts back into their human form including Wolfie and Leo.

"I got through to Mavis, he said Kristofer is injured and unconscious. We need to go check on him once it's safe". Cassius comes up to me and pets my fur. Everyone is shifted and already leaving the basement except for me. Iris doesn't want me to move or shift. I whimper and place my head down onto my paws. Iris is scared. So scared she would rather hide in plain sight.

Let me know when it is safe, I'll go in Iris' place. I ask Luna Cassius through the link, and he nods without further questioning.

"What's wrong with her?" Atlas kisses Cassius on the cheek.

"She is going through something, and Iris needs to figure it out on her own. She'll talk when she's ready." Cassius leads Atlas back upstairs leaving me in the dark basement floor alone with my crying human. The best I can do to comfort her is to lay here in the dark silence.

Chapter 4
Nora

Hey, Iris?

Yes, Nora?

It's almost time to visit Kristofer.

I know but I can't face him right now.

Iris... I am sure he isn't going to hate you for it. If he did, he would have rejected us by now.

I guess. But not tonight, please Nora?

Okay.

Three hours go by. It is inching to midnight and most of the pack is sleeping or at least in their homes. What is supposed to be a joyous night turns into an exhaustingly scary one. Iris of course is still hiding, refusing to shift using me as her hideaway.

"Nora! Let's go", Cassius calls up the stairway. I bark to let him know I heard and make my way down much to Iris' dismay. He ruffles the fur on my head and opens the door for me to head out to the car. Atlas follows behind me and then Cassius.

The drive over to the house is short. Yet with Iris quaking inside of me, I am sure it is like an eternity for her. We park next to one of the cars by the pack house, making sure to check the area before going inside. The house is relatively quiet with a television playing softly upstairs somewhere and Cecile turning off the teapot that is going off in the kitchen.

Demetrius waits by the door to take us to the room where Kristofer is resting. With gentle steps, I follow into the room and whimper when I see him with the bandage around his leg and an IV drip in his arm. The bag hangs with an orange transparent liquid inside which I can only assume is something to help him flush out whatever is in his system or medicine to aid his healing.

My eyes widen when his scent hits me like a freight train. I thought his scent was strong the first two times Iris smelled it but now it is much more intense, maybe even untamed and potent. Freshly ground coffee with a hint of cinnamon engulfs me and every inch inside of me. Iris moves inside of me feeling the effects of her mate wrap around her in a hug of pure euphoria.

I think the bullet was laced; I mentally whisper to Iris, but she doesn't respond. Yet, I feel her watching.

Cassius walks over to Kristofer and gently squeezes his arm to stir him awake. Kristofer hisses a bit and opens his eyes, squinting at the dimly lit room. His movements seem stiff, but he does his best to scoot himself up to a seated position. They talk a little with Atlas chiming in as he passes looks my way unsure of what to make of my presence. Kristofer jerks his head in my direction, as he was only just realizing who I am to Iris. His eyes bore right through me in search of his mate and the intense stare that makes its way through me, tells me that he found her behind my eyes. It is as if he is not looking at me but at Iris instead.

I take a step forward and he nods his approval. Kristofer sticks out his hand and I walk until my head nuzzles right under it. He runs his fingers through my fur sending waves of little electric bolts through my body. This would feel more intense for me if he was in his wolf form. Iris stirs inside reacting to his touch and I can hear a sigh escape her lips as if she let go of something. She calms down and settles against his touch. Kristofer continues running his fingers through my fur and there is no denying how much he wants the bond to work.

"Hello beautiful", Kristofer continues combing my fur with his fingers. I rumble in response.

"We will give you guys a minute", Cassius steps out of the room with Atlas and closes the door. I return my gaze to Kristofer who is now looking at me a bit concerned and sad. His deep eyes reflect the sorrow I have been feeling all this time and a bit of hurt forms in the lines of his furrowed brows.

"Is it okay to ask, why you haven't shifted back?" Kristofer's voice is deep but gentle. I yelp a little in response. We can't communicate through the mind link because our bond isn't strong enough yet to allow it. If anything, the bond is weaker than the day we first realized we were mates. "How about I ask yes or no questions? Tap your paw once for yes and two for no. If you don't want to answer, then don't tap." I like this human; he is trying to understand us without getting upset. I tap my paw once.

"Do I scare you or Iris?"

Two taps

"Hmm, okay. Then does it have to do with what recently happened?"

One tap

"Are you or Iris going to... r-reject me?" He chokes on his words trying to stifle his emotions.

Two taps

"Can I see Iris right now?" His expression softens at the realization that he won't be rejected. Iris may not be ready right now, but I doubt she wants to lose this opportunity as well. I pause at his new question. Painfully I need to say no.

Two taps

"Okay...last question. I will wait until Iris is ready to trust me but for right now, Miss Wolf, can you lay next to me until I fall asleep? I promise I won't touch you." Kristofer says those words with his eyes closed almost as if in prayer. Or maybe fear of a possible rejection. I like how he called me Miss Wolf though. He doesn't know my name yet, so that was cute of him but the fact that he feels he needs to tread so lightly, breaks my heart.

Is it okay, Iris? I won't do it if you say no.
It's okay, Nora. I know you want to bond as well. Iris whispers.
Thank you.

Instead of tapping my paw, I jump onto the bed. Kristofer almost has a heart attack from the impact and I'm sure his injury doesn't appreciate being jostled either. After a slight groan, Kristofer relaxes and all the worry from his eyes fade, and for the first time, I see how soft his features can be. A smile spreads across his handsome face. As promised, he places both his hands on his chest and laces his fingers together.

"I hope you don't mind but I would like to tell you a little bit about myself. Maybe it'll help Iris or maybe it won't, but I'd like for both of you to get to know me a bit. Once I'm better I can introduce you to my wolf, Zeus." Kristofer looks over to me waiting for a response. So, I make myself comfortable by placing my head on his stomach and rumble softly. He chuckles making my head bounce and begins his story.

"Well in all honesty my life isn't too exciting. I grew up in this house with two amazing parents. When my dad died, I pretty much started keeping to myself and focused on strengthening what now is my pack. Pretty much what Atlas had to do as well. I've also never been with anyone, either emotionally or... sexually."

I pop my head up and look at him tilting my head to the side. His cheeks flush multiple shades of red at his admission. "Yes, it's exactly what you're thinking. I'm as virgin as it gets." I place my head back on his tummy. "I've also been struggling with something that I haven't told anyone in the pack."

My ears twitch in his direction to indicate I'm listening. "I still don't know how I feel about my mother and Martha being together. I have never felt so selfish in my life, and I hate myself for feeling this way. I want both of them to be happy, shit, they deserve it after all they've been through but seeing them together makes me think of my dad. And, well more importantly, how I don't have any of that." His voice trembles. I can see where he is coming from. I don't think Iris has had a moment to even process her mom and Cecile rekindling their relationship either. But she might also not have as much a hard time with it being that she already knew about their romance long ago.

"I move my head up to his chest and with my snout, I try to pick up his hand. He hesitates a bit but starts petting me, running his fingers through my fur again. I know he feels the same electricity I do, so in turn he should feel more relaxed like I and Iris feel under his touch. It's the least I can do since we can't communicate properly, and he continues.

"I want them to find in each other what they lost when their husbands died but I need time to get my heart to understand that she isn't betraying my father's memory by doing so. The more I think about it, I'm sure if it were my mother and Martha who died... maybe my dad and Raven would be finding comfort in each other as well. Guess either way I'd be in this predicament." He chuckles making my head bounce a little on his chest. "Oops sorry, I'll try not to laugh."

Kristofer goes on to talk about his new tattoo and his ideas for other ones. He tells me what he does in his spare time and the diner he loves to have breakfast in.

The sound of his voice changes and reveals the depths of him as he shares a bit of himself with me and Iris. Kristofer laughs at something, and it pulls me back into what he is saying, and I realize he is describing the waitress Jodi and how she is his therapist.

He then apologizes again for laughing as my head bounces, but I don't mind. I'm enjoying watching his expressions change and the multitude of emotions behind his words.

I rumble against his chest again in response to his hand not moving. A protest of sorts that prompts him to look at me and smile before he returns to caressing my fur while confessing how he made a promise to touch or love no other person but his mate which has turned into his long virgin club membership.

Just as he goes on to say that he is resigned to being alone forever, he dozes off. His breathing slows down falling into a deep sleep. Poor Kristofer must be exhausted. His hand eventually comes to a stop resting on my back and I watch his handsome face lose all its anxiety from revealing his deepest thoughts. My head moves up and down in a slow steady rhythm. Surrounded by the smell of ground coffee and cinnamon, I drift into the best sleep I've ever had with Iris and my human mate.

Chapter 5

Kristofer

A slight shiver wakes me from my deep sleep. I no longer feel as warm as I did earlier. With a quick stretch, I notice my leg is pain free and almost new. I've healed enough to move freely and easily. Looking down to where my chest is vacant, I sigh at the fact that she is gone. Not that I expected her to stay but I wish she stayed, nonetheless. Her scent, however, slightly lingers in the sheets and on my shirt. It's comforting notes cling to my senses and calm the storm trying to brew inside me.

Another sniff of her scent allows my body to release the tension it's building from knowing she left. I know she hurts but I am grateful her wolf stayed with me. It is a step in the right direction, and it gives me hope. That little bit of hope is exactly what I need to keep strong for us. I just want her to know that whatever it is that she is going through, I will be here. There is nothing I wouldn't do to make sure she is okay, but I can't begin to imagine or pretend to know the experience she had. I hope she understands through her wolf that I won't do her harm. *She wouldn't have stayed if she didn't know, right?* I try to reassure myself.

I mind link with the doctor to come and remove the IV that he left in my arm. The bag is already empty and I'm too restless to stay in bed and rest. The need to check on my pack to make sure everyone made it back outweighs my patience. Then there's Alex that I need to make sure survived. The last thing I remember seeing is his unconscious body being carried off by my Beta.

I gag as the image of my Beta's dick swinging in my face resurfaces. I still can't believe that thing was that close to me, and it makes me almost feel sorry for whoever his mate is. I kick the covers off and impatiently wait for the doctor so I can find Alex. He isn't in the infirmary with me which I hope can only mean that he is up and about.

Dr. Michael walks in quietly, interrupting my thoughts, and checks my vitals before removing the IV. He must be enjoying the way my finger is tapping on my leg anxiously for him to continue with the speed of a snail. He gives my thigh a once over before being satisfied with how I healed.

"Thank you", I smile at the doctor, but I am sure he knows it is out of courtesy. "Where's Alex?" hopping off the bed and straightening my clothes, waiting for an answer.

"He is limping but moving around on his own. He should be in the kitchen with Cecile having breakfast". I nod in response and make my way over.

Nothing Stays Buried

The house is quiet and that tells me it is either pretty early in the morning or the pack is tuckered out from an eventful night and is sleeping in late.

"Good morning, mom... Alex," I smile at them both but only Alex returns the smile. Mom must still be upset by the looks of it.

"Good morning, Alpha. How are you feeling?" Alex tries to cut the thick air, evidently growing between me and my mother.

"I was going to ask you the same. But me? I'm okay. I'm already healing well. I think you had more silver in your system than I did but don't worry, I'll get the pricks that did this to us, you'll see." I take a seat closer to Alex.

"Well, good riddance to them. I hate that I'm limping still. I've never taken this long to heal before, and it makes me pity humans even more knowing that they last months with a cast and are unable to quickly bounce back. But whatever the hunters are lacing their weapons with is a nasty little thing. They are learning too quickly how to hunt us." Alex finishes off his sandwich and clears his plate. "I am going to check on Demetrius." He leaves the kitchen before I can ask what is wrong with Demetrius.

I turn to my mother sitting across from me and watch her push around her scrambled eggs. Her silence is terrifying.

"Mom?" I do my best to sound calm but the crack in my voice gives me away.

"Yes, Alpha Kristofer," she snaps.

"I want to apologize. I have been selfish and ignorant towards you and Martha. I honestly and truly do want you happy and if Martha does that for you then great. I, myself, need time to adjust. I still miss dad, but I will do better, mom. I promise." A tear trails down my face. I do mean every word but didn't expect the tears to show so easily.

Mom's expression softens, "Son, I still love your father. I will continue to love him until my dying breath. I just want you to know that the love I have for Martha isn't new either nor is it replacing your father's memory. We were all one and we both lost our other half at the same time. I know you were in the dark until now but give her a chance." My mother stands up walking around the table to place a hand on my shoulder. "I want to be happy with you by my side." She walks away leaving me in my guilt to sit in.

***

The next few days go by in another blur. It truly does seem to be a norm for me now to go through periods like a robot. As if on autopilot, I go about my day, and it just melds into one another. All I know for certain is that tomorrow is Thanksgiving. Now of course we don't celebrate it with the same intent as the humans do, but living amongst them for so long, we picked up the habit since life in the city tends to shut down regardless to celebrate.

The television continues to flip through channels as I hold down the button to get to the news. I am curious if there is anything involving hunters or if the protest has settled. Cassius opens the door to the house and walks by with Martha close behind him and I greet her with my best smile. If I didn't know any better, I'd say she didn't buy it, but she smiles back, nonetheless.

Cassius zooms into his room as though on a mission and the sound of drawers opening and closing filters through from his room. He is most likely grabbing some clothes and stuffing it into a duffel bag. Confirming my suspicion, Cassius steps out of his room and drops the bag by the door.

"When are you moving out? Half your stuff is over there already." I chuckle at his exaggerated expression of shock.

"When I marry the man. Why? Are you kicking me out?" He points an accusatory finger with a hand on his hip.

"Shut up." I ruffle Cassius hair laughing and leave him with the television talking about the stock market.

The day then suddenly booms into chaos. All the female wolves and a few of their husbands are in the kitchen or dining hall cooking desserts and decorating for the big day tomorrow. It is funny to see, and something I never tire of no matter how many years we have been doing this. Watching everyone compete over dishes they try to perfect every year while laughing and making memories is what this holiday is truly about for us.

My mother slaps on an apron and takes charge of multiple turkey's using seasoned buckets of water to brine them in. At this point, I step away and lock myself in my office to do some paperwork. Being out of the way is best right now especially since I have nothing to contribute to the kitchen. Besides, now might be the perfect time to draw up the proper documents that will bind an alliance between my pack and Alpha Atlas. Might as well get it done now since they will marry soon enough.

The amount of paperwork I stack to the side is only proof of how much work I am neglecting lately to wallow in my own self-pity. I haven't even started the draft for the alliance because I keep finding other things that require my immediate attention. My eyes strain to see the words on the paper and only then do I notice that my office is darkening from the setting sun.

I look up to check the time with a chest filled sigh that escapes my lips. *I wish I could see you, Iris.* I call into the void of my mind and lean back in my chair closing my eyes. Tears leak from them once again as pain consumes me and then turns to sadness. But oddly enough, these tears and emotions are not my own. I can feel her. It's Iris.

I take a gamble not sure if our bond is strong enough to mind-link. Maybe the little bit we shared in the infirmary is enough to reach her.

Iris, are you okay? I wait but nothing comes back in a reply, so I try again. **Iris?** I slump in my seat with the silence. *I guess it's not strong enough.* I think, almost hating myself for hopefully trying, knowing that it never worked before. I should know by now things never go my way.

Yes? Her beautiful voice echoes in my mind. I had to look around my room to make sure I was alone, and I really did hear her. My body relaxes into the seat, and I smile in excitement but now isn't the time to feel this way. Something is wrong for her sadness to overwhelm me the way that it does.

Are you okay? I ask in almost a mental whisper.

I was sleeping and had a nightmare, that's all.

Want me to come over? We can talk about it or just talk about something else. I'll bring my famous hot chocolate, and we can sit on opposite ends of the room if you like. I sing the part about hot chocolate and then kick myself for sounding so pushy. She needs time and space, I know that, but I also can't help wanting to be near her.

Of course, if she says no, I will respect that as well. Iris' long pause leads me to think she is either contemplating the idea or doesn't know how to let me down gently.

Do you have marshmallows?

I chuckle, **yes.**

See you soon. She replies and I half jump out of my chair with excitement.

The fact that I am seeing her soon fills me with a sense of joy that only a child can express at Christmas. I run to shower first to make sure I smell pleasant and not like the ball of stress and anxiety that I have been. Of course, nothing is going to happen, but I still must smell clean, right?

I run downstairs and into the kitchen almost bulldozing the people out of the way. The chaos from earlier has died down and I have just enough space to prepare two canteens of hot chocolate. I pull out a picnic basket and pack both the canteens, marshmallows, and some buttered croissants. My heart accelerates a mile a minute, but I can't help it reacting to me finally getting to spend time with my mate. We are making progress, and I have a funny feeling I have her wolf to thank.

Are you running here? Iris pops into my head almost making me drop the basket.

No, why?

No reason. Is all she says.

Did she want me to run there? Confused by her question I make my way to the car and look at myself in my rear-view mirror before readjusting it, but it dawns on me why she asked. She can feel my racing heart and assumed I was running because of it.

I pull into the driveway and walk up the stairs more nervous than I should be. But I link with Iris that I am here and wait. After a couple minutes, she opens the door with a smile. Finally, in all her human form glory she stands before me like a goddess. Her sweet scent of freshly baked brownies and toasted marshmallow swarms my senses.

The scent comforts my souls in ways that makes it hard to breathe. Standing frozen under her gaze, I forget why I stand before her in the first place. Transfixed by her beauty and the insane sweet tooth she gives me, the big tough Alpha in me disappears. Iris steps to the side to let me in and I almost smile like an idiot ready to drool. I'm not sure if I make a face at this point but somehow, I manage to move my feet and follow her to the family room. She grabs a few pillows from the couch and throws them on the floor by the fireplace.

Iris then closes the door, so we can have some privacy and motions for me to sit with her. Placing the basket before us, I take out the contents, one by one, and line them in front of us just to keep myself from acting like a bigger fool. Next, I grab the poker stick next to the fireplace and pop a marshmallow on the tip. Iris watches me while I begin to roast it slightly and letting the white fluff catch on fire before popping it in the canteen cup Iris holds out for me. I pour her share over the roasted marshmallow before pouring one for myself.

My eyes follow her hands bringing the cup to her lips and I watch expectantly as she puckers and blows the hot liquid to take a sip.

"Mmm," her eyes close enjoying what she feels from the sip. And goddess, her moan of delight does something deep ad low inside of me.

"Do you approve?" I sip mine and watch her have another taste before scrounging her nose.

"Meh, it's okay." Iris peeks with one eye, a wicked smirk, and a shrug. My face grows in horror prompting her to giggle. "I'm kidding, I approve. It's delicious. I would have never thought to roast the marshmallow first". She adds a few more marshmallows and stares at her cup for a bit. "I'm sorry for how I've been. I know it's probably not how you pictured meeting your mate. I spoke with Nora, and I agree with how she perceives you, but can I just ask that we take this slow?" I nod at her question with relief knowing that we have hope.

"We will go at your pace. Just lead the way." We clink our cups and finish off the rest over light conversations about each other.

Chapter 6

Kristofer

THANKSGIVING IS A SUCCESS. I didn't get to spend as much time as I wanted with Iris but at the very least, we did chat here and there. Even sitting across from each other during dinner, stealing glances is worth my current state of solitude. Being alone now and longing for her only proves how much I enjoy her company and how I want her to give us a chance.

I'm honestly still high from the long conversations that night prior. We spoke about the little things that make us tick. Our likes and dislikes, our favorite places to hang out, and childhood stories.

I learned a lot about her and her dreams. The fact that she stands as the liaison between two worlds, fighting for our rights among these ungrateful humans, amazes me. She also admitted that she knew about her parents and mine being together. She was the only one that did since she had caught them in the act once.

That might be how they ended up with the shack in such a secluded area. She smiled when she said she was fully supportive and the guilt for not feeling the same settled in my stomach. And yet I couldn't help but feel my heart tug at that moment. If she could hurt so deeply and still find it in her to accept her mother's relationship, then why can't I?

The conversation prompted me to tell her about the conversation between my mother and me. Other than the waitress, I haven't told anyone about how I truly feel. But telling Iris makes the burden of my secrets somehow less to bear.

It's now Sunday night. The pack is still raving about the amounts of food that both houses prepared. Some I swear are hibernating from the continual gluttony like Lenny for example. That man is a bottomless pit yet strong as an ox. With all the food left over, everyone keeps reinventing the wheel as they form new dishes with the scraps. Sandwiches, soups, casseroles, and stuffed cabbage rolls are just a few new items on the menu. It's comical really.

I set out with my shovel to make a path to the cars out front. The snow is steadily falling and piling up fast. If I were smart, I would have done this last night, but I was too lazy having a third serving of casserole. Then again if I didn't give myself a third serving Lenny would have stolen my food. Every time that wolf comes around, food goes missing.

The white blanket over the property makes the place seem so serene and quiet. There's no scurrying of animals, no birds twittering, and the calm wind adds a subtle white noise in the air. Now, I regret it since the snow is at least up to my ankles deep and I have a funny feeling my back with be paying for it later.

Working up a sweat, I begin clearing the snow leading around back. After two hours of shoveling my muscles are feeling the warmth as I continue to widen a walking path. This will make things easier when it is time to take out the garbage cans later. The salt we bought did little to deter the snow from building up. I stand the shovel and lean on it admiring my handy work when a crunching sound of snow echoes from a distance.

My ears perk but I continue to shovel to not give away that I'm aware. The sound of approaching boots becomes increasingly louder, and I am now certain that it is more than one person. *Why are these assholes active so early in the morning?* I ask myself, referring to the Hunters who are worse than roaches. I stop shoveling to adjust my gloves but really, I am listening to the direction they could be hiding.

Kris, move now, Zeus shouts just as the impact of a bullet hitting the tree behind me forces me to jerk out of the way. A soft pop from a gun forces me to duck out of the way in hopes that I dodge wherever they were aiming.

On instinct, I crouch down, and crab walk closer to the house and behind the garbage cans. My breathing quickens and forms against the cold. Puffs of cold breath give away my location like a smoke signal. Doing my best to scan the area I blink out the tears stinging my eyes.

The sun's reflection off the snow burns my vision causing me to narrow my eyes. I wipe my face to clear my sight, but it does little to help. My frozen hands fail to clear the tears and the wet glove from the snow leaves no more room to soak up the tears. I close them instead, trying to let them reset and stop watering while I think.

Whoever they are, they are not here to talk and are willing to shoot first. Either they know who and what we are, or they are simply playing Russian roulette. The bastard shooting at me must be using a silencer because I hear the soft pop and then the impact.

The second bullet grazes my cheek and with a hiss, I flinch. The men must not be professionals to miss their shots the way that they have. Either that or they are having snow blindness affecting their aim.

I mind link for everyone to stay inside and be on alert. Some respond they are already on it because of my Beta and are locking the windows of the house while others scurry to the basement. I reach out to my Beta to cover me as I slowly open my eyes and look in the direction the bullet came from, squinting at the brightness before me.

Small movements catch my attention in the distance. A man dressed in all-white camouflage is lying real low on the floor aiming towards me and another two behind a tree. They are using distance and the glare from the snow to their advantage. These hunters are more cunning than the last. Just not cunning enough.

Fucking hunters. I curse in my mind loud enough for the pack to hear. So tired of these human bastards thinking we are game for their pleasure. I mind-link one of my warriors to go to the top floor and snipe out the man behind the tree.

Another shot hits the trash bag next to me, but it does little to stop it from clipping my shoulder. Only being able to notice the bullet until impact puts me at a very dangerous disadvantage. I wince, only then noticing that the wounds aren't healing. *Shit the bullets are laced.*

I slow my breathing and lay down in the snow minimizing myself as a target. With my large frame, this is no easy task but right now it is all I've got. I need to get out of the line of fire. So, I army crawl backward until I reach the front of the house while keeping my eyes in the general direction that I saw them hiding in. I hiss at the pain in my arm, but it is a relief to finally be out of sight.

Just then a pop echoes behind the house. Silence follows but my adrenaline has me looking around the corner to see the man behind the trees fall slowly. The man hiding in the snow then rolls over to take cover revealing his location and another pop goes off as well revealing a crimson spray before a third shot goes off.

Thank you. Great job, I tell Demetrius and make my way over to the men to check their bodies for information as I am joined by Demetrius and... "Alex?"

"Yea?" His head tilts at the confusion in my voice.

"Since when do you know how to shoot?" The anger slightly rolls off my tongue. No decision is made without my knowing yet here is one of those decisions making themselves known. This pup is wielding a gun without my knowledge of it and although I am grateful, my Beta should have told me. Of course, I applaud being able to defend your pack and having the proper skills in combat, but this pup is barely eighteen, lacks discipline, and most of all didn't consult me for weapon use.

"Well, I told you last week that I would be training him, or did you forget? When we began, I gave him a gun out of curiosity and had him hit a couple of targets. He nailed everything like a natural, so until he is up to par physically, he will stand alongside us as a sniper." Demetrius announces proudly. "Besides, you gave me full control in how I train my men and women." The Beta lifts a brow waiting for me to agree.

Alex blushes at Demetrius' words but holds his gaze on me. It's a bit of how he blushes when he is near Cassius but even more so. *Interesting.*

"Must have slipped my mind and yes you have full control. Guess, it was unexpected to see given Alex likes to skip his training." My Beta is not one to overstep me so I guess I really must have been in my head at the time.

Usually, I let him handle any decisions involving training but when it comes to pups, I need to approve, and he knows that. Until the age of twenty-one, decisions in combat go through me. "Thank you, Alex.

I don't know who you shot but it saved me." I wipe the blood dripping from my cheek. The wound is finally healing. Since the bullet only grazed the skin not letting enough toxin introduce into my system, it's healing nicely.

"I shot all three, Alpha," Alex proudly puffs out his chest with my Beta nodding in approval.

Demetrius' eyes linger a little too long on Alex and a bit of color flushes his cheeks. Something is going on, but I am too shocked to care at the moment.

My eyes just about fall out of my head at the admission from Alex. He barely turned eighteen and is already a better shot than most of our men. I give him a smile and a nod before returning to check the pockets of the deceased humans. The first two men had nothing, but the third hunter had a piece of paper and a map of my property. The folded paper was a kill order for me and... *Iris?* There is no other information on it, just our names in ink.

"Someone put a hit on us." Handing the paper to Demetrius, I stand up.

"Us?" Demetrius looks the paper over and gasps. "Do you think it's one of her legal clients?"

"I don't know. She isn't home yet. She had to pick up some documents from her office in town today. I'ma head over to Alpha Atlas then give her a call." I put away the paper and map, "Handle the bodies, I'll be back". I jump in my car and make my way to Atlas' pack house.

Driving as best I can in the snow, I try to give Iris a call through our link. Nothing but silence answers back and either she is really busy, or she cut off the link like she did that one time at the cabin. I wasn't able to get her number so calling her cell will have to wait until I get to Atlas.

I pull into the pack house's driveway and run inside to find Atlas in his study with Cassius. I explain everything, showing them the kill order and map. The only hint we have to go on is the crest watermarked on the corner. The crest consists of three arrows over a crescent moon.

"Do you know this crest?" Atlas looks over at me and then at Cassius. We both shake our heads clueless. A knock turns us over to the creaking door and Martha steps in. She is bundled up to the top with her coat and scarf. Gloves hang from her pocket and her purse hangs in the crock of her elbow.

"What's wrong, mom?" Atlas looks back down to the crest.

"I am running into town to get more salt for the snow. Do we need anything else?" Martha stays by the door waiting for a reply.

"No, but take a couple of men with you... um, hey mom?" Atlas looks over at Martha. "Have you seen this crest while traveling?" Atlas folds the paper, so Martha only sees the crest. She walks over to his desk and drops her car keys with a gasp.

"Where did you get that?" Martha picks up her keys shaking.

"What is it? How do you know this crest?" Atlas stands up worried about his mother's reaction.

"You wouldn't believe me if I told you." Martha takes the seat that Cassius offers.

"Try me, it's important." Atlas sits back down. The tension in the room thickens but the pheromones reek of fear and disgust.

"Well, a very long time ago before Iris was born and you were just a toddler, I had gotten very sick. The fever wouldn't go away which is unusual for werewolves and eventually, I blacked out. Your father, Raven, insisted it was the tea I had that was treating my insomnia. I stopped taking them, but nothing changed so we hired a supernatural healer. Your father, Raven, called in a very high-ranking elf to treat me as a last resort. These elves are very rare. By the next day, my fever was gone. However, I started having nightmares..."

"Wait I thought high elves were extinct." I interrupt remembering I had read it in a history book when I was in elementary.

"It's how the books make it seem, but they still live. Scattered across the world. Elves have an extraordinarily long lifespan compared to us. They keep themselves hidden. In fact, you know of one."

"We do? Who?" Atlas and I almost say in unison.

"Ithil."

"Uh, no. Isn't Alpha Robert's son from elf tribe in Crescent Hills?" My voice did little to hide the shock.

"He was adopted in secret by Alpha Robert from the elders." We all nod in shock and let Martha continue.

"These nightmares were always random images and one of them was that crest. I would see that, and blood, and piles and piles of bodies. After two weeks suffering with these nightmares, Raven gave me a sleeping medicine that Jude had given him. I was finally able to sleep for the first time in a long while.

I dreamt I was tied up to a bed, stripped of my clothes. The healer walks in with a grin as if saying he finally had what he wanted. He whips me over and over watching my skin break and then heal. After what felt like forever, he climbs the bed laughing at me while I'm writhing in pain. He then places a hand on my stomach and suddenly, I look pregnant and ready to burst.

He pushes down really hard forcing me to give birth and through all that blood a baby girl laid between my legs crying hysterically." Martha is trembling even more now recalling everything. I felt my stomach clench. Nausea beckoning at my throat.

"A week after that I found out I was pregnant with Iris. At that point I told your father about the nightmare. He shrugged it off saying it was hysteria from the stress and not sleeping properly." Martha wipes her tears and takes a deep breath. "The healer went by, Liber De Buer but I never looked into it further since your father dismissed it." Martha stands up sniffling and leaves dismissing herself. I feel my stomach twitch. Something is wrong. I look at Atlas and his Luna, unsure of what to make of what we all just heard until Atlas breaks the silence.

"What the fuck?!"

Chapter 7

Iris

"MR. KLINE, WAS THERE anything else you needed before I go?" I run my finger over a list of things I finished and things I need to get done. If I hadn't cut off my mind link, I wouldn't have been able to complete anything.

It's not easy going to law school and doing consulting work as a liaison between my species and humans. Yet, I love it. It gives my life purpose and at this point, I need all the distractions I can get. Life isn't all rainbows and butterflies and that's not including the things I deal with simply because I am a wolf.

I need to get out of my head so I can forget what I went through as a victim. However, I hate that I had to ask my professors for an extension. By next week I should be caught up and enjoy the rest of December without having to worry about schoolwork.

"Can you pass me the Turner case file?" Mr. Kline calls out from his office. Ah yes, the Turners. They are something of a headache. They claim their livestock were killed by my kind and are trying to sue the pack that lives one property over. Of course, this is handled carefully because there is no room for bias.

However, the Turners have no proof of the number of livestock they had prior as opposed to what they have now. At this point its hearsay. When I spoke to the Alpha of that pack, they denied it but also told an interesting story of how their daughter is smitten with one of theirs. When the parents found out, that's when talks of the lawsuit came about. Unless the daughter comes forward and testifies against her parents, this will be a drawn-out case and a waste of taxpayers' money.

"Okay!" I call out to Mr. Kline who is nose-deep in the newspaper catching up on a trial from a competing firm. It's funny watching him read the paper because he practically puts it against his face. The man is blind as a bat and always forgets he puts his glasses on his head.

Mr. Kline is a rather nice old man despite how cold he is in the courtroom. He keeps to himself and doesn't bother me with unnecessary questions. He respects my space and defends me when people make crude remarks about werewolves. For a man his age, he is more open-minded than the younger crowd. You would think that a man who has lived more than half his life would be set in old ways, but he and his wife have been nothing but kind. They treat me like a daughter at times which means a lot considering they were never able to conceive.

"Here you go", I hand him the case file. "Anything interesting in the case?" I nod towards the newspaper.

"No, but it's pretty much a done deal. The defendant managed to produce a witness and there is evidence that supports the claim but enough of that my dear. How come you look so pale? Are you eating properly?"

"Yes, Mr. Kline. I eat very well. Maybe you're seeing things." I chuckle.

"Don't get sassy with me now. I'll tell Moira to bring in some of her famous pot roast for you next time. If I am to have grand babies, I need you to reel in a good man." Mr. Kline waves me away and begins to flip through the file I handed him.

It never fails that our conversations always end with him trying to get me married. I guess he really does look forward to me having a family of my own if only to live vicariously through me. I sigh with a smile and leave for the day. The office may be a safe haven for my mind, but it can also pull me under if I let my work consume me. To constantly be knee-deep in paperwork, reading nothing but animosity for my kind, can really dampen the mind if you're not strong. You need more than thick skin. And thick skin is one thing I literally do not have.

The cold air hits my cheeks reminding me of how quickly winter came. The amount of snow that now piles outside makes me groan as I trudge through it. It's only lunchtime but I have been in the office since five in the morning catching up on things I've missed because of the holidays. "I should have worn my other boots," I mumble, feeling the cold seep to my toes through the boots and thick socks. Luckily, I didn't park far and shove my body into my car to put the heater on full blast. My toes froze into mini-popsicles in the short time it took to walk from the office to my car.

Wolves are naturally warmer but for some reason, I feel the cold easier than the rest of us. I'm still warmer than humans but not as warm as wolves. It's odd really and no one could really understand it. By the time my mother got tired of me complaining and offered to have me tested, I declined and refused to go to the doctor. I just couldn't be bothered anymore.

I rub my hands and put them against the car vents. *Oh yeah, that feels nice.* The warmth spreads through my fingers and I hum in pleasure as it filters through my body chasing away the goosebumps from my skin. A shadow behind my car shifts quickly past. I flinch from the sudden movement but cannot see clearly who or what it is. Looking through all my mirrors, no one is there but my breath that fogs the mirror. A knot forms in the pit of my stomach as I do my best to discreetly check if my door is locked. *I need to leave,* looking around grateful that the streets are mostly free of snow, I get myself situated quickly.

As if put into high gear, I pull out of the parking with my tires skidding a bit. I try to will my car to go faster but my small car skids every time I accelerate. It's impossible to get away quickly in this kind of weather and if I am followed and the car has better tires than me, then I am essentially screwed. Tapping on my breaks, I slow down enough to gain proper traction before my car ends up spinning out.

An SUV appears behind me. At first, I think it is nothing, but the lights are growing brighter and closer. I panic with every fear I have within me coming forth. The SUV rams right into my car pushing me forward and to the right. I swerve a bit, forcing me to counter-maneuver the wheel but I manage to regain control. My heart is racing with adrenaline as I turn onto the main road. I pick up my speed and mind-link with my brother.

Atty, I'm being attacked. What do I do? There's nothing but silence for a few moments.

Where are you? Atlas asks calmly but panic is clear in his words. My brother is scared.

I am on Livington St.

Okay, don't come home. Meet us at the old lodge on Brighton Rd.

Okay. A deep breath slips from my lips, but I know it's too early to feel relief.

At this point I gun it. The headlights, however, aren't going away and I need to put as much distance as I can between us. They manage to catch up and are almost close enough to tip my car. They are better equipped for this weather. I spot Eagle Road and make a hard left. My car screeches and makes the turn drifting as I go but for an SUV, they need to slow down considerably so they don't roll. This road isn't as clean, unfortunately, so I slowdown in hopes that it means the SUV must slow down as well. The lights appear behind me again but far enough for me to have hope. This is my chance to place some much-needed distance.

I make two more turns with the SUV managing to keep track but slowing down. The cabin comes into my line of sight, and I pull into the parking noticing my brother's pickup already there. I run to the back of the cabin to knock but Atlas opens the door and pulls me inside into a hug.

"You, okay?" Atlas checks me to see if I'm hurt anywhere.

"Yea, but my car got a beating." My eyes flick over to my mate watching me with worry. I can't deny the butterflies he gives me or the relief knowing he is here as well. His stare alone burrows deep into my soul making my wolf whimper inside. I know Nora is longing to meet her wolf mate, Zeus. She likes Kristofer running his fingers through her fur like he did that night, but she yearns for Zeus and his fur against hers. Kristofer turns around when Cassius pulls his attention with my heart faltering at the break of our eye contact.

"I see them, they have handguns and they're following her snow prints here." Kristofer and Cassius, walk away from the front windows and wait by the back door. Two other men stand by the front and Atlas takes me to the bedroom locking the door and listening.

Silence screams at me. No one is moving. No one is breathing heavily but me. My brother sticks out his hand to warn me to stay back. My hearing isn't as keen as theirs either which is why he sometimes gestures to me instead. Another one of my many flaws. None of my wolf attributes are as keen as the others. It's why I always come in last in training.

A door creaks open and if that isn't the sound signaling the beginning of a horror movie, I don't know what is. It is the loudest sound in the cabin besides my blood rushing in my ears.

My heart is pounding almost painfully against my chest and sweat is beading on my skin faster than I could wipe it off. The cabin breaks into chaos the second my sweat drips down my nose. Shots fire and furniture smashing to pieces echo through the thin walls. Through all the commotion the bedroom door breaks open.

"There you are, you stupid bitch," the human adjusts the silver knuckles he is holding and gets into stance.

"Don't you dare speak to my sister that way, asshole." Atlas charges toward the man being sure to avoid the silver knuckles. The human swings with his right arm and Atlas ducks under it but the unrelenting human manages to catch my brother in his ribs with a left hook when Cassius screams in the other room.

In the split second that Atlas loses his focus, he falls to the ground gripping his side. The human tries to land another punch, but Atlas blocks his head causing the knuckles to pierce his arms instead.

All I see is the massive amount of blood splatter onto the knuckles and down Atlas' arm. I lose it. My heart erratically skips trying to find its normal rhythm. I want it to stop. The human lifts his fist one more time but I can't watch him hit my brother again. My poor brother. He is bleeding out because of me, and I am just standing here doing nothing. With a mental snap, I scream with everything I have. Scream as if my life depends on it and it does. I close my eyes with tears burning my face like streaks of lava from the eruption of my fear. Screaming over and over, I open my eyes to the sudden silence. My voice does not register in my ears. I stop and take a deep breath.

The room is in disarray. Everything is thrashed around like the aftermath of a storm. You would think a tornado hit the room. I look over to my brother who is in a fetal position on the floor with his hands over his head in protection. Everything conveniently avoided him, unlike the humans. The bedpost is shattered into pieces and some of those pieces are staking the man through the chest and limbs. Confusion fogs my every thought as I stand there petrified by what I am seeing. *How did this happen?* My brother stares at me wide-eyed with the same question in his eyes while the others walk into the room.

"You guys, okay? What was that?" They scan the room and take note of me and my brother. Atlas lifts a hand and points at me shaking in fear. It is the first time that I see such intense emotions in my brother's eyes, and it is all because of me.

"You did this?" Cassius steps into the room to help up his mate while Kristofer walks over to me.

Kristofer wipes the tears from my cheeks with the pads of his thumb. Tears that I didn't realize were still falling freely. I pull away shifting my eyes to him with vexation. *Why is this happening?* I repeat over and over in my mind. My lips quiver but the words won't form.

"It's okay, I won't do anything." Kristofer tries to assure me, but it doesn't matter. He reaches over again to wipe my other cheek, and I slap his hand away.

"DON'T TOUCH ME!" I yell but Kristofer's scream follows mine as his finger snaps back in two. Tears sting his eyes, yet he doesn't look away from me. He doesn't show anger or fear. Instead, he is looking at me with understanding and plea despite his finger slanting to the side.

"I'm...I'm sorry. I didn't...I", I stumble over my words realizing that it's me doing this. I am doing all of it. The truth hits me and all I can think to do is run. And I do. I run toward my car and drive away scared of everything. Scared of who I am and what I did.

Chapter 8

Iris

"WHAT THE HELL? What the hell? What the hell?", I run to my car. "What was that?" The question keeps circling my mind as I fumble my keys. With a shaky hand, I open my car door and drive off before anyone can follow. That couldn't have been me. No way that I'd cause that.

My chest rises rapidly as I call my friend and ask if I can stay over. Without hesitation she happily says yes and off I go to Jesika's apartment. The idea of being able to spend time with her eases my tension a bit but not enough to keep me from spiraling. But I need to get away from it all and as my best friend, sometimes she is all I need.

Flipping through the radio using the buttons on my steering wheel, I scour the vast frequencies of stations. The silence of the drive is not helping prevent my thoughts from going in weird directions. But the snowstorm isn't allowing anything to come through the radio. *Ugh.*

I hit my steering wheel in frustration. Every station is filled with white noise as I continue to flip through the radio. Something has to give at this point, I am fine with anything as long as I can have something to sing to. Finally, after a few more presses on the next button, an old R&B station plays clearly enough to enjoy. Bruno sings one of my favorite songs and I sink into my seat a bit. The tension leaves my shoulders just enough to have me humming to the lyrics but bits of what I saw keeps forcing their way to the forefront of my mind.

The snow picks up and is piling up high enough to make the roads slick. The road is barely visible and finding the lines that divide the lanes is becoming a challenge. The storm must have caught the city by surprise for the streets to be this ill-prepared. Either that or the city is becoming slack with what to do with our taxes. Even a bit of salt on the roads would have gone a long way.

I turn down the radio to see better because everyone knows that's how it works. A thirty-minute drive is what I need to clear my thoughts and now that I arrived, I can cry with my bestie while she feeds me junk food.

The streets look untouched which only means that parking will be horrendous. A blanket of snow is covering everything in sight and the untouched fluff makes it difficult for my tires to navigate me safely through the neighborhood.

I scan through the snowfall for an open parking spot, but everything is either taken or filled with snow. If my car wasn't so low, then I can try parking in one of those spaces, but I am sure all I will end up doing is getting stuck.

Driving a block down from her building, I manage to find a semi decent spot that is relatively clear. A car must have just left for it to be so clean. I park and try to make a mad dash to Jesika's building while I text her that I am on my way. She also better have her door unlocked so I can mad dash inside.

The tips of my fingers grow numb with the cold seeping into my bones. Each tap on the screen reminds me of the numbness taking over and it hurts. So, I put away the phone and squint up at the building as I shove my hands in my pockets. My eyes water from the cold wind that picks up. It whips and lashes against my skin, cutting me with pain. This is the kind of weather that gets you sick. I pick up my speed and huff, running against the wind in the thick snow.

Jesika, I guess, decides to wait outside for me instead because in the distance I can see a blob in front of her building. Her body is lost under big orange sweats, black snow boots, a blue bubble coat with a brown fur hood, and a pink scarf wrapped around her neck. Oh, let's not forget the neon green mittens she is waving at me with that could bring down a plane in this weather.

I giggle at her appearance but it's why I love her so much. She is such a carefree spirit. Jesika accepts me as a werewolf and finds it fascinating in fact, but the real reason I love her is because of her heart. She is such a pure and loving soul.

Excited to see her, I run so fast that I can't stop myself in time and lose my footing. We both topple over into the snow in a fit of giggles.

"Aww I missed you too darling but next time take me on a date first." Jesika jokes giggling.

"Sorry, booger butt," I push myself off and help her up laughing at our failed attempt to keep our footing once again. This time she lands on me, and I almost lose my footing a third time when she grabs my arm. With another fit of laughter, she calls me clumsy nuts and I curtsy. We have weird nicknames for each other, and they constantly change but it's how we show our love for one another. She is like a sister I never knew I needed and glad that I have. "Let's go inside dum-dum, I got a long story to tell you."

We slip and slide our way into her building and stomp our feet to rid the snow off our legs. The hum of the elevator grows closer and then opens its creaky door to lift us to the fourth floor. Two doors down from the right is her oasis. Her apartment door is creaked open but just one foot in and I can feel how warm it is. It feels like home.

My skin melts the instant we step inside, and I start to strip my wet clothes by her door. Jesika follows suit and both of us carry our clothes to her bathroom in our undies. We hang our clothes on her curtain rod and the edge of her tub to dry, smiling at the pumpkin candles in her bathroom.

"Come, we can slip on some pajamas. I already set up Netflix and put out some snacks. Just gotta make some hot chocolate." She hands me a pajama set and I slip into the cozy cotton fabric covered in witch's broomsticks. Of course, she would have pajamas like this. She deems herself a practicing witch after all. I probed her when we first met to see if she was one from lineage, but she isn't. At least not from any lineage I am familiar with.

It began as a hobby after she became obsessed with a TV series that ran for a few years. Raised by two mothers, one being her birth mother, she never knew her whole family. So, it wouldn't be too far-fetched if she was a witch in blood.

I remember when she found a funny-looking book in a shop that sold candles and stones. She was so excited to try the things it had. Yet, I was the shoulder she cried on when nothing worked. Ever since then, she tries to do whatever she reads on the internet and buys from crystal shops. All of which is a gimmick really, but it makes her happy. Although every now and then, it is possible to come across real witchcraft. Jesika knows this and always keeps her eyes peeled for that fateful day.

We go into the kitchen, and I pull out a small pot and milk. Jesika happily grabs powdered chocolate mix, nutmeg, cinnamon, and waits for the milk to simmer before adding everything. She stirs and goes on about some new crystals she found and a stone for centralizing her energy. She points to the dinner table where the stone is entwined with some wire. She mentions something about turning it into a necklace. I nod but I'm not actively listening. The images of the cabin and the impaled human dance in my mind. I grab the mug she offers and make my way to the bundle of blankets on the couch.

The warmth from the mug filters through my fingers as I stare at my drink and take a sip. *It's not the same.* I note and let my mind drift to my mate. He must be so worried about me right now or maybe he hates me for being so flippant. I don't know at this point. I can't believe I broke his finger by simply shouting. He was the only one that didn't look at me scared before I left, even with the injury he clutched to his chest.

His hot chocolate is way better, I decide, sipping from my mug again and grabbing a handful of mini marshmallows. *I wish I could roast these.* The memory of Kristofer putting a large marshmallow on the poker and over the fireplace invades the corners of my mind. He has shown nothing but kindness and patience with me.

"Taste good?" Jesika hums with the sip she takes.

"It's delicious," I answer trying to hide the lie in my voice.

We flip to something random on the television and I begin telling her about my day. I trust this woman with my life. She knows everything. Even about what happened with Rick and then Kristofer being my mate. She has been helping me cope when I wake up from nightmares and I call her in the middle of the night. She comforts me and gives me advice. It's helped me be more open to the idea of Kristofer as well.

In the middle of my story, the power goes out along with the sound of the transformer popping outside the window. The thought that more hunters were watching lifts my hairs on end. Although with the storm, it could simply be an outage from the disastrous winds but the thought pricks at my mind, nonetheless.

Jesika scrambles to light her candles, which is a lot, and I mean... everywhere. She has several lined up on her shelves and more on the counters and coffee table. A few lay scattered in her room and another two in the bathroom. A howl echoes in the distance sending a chill crawling up my spine as if it were counting each and every single vertebra it covered. *Shit, it's my brother.* Jesika senses my panic despite her not being able to hear the howl as I can. That brother of mine is as tenacious as they come. Luckily with this blizzard, my scent is scattered more or less. The howl echoes again against the wind and this time Jesika hears it. Now, understanding my panic she grabs her sage and gets to work.

"I am going to smudge the building." Quickly, she leaves the apartment and runs down to the first floor. I can smell her as she speeds through the lobby and goes up one floor at a time smudging the hallways. She has the right idea, but it'll make it obvious that someone is trying to hide something with the scent. After what seems like forever, she comes back down from the fifth floor and speeds into the apartment out of breath just as another howl comes closer.

Jesika runs the sage over me, and her, then the apartment. I am so grateful for her, but I must admit that I hate the smell and being in the very center is making me want to run. However, I didn't even need to ask, and she understood the assignment. Bless her soul but damn the strong smell to hell.

She peeks out of her window and shows me three fingers. I'm assuming she sees three wolves and they must be close enough to hear us. However, I have tried to explain to her that while our hearing is exceptional, we can't hear through walls from long distances or through bad weather if speaking normally. But seeing her take it seriously keeps me from reminding her for the umpteenth time.

The fact that I am in an apartment building is enough to hide my voice among the many. I slump my shoulders at the thought of three wolves being outside because I didn't consider that Kristofer could lead them to me through our bond. I peek as well and watch them pass the building flinching at the strong smell of sage. They continue down the block and I freeze as my brother links in my mind minutes later.

We found your car; we know you're here somewhere. Let's talk. Atlas sounds desperate.

I stay quiet.

Sis, please. I know you're scared, I'm sorry for how I reacted. We can figure this out together. It might have to do with mom. Atlas pleads but begins to tell me about a dream that mom had and how it freaked her out. She found out she was pregnant with me soon after.

What the hell does mom being promiscuous have to do with me going Matilda back there? Just go away, please. I beg.

Iris, I can smell you even with all that Sage, but I feel like I'm going to hurl. Please come out so I can explain better.

GO AWAY! I close the link so no one can get through.

What does mom's dream have to do with it? That doesn't make any sense. Jesika and I wait for a while to make sure that my brother leaves and cuddle on the couch before continuing my story.

"Oh my god! Could you be like a half-witch?" Jesika is excited by the idea.

"Impossible, both my parent's families have only ever bred with humans or half-breeds. There's nothing magical or special about me." I sigh and bite my lip as the words Atlas told me sink in a bit deeper.

"Then how do you explain what happened?" Jesika slumps in defeat.

"I don't know, my brother just told me it might have to do with mom. Something about a dream." I throw my hands up in frustration. It's all so confusing.

"What dream?" Jesika scoots closer to me so I tell her what my brother told me.

My best friend in the whole world just sits there hugging me. I don't cry though. I just stay in her arms in silence. "What if you're not a witch like I thought, but an elf?" Jesika pulls back.

"Now you're just as stupid as my brother."

"I'm serious here." Jesika slaps my leg.

"You really expect me to believe I'm not just a wolf and that I am a mixed breed?"

"Yes. Now let me try a spell," she squeals as I pull away from her with a questioning brow. She should know by now that her spells never worked before. I am witness to the failed attempts one too many times now.

"You know the spells you find on the internet are not real right?" I roll my eyes, but she suddenly lights up as if I am saying something grand.

"Not this time. I found a book in a used bookstore. It's extremely old and in leather binding. It's even all written by hand. I tried one already and it actually worked." Jesika grabs the book from her room and hands it to me. There is nothing on the cover but a crest. Three arrows and a crescent moon is engraved into the leather.

"Wow, this does look old." I hand it back, impressed but still skeptical. Even if the book is real, she will still need to be a descendant of witches to practice it.

"Wait, you said it worked?!" I eye her.

"Shut up and listen. I saw a spell in here for revealing secrets. Maybe we can use it to figure out what happened." Jesika rearranges some candles in a circle and draws a symbol of a heart, a question mark, and a crescent moon. The symbols are drawn on top of one another. She grabs my hand and nicks my finger with a small dagger. A drop of blood is squeezed over the symbols.

The flames that were just crackling, steady themselves as if obeying a command. My friend reads off a spell:

"Goddess of the moon,

Spirit of the night.

Reveal what is true,

Show me what is right.

I offer this blood,

Bring the truth to light."

The flames shoot up into the air turning shades of blue, purple, then green. Dancing in a seductive swaying motion, the flames settle, and my skin begins to itch. Looking down a small crescent moon begins to form on my inner wrist with one arrow through the middle. Jesika gasps and points to the floor. The blood on the floor begins to move and spells out were-. The words stop forming leaving the girls in suspense.

"WERE WHAT?!"

Chapter 9

Kristofer

IT'S NOW FOUR DAYS since we last saw or heard from Iris. With the storm turning for the worse we can't continue to wait for her to change her mind and come home. If we do, we may very well end up waiting a long time. After arriving home that day and telling Martha about Iris and everything that is happening, she freaked out and made calls to everyone she has contact with from other packs. It is of no surprise that she decides to rally everyone. But because of it, now everyone is aware of the name, Liber de Buer.

This elf is not just a threat to us as a family but a threat to everyone as a species. He is someone that cannot continue unchecked.

Pacing back and forth in my room making calls to the few leads we managed to find. My mother, Cecile, has her head nose deep in dad's old books trying her best to find something that can help us track Liber. She has been at it none stop right along with me.

"I knew it!" She yells from my office where she sits in the center of piled-high open books and paperwork she is using to cross-reference.

"What is it mom?" I walk into the room after leaving a voicemail, half-awake from sleepless nights. If I don't get rest soon, I may very well fall asleep where I stand.

The coffee I keep ingesting is doing little to keep me awake and may be contributing to my system crashing even harder. If anything, I am sleepier now than I was when I had my first cup.

"I found the bastard in Jude's ledger. After hearing the name, it kept bugging me. I then remembered that while traveling south your dad and I went to a supernatural conference." Mom looks excited as she gets up from the floor with the ledger.

"We ended up meeting a very distinguished looking man there. Porcelain skin, eyes dark as coal, long dark blonde hair, and a slender build. He struck up a conversation with us first saying he was looking to move to a new territory with his family. We told him of this area and how nice it is and perfect for raising small children. We assumed he was a witch but later found out he was a high elf when Raven hired him through a third party to help Martha when she was sick." Cecile takes a deep breath. The wheels in her head, turning quickly as she spoke.

"Wait how did you not recognize that he was an elf?"

"I had never seen one before and his ears were covered with the long cloak he wore." Mom shrugged.

"So why would he be in dad's ledger?" I ask almost certain about my suspicion.

"He offered us his services a couple of times as a teacher when Michael was first learning to use medicinal herbs." She steps out from the circle of books she created. "We can use this to track him down. We have his number and account information. It's old but it's something." She runs to the phone and puts in some calls to begin the search. While I am not sure it would turn anything up, she is right in that it is our only lead at the moment.

I walk out of the room rubbing my neck in hopes that the search pans out but it's a stretch considering how long ago it was. *I need to sleep desperately.* My thoughts drift as the weight of my eyes is too much to ignore any longer.

Kristofer? My step falters walking up the stairs. Thankfully I am grabbing the railing.

Iris? I honestly can't believe she reached out to me first.

Yes. I want to see you. My wolf starts to flip inside at those words and so does my heart.

Tell me where and I'll be there. I'm already in my room going into the shower to wake myself up before dressing in something proper.

Don't tell anyone. Meet me at Maricott Hotel on Clermont ave, room 506.

Okay I'll be there soon. I reply and that is all it took to completely snap me out of my sleepiness.

I can finally check on her and make sure she is okay and spend the time my heart craved to be near Iris. My body is vibrating with anticipation of spending time with her. Of course, I'm not expecting anything sexual to happen but just the thought of feeling her warmth sends me to the moon and back. The flutter in my stomach increases with each passing second and leaves me almost rushing to finish getting ready.

I sneak out of the house to avoid questioning from anyone and head out in my truck. The snow is still packed high, but we did a good job clearing out a path to the main road. The road salt crunches beneath the tires and I am certain that it's just giving away my departure with how the sound echoes. I rush towards the location going over the speed limit in what feels like the longest forty-five minutes of my life.

The hotel comes into view, and I speed into the parking lot making my tires screech a bit from the sharp turn. I may have almost clipped a couple that is crossing the lot to their car, but I couldn't care less at this point.

Finding an empty spot, I throw the truck into park and go straight to the elevators of the hotel. It doesn't take long to reach the 5th floor, but it could have been a bit faster if the elevator did not have to stop on the second floor first and then the third. Who gets on an elevator that is going up when they clearly need to go down? *Simpletons,* I think to myself and stare at the number five lighting up above the doors.

The bell goes off and the reflective doors open. My feet trip over themselves as I rush out of the barely open elevator and speed walk over to room 506 with a bit too much of a pep in my step. With a deep breath, I try to calm my nerves. Being in a hotel does not help the wild imagination running rampant in my mind.

The cameras in the hallways must be having a field day as they watch me approach the door and hover my fist but unable to knock. **I'm outside the door.** Announcing myself like this may be a better option since I figured she wouldn't feel jumpy if I linked her instead of knocking overly excited. I might have ended up knocking so hard that the door would have come off its hinges. The door unlocks and opens slowly revealing a beautiful smile upon rosy plump glossy lips.

"H-Hi", I stutter like the love-struck fool that I am.

"Hi. Come in," Iris steps aside and giggles. She must be sensing how nervous I am. At least I think that's why she is giggling. "Thanks for coming last minute". She fiddles with her fingers and almost averts my eyes.

Even shy she is gorgeous. Nothing can take away from her natural beauty. I trail my eyes over her soft skin, noticing how it looks dewy. Her hair is partially dry from an apparent shower. Her jeans hug her nice and voluptuous curves, and the top accentuates her breast perfectly.

"Anything for you," I mumble. She walks over and sits on the bed motioning for me to do the same.

"I've had a lot of time to think and in light of what's going on, it makes this bond seem not as scary anymore. So, I want to try. I want to work on us. I know I'm attracted to you, and I can feel how you care for me and how our bond strengthens whenever we spend time together. So, all I ask is, if I say stop to anything, a kiss, a conversation, a touch, anything, promise me that you'll listen and actually stop." Iris moves closer to me with a hint of fear in her eyes. It almost breaks my heart that she needs to say this out loud, but I am so proud of her for doing so.

My lips part slightly, and I want to steal a kiss. We are going from barely a few conversations to her opening up to the idea of us fully. Aside from that one night before Thanksgiving, we haven't had some real *us* time. But I'll take it.

I'll take the rope she is giving me even if she later changes her mind and hangs me with it.

"I promise," I whisper, almost afraid that my voice would break the fragile moment suspended between us.

We linger there in silence and I want to ask her so many questions about what happened that day. I want to know if she is okay and if she wants me to do anything to make this more comfortable for her. The last three days I was restless with the idea that maybe Iris is crying herself into exhaustion alone or maybe something like what happened before had happened again and she trashed another room.

Then I get angry with myself wondering if she is with another man and if he is comforting her even though Atlas assured me that she is with her female friend. He knows that his sister has a best friend she often spends time with but doesn't know what she does for a living. I stare at Iris' beautiful eyes that are searching mine for something. She looks well rested and not at all like what I expected to see on my way over. It scares me a bit to think that instead of processing anything, maybe she is pushing it aside and ignoring everything instead.

"Kristofer?" Hearing my name on her lips makes me blink into focus and smile at the raised brow she is sporting. But before I can ask her to talk to me about what her last few days were like, she surprises me.

"I'm too nervous, can you kiss me first?" Iris closes her eyes and waits.

When did the moment turn into this? My palms grow sweaty, and I swipe them on my jeans. Despite me being the one to initiate the kiss, she is in full control and my heart is ready to burst.

I take a deep breath forgetting every thought I just had in the last five minutes. *Shoot*, who told her that I wasn't nervous too? I'm the virgin here but I take another deep breath in and out. It's now or never. I turn towards her and gently place my fingers behind her neck and through her hair. She flinches but relaxes after I rub her cheek with my thumb. All I can hope is that I look like I know what I am doing and lean in until my lips feather against hers. Sparks course between our lips.

"Are you sure?" I whisper against her lips sending more sparks where our skin touch. She nods and I close in again. Pressing against her lips, I'm slammed with waves of pleasure. She feels it too as she returns the kiss a bit more assertively. The way I moan into her mouth and suck in a breath robbing her of air, ignites a smile when she gasps against my lips.

Her tongue slides across my mouth and my eyes shoot open in surprise but she grins peeking at me as well. I feel something I my burst to life and most likely the green in my eyes flare. *Fuck.* Accepting her tongue, we play. A game of joust. It only fuels my need for her further. *Shit...shit.* I jump off the bed and run to the bathroom locking the door.

"What's wrong? Did I do something?" Iris calls through the bathroom door.

"Trust me you did nothing wrong. In fact, it was too good, and I don't want to lose control. I don't want to scare you. I...I..." Fear catches in my throat. I want her so bad, but I don't want to lose my virginity in a fit of lust and break the effort she is making towards me. Such a strong woman willing to fight her trauma to give us a chance. She is an angel. While I'm just a horny virgin devil in wolf skin. *Fuck!*

I slap my boner annoyed at how it is raging at attention. Pain explodes making me buckle to the floor. Reminder to oneself, never slap a boner unless you want to risk breaking it off.

"You won't scare me or hurt me. I've learned that much from you already. Please come out Kris." The sound of my name on her lips makes my dick throb harder. But the good kind of throb.

"Not until it calms down."

"Kris, why would you want that if it's only going up again after? Open and let me help you?" I gulp and beg my wolf to behave. I don't want to mess this up. The fact that I am acting like this only emphasizes my virgin mentality and I am sure she is wondering if I am worth the trouble.

I unlock the door anyway and wait for her to open it. She steps into the dark windowless bathroom and closes the door.

"I want to try and help. I won't heal unless I am willing to trust you to keep your promise." Her hand reaches out to my chest. My eyes slowly adjust, and I can start to see her perfectly in the dark.

"I just don't want you to feel like you have to rush us. Anything sexual can wait. I've gone this long without it. I'll be fine."

She smiles at my words. But I am becoming oddly aware that while I do mean what I say, I think I am beginning to panic over losing my virginity after so long. What if I come too fast or what if I can't do it in a way that she is satisfied?

"Well, I do feel this is fast, but I also don't want our bond to die because we didn't try. I am not saying we have to have sex right now. Just small steps of intimacy." She must have adjusted her sight as well because the other free hand goes straight for my erection.

"Mmm," I growl and moan at the burst of sparks now flowing from her grasp to my member. Even through my jeans, I feel her completely. "I won't do anything. Do whatever you are comfortable with. You have full control." I give a strained whisper.

Her grip suddenly tightens around me. I flinch at the onslaught of pleasure, and something changes in her eyes. Something sexy that says she is the master of this moment. A soft light turns on and Iris lets go of the switch she flipped on just beneath the vanity mirror.

Through the glow of the light, I can see her in all her magnificent beauty. Her damp hair sits over her shoulder framing her rosy cheeks. Iris is breathtakingly beautiful. The way her features changes when she looks down the length of my body makes me cower under her touch. Without words, the message she is sending me is that she is Dom of this relationship and my wolf and I, willingly submit.

She pulls down my pants and backs me up until my bare cheeks hit the cold of the sink. I yelp at the ice against my skin. If I wasn't about to have my first intimate experience with someone, I would have lost my erection from the cold. With the heat coursing through me, the cold did little to deter my hard on.

Her soft hands stroke my length, coaxing moans out of me in uncontrollable waves. I've never had a woman's touch or anyone's for that matter. The only hand my dick has had is mine on lonely Friday nights. The intense feel of her touch has me edging on the brink of release.

"I'm close", I whisper between breaths with gravel I never heard in my voice before.

"No, not yet." Iris stops and I whimper at the loss. I leak from my crown the preshow to the main event. She rubs the pre-cum spreading it all over my tip inducing shivers of pleasure as it over stimulates every nerve ending in my dick. The look in her eyes tells me she is enjoying what she is doing to me, and it excites me even more as I watch her lift her sullied thumb and lick it clean.

"You're killing me, Iris." My voice, husky and aching to catch the moan she lets escape from her lips at the taste of me on her tongue.

"Turn around and bend over the sink for me," she demands with her hazel eyes aflame.

"What?"

"Do it!" She demands a bit louder. Her authority sends a rush through me and straight to my balls. *This. Is. Fucking. Hot.* I obey my mate and bend over the sink with my pride by my feet along with my pants.

She rubs one of my cheeks and slaps it hard. I jump and almost straighten with the impact. What initially stings sends warmth and arousal within every fiber of my being. She does the same to my other cheek but this time I moan into it. Who knew I'd like this type of degradation. Or would this be considered punishment? She stands directly behind me which is hilarious considering how much bigger I am compared to her. I am six feet three inches, and my sassy mate is five feet seven. She reaches over and jerks me off slowly.

"Beg for more", Iris squeezes my shaft, and I shudder within her grip.

"Give me more," I whimper and my wolf inside is living for it.

"Where are your manners? Ask properly," she slaps my ass harder than last time. I grunt at how much it hurt yet at how much I'm enjoying this and do my best to not cum from that alone.

My dick twitches in her hand as it starts to drip onto the floor. Why haven't I ever realized I liked to be dominated? I should have noticed from all the porn I watch. Surely some were BDSM in nature.

"Please may I have more, Madame?" I respond and earn a moan of approval from her lips.

"Well since you asked so nicely," she rubs one of my cheeks and continues to jerk me off but just as I think I'm getting another slap, she places a wet finger on my forbidden spot, and I tense. Gently she massages it and stops as if silently asking permission to continue. I nod and try to relax as she slowly pushes in my just as virgin tight ring of muscle. The pleasure catches me so off guard that I shoot ribbons of pleasure on the floor.

"Holy shit", I shake as I never had an orgasm before, and the action causes me to clench down on her finger. My knees go weak as Iris removes the intrusion and watches me pathetically slump to the floor to catch my breath. "That was the last thing I expected," I look up at her not-so-innocent face. She giggles unapologetically and turns on the overhead light.

"Well, I guess I'm a lot more comfortable touching you instead of being touched." Iris stands over me with her crotch directly in front of my face so she can wash her hands in the sink. *This sassy little tease.* "I hope that's okay with you. I want to be comfortable with sex and I feel safe with you so it's a bit easier not to think and just do the controlling instead."

"Of course, it's okay but I want to satisfy you too." Not that I would know where to even begin but I don't want her to not get any gratification.

She contemplates it for a moment. "Okay, but no hands though. I'll let you be my first in this, well I guess I'll be yours as well." I look up from her crotch, which I apparently am staring at, confused by what she means. Iris pulls down her jeans and takes out one leg. The action is so simple, yet seductive and has me ready for action once more. My eyes grow wide in realization of what she is offering. She places her free leg on the edge of the sink providing the most magnificent invitation, which I gladly accept. Let's just pray I know what to do as I get ready to lap up the dessert before me.

Chapter 10

Iris

I AM COMPLETELY out of my mind. Nora, I don't do shit like this. Taking a deep breath, I look down at Kristofer panting on the floor. *Damn, he looks so good beneath me though.* I close the space between us to wash my hands.

I may have been brave when I decided to try something with Kristofer but now with the lights fully on, I can see his nose touching my crotch over my jeans and my knees struggling to keep me up.

"Of course, it's okay but I want to satisfy you too." He replies barely moving an inch from my core. It's hilarious how he is practically talking to my vagina instead of me.

My core heats up with how close he is to it as I contemplate just walking away but I can't deny how riled up he gets me. Nora is pleading inside me to continue being brave and I am not too opposed either. Nora has been holding my hand through this, but I would be lying if I didn't say I was on edge as well.

"Okay, but no hands. I'll let you be my first in this, well I guess I'll be yours as well." I pull away just enough to pull down my jeans and release one leg.

Nora, I'm trusting you here.

I know, just do as I say Iris. Now, lift your leg over him and rest it on the sink. I listen with my nerves on full blast, but I can't let it show.

My confidence needs to show through, so I throw my head back to avoid the embarrassing eye contact. *I can't believe I am doing this.* His nose rubs against my clit sending sensations to burst to life from the contact. My breath hitches. Everywhere our skin touches, a jolt of electricity rushes through me in overwhelming waves of pleasure. This is his first time as well so I can only imagine he is much more nervous than I am in this but with how his tongue is working my bundle of nerves, I wouldn't know.

Nora this feels amazing but I'm honestly freaking out a bit. I admit.

Just take a deep breath. Focus on the fact that it's Kris. Your mate. He won't hurt you. We know he loves you even though he hasn't said it. Nora assures me.

Nora, I might make him stop. What if...

Hey, just focus on the feeling. Take back control. But if you must stop, it's okay. Nora calms me a bit.

Okay, you're right. Take back control.

I relax a bit and recount to myself everything Kristofer is doing. His tongue swirls around my core tasting every inch he has access to. All that echoes are the slurps against my growing wetness and the moans he delivers against my flesh. I moan in return, allowing the sensations to work their way within me. This is so foreign to me. So new and nothing like the horrid experience I had not long ago.

I've never felt something so good like this before. Wave after wave, my body crashes in the pleasures that this man is providing. He sucks me, licks me, and nips at my thighs with a fervor so eager, it causes a head rush I'll never forget.

How is a virgin so good at this? Or does he suck, and I only think it's good because it's my first time having someone go down on me? The thought almost makes me giggle but the suction this man has against my clit almost makes me knee buckle.

"Kris," I breathe out in a groan so deep it matches my climbing climax. He grunts in response and almost sends me over the edge with the vibration of his lips. I look down at his closed eyes and how he is enjoying my core while he jerks off almost desperately. Frantically. As if it were his last nut. It truly is a sight to behold. "Kris, more," I whimper and lower my weight against his lips. His eyes fly open and lock on mine, taking in what I am requesting. Letting my words dance in his ears as understanding settles in.

The intensity of our stare only lends to how amazing it all feels and how quickly my release is about to peak. "You can touch me now," I lean on the sink because my knees are weakening with each lap of his tongue.

His hand finds its way up my leg, scorching my skin with the heat of his fingers. Kris rests his hand on my pubic bone letting the heat of his hand invade the depths beneath my skin. With two fingers he spreads my lips so he can nosedive deeper into my core. "Mmm, yes. Right there." I can't believe how erotic my voice sounds against the bathroom walls. I barely recognize the seduction in my voice. This is the first time I hear this version of me. A version I want to explore further.

Kristofer smiles against me and I keep my eyes fixed on his. Panting and not caring what face I am making in the process. He pulls away and runs one of his fingers down my center, entering my folds. I gasp with my eyes rolling back for cover.

Nora? NORA? I call out to her.

Yes?

I don't know if I should stop. I admit it. This feels different, amazing, exciting, and it scares me. It's too intense.

Hun, only if you truly want to. I don't want to push you too much in one day.

Yea, but it feels good. This is so confusing. It's nothing like Ri...

I open my eyes realizing that nothing is happening. The sensations, the vibrations, and the moans have stopped. Kristofer is looking up at me with his brows furrowed.

"Do you want me to stop?" He whispers in a husky voice and glossy lips. He wants to continue but is restraining himself out of concern for me. He senses my hesitation.

"I don't know actually." I want to be honest, and the truth is, I don't know.

"Then I'll continue slowly. If you decide that it's enough, I'll stop. Don't be afraid to tell me how you're feeling. Remember, you are in control." He waits for my approval. How did I end up with such an amazing wolf as a mate?

"Okay, slowly then."

His lips get back to work and his finger gently pumps in and out of me in a slow rhythm. Ripples of pleasure accumulate with each thrust. The buildup of pleasure drips down his hand as I moan louder than before. My hips rock against his hand trying to ride him. The urge to chase my climax overrides the tightening in my chest. Without a care in the world, I am smothering my core on his face, and he looks like he is on cloud nine because of it.

A second finger goes in, but he stops. His eyes lock back onto mine and holds me there. Kris most likely feels me tensing up at the tight intrusion. His tongue makes work with my clit and flicks it until sensory overload. I gasp and relax against him again when he stops with his tongue and continues with his fingers. A slow thrust in and out works up to speed. Now this... this feels like heaven. His thick fingers fill me enough to truly feel pleasure.

"Bend your fingers," I demand, now grinding harder against his mouth. His brow arches in question.

"Your fingers inside, hook them and you'll find my g-spot." Understanding immediately, Kris sets his fingers in position. "Oh, yes. Kris. That's it." He makes work of my g-spot and sucks my clit like a fucking vacuum.

"Oh, don't stop."

An odd sensation builds but I ignore it. I don't care anymore. I just want to release. My breathing quickens with each thrust forcing me closer to coming undone.

"Right there, Ah...Kris"

I pant, griping his hair. His tongue whips back and forth violently against my swollen nub. My core is clenching his fingers, holding them prisoners in my wet cave of impending fucking orgasm.

"I-I'm coming", the intense sensation bombards me like a floodgate breaking open. I'm incomprehensible. My legs shake violently from the orgasm, and I lose all my strength. *Oh shit, I think I know what's about to happen.* Before, I could pull away from his face, I cum in the form of a shower. The scream he provoked with his final thrust made me squirt right on Kristofer's unsuspecting face.

I hold onto the sink scared of falling while I drip down my thighs. My legs are like jelly, and I can't seem to get my breathing in order to tell kris how amazing that was. I drop my leg from the sinks ledge and look over to Kristofer when reality sets in.

"Oh my god, I am so sorry." I panic. Kristofer's face and shirt is drenched. His eyes are shut closed and so is his mouth. This is the first time that I squirt as a result of someone else. No one has been able to do this to me and I am mortified. I grab a towel and hand it to him as he blindly reaches for it.

"What just happened?" He asks with his eyes still closed. Poor thing is in shock, unsure what to make of it.

"It's the first time I've done that." My face most likely looks like a tomato right now and I want to die. Just carry me out back and place me in the dumpster. He doesn't need to know that I can make myself squirt with a vibrator.

"Wow, I've heard of it but never seen it before. That's intense. At first, I thought I made you pee until I noticed it didn't really smell like it nor taste like it… Some got in my mouth."

I blush even harder at his innocence. *He thought I peed, and it went in his mouth.*

Nora, kill me now. I shriek internally.

Haha, thank goddess it's you and not me. Nora replies laughing at me.

Ugh shut up!

Maybe I really should just trust him with my body. He is the complete opposite of that asshole, Rick, and obviously knows how to play my body like an instrument of his own making. But most importantly, he listens to me.

Kristofer wipes himself and I help him up as best I can, but I am still jelly from the orgasm. "Hey, do you maybe want...to shower with me?" I can't even make eye contact with the man. It may be his innocence, size, or the simple fact that he is my mate that is. Making me embarrassed. Maybe it's everything combined.

"Only if you're okay with it." He answers and drops the towel. I nod and turn on the shower before I finish stripping and step in.

The devil water feels amazing against my skin. It pounds away at everything. Kristofer opens the curtain, and I step aside to give him room suddenly feeling crowded in what I thought was a decently sized tub. I couldn't be more wrong with how much he fills the space.

My eyes trail his chest tattoo down to his abs and then his deliciously enormous package. *How in the world is that going to fit in me?*

"A picture might last longer", he chuckles. I snap my eyes to him causing a burst of laughter, turning me twenty shades of red. "You are absolutely stunning. Have I ever told you that?" He smiles and I shake my head no. "Then I shall tell you every time I see you." He grabs the soap and most seductively begins lathering his hands. "Can I?" He makes the motion of wanting to lather my body and I smile.

I grab the soap from him and do the same. He bites his lip knowing full well my intention. I put down the soap and begin to circle his chest with my hands making sure to lather every inch of skin I see. His soapy hands trail up my arms and I do my best to ignore the half-erection knocking on my thighs. If it's already knocking like this at half-mast, then what is it like at full sail?

Even though I looked at it earlier and had him in my hands, the dim lighting did him no justice. I run my hands down both arms and back up to his neck, not once does he look away from me all while doing the same to my body. He works his hands like magic.

Every time I gaze into his eyes he holds me there. He captivates me with pure warmth and love. Never does his eyes seem judgmental or harsh. Never does he look disgusted or ashamed. Just love. Pure innocent unhinged love. It's what calms me down more than anything. I break away and turn him around. Looking into such depth almost makes me choke. It can be overwhelming, like a confession of his undying love. I don't know if I can handle that kind of level yet.

I lather some more and work on his back, down to his plump and firm butt.

"I am pretty sure it's clean now", he chuckles again at my excessive soaping of his ass.

"I need to make sure. Gotta be thorough." I reply but he erupts in laughter. I smile at the beautiful sound. "I think your laugh is my new favorite sound in the world." The words come out of my mouth before I can think myself to stop. He stays quiet but hums in appreciation. If he ever hummed like that against my skin, I am sure I would squirt again.

I reach around his waist satisfied with his soapy butt and find his erection now at full attention. Kristofer tilts his head back and I finish him off. Hot white ribbons shoot onto the tile wall and drips slowly.

"Please don't rile me up any more than this babe."

My ears feel like they are on fire. "What did you say?"

He turns around to look at me with droopy lust-filled eyes, "I said please don't ri-"

"No, not that, the last part", I cut him off with a smile.

He smirks, "you mean, babe?"

I nod, permanently maintaining a red hue on my face. "I like how that sounds," I hug him wanting to hide the never-ending pigment of embarrassment.

"Me too." He whispers against my neck sending chills down my spine. We stay there with my back in the scorching water and feeling the safest I have ever felt.

Chapter 11

Kristofer

WAKING UP WITH MY MATE in my arms has to be the best feeling in the world. I slightly readjust myself to see her gentle angelic face in slumber. If only I could burn her image into my memory and keep it there the way we keep dried flowers between pages of our favorite books, I'd die a happy man.

Iris squirms a bit and mumbles something I can't make out. *Goddess, help me keep it in my pants until she's ready,* I pray in silence as I kiss her forehead and wake her, "Morning sleepy head". Iris stirs a bit before she opens her eyes slightly and nuzzles into my neck giggling.

"What has you in tickles?"

Iris inhales my scent and pops her head up. Her warm hazel eyes look at more than just me. They see all that I am. My deepest desire. My secrets and I feel exposed yet wanted under her soft gaze.

"This is the first good sleep I've had in a while." She admits and gives a slight stretch before placing a kiss on my cheek. *Crap this isn't good.* I groan at my arousal. "Oh my!" Iris gasps and I already know why.

Ooooooh goddess of the niiiiiight.

What the hell are you doing? Zeus interrupts my mental singing.

Shut up Zeus! …Who shiiines her light down, briiiiiiight-

Dude, that's an elementary song. Stop singing. Zeus continues trying to cut me off, but I ignore him.

Be the guide I neeeeed, when you find me, through the wolf I seeeek.

Kris, you're getting harder. The song ain't working. Zeus laughs in amusement at my failed attempt to bring down my boner.

Fuck! Shut up, Zeus.

The tenting beneath the sheets twitches and I can no longer deny that my erection will not go away. I cover my face, feeling the heat in my cheeks rise.

"Please act like you didn't se-", warmth wraps around me, and it traps the words on my lips. I look down to her beautiful head bobbing on my erection. "Iris, wait, you don't have t-". I moan at the flick of her tongue across the slit of my crown. *How is she so good at this?* Her hand twists and jerks my length in rhythm with her lips. "Shit, Iris. I-I'm...", I release everything into her mouth watching as she gladly accepts what I am giving her and swallows.

"Thanks for the meal", Iris licks her lips, hops off the bed, and goes into the bathroom.

I am pretty sure my mouth is catching flies at this point. This woman is a freak, and I must be the luckiest virgin in existence. *Wait does that mean she isn't a virgin. Wait, did she call my cum a meal?!* My mind swirls between elation and jealousy of those before me. The fact that she even considers it a meal must mean she has had it before. *Right?*

Kris don't even go there. Even if she isn't, that doesn't matter. You are the one she wants. I say let her have her way with you. I'd submit for Nora anytime if you ask me.

Of course, you would. You're another freak. I reply with an internal eye roll.

My wolf laughs. He is definitely already whooped by Nora, and he hasn't even had time to be alone with her yet. Well, maybe I am whooped too if she keeps doing what she does. But if anything, Iris has shown me the power behind sex. It's more than just the bodies connecting and enjoying the sin of flesh. It's mental as well.

I dress myself by the time she steps out. The way her hips sway as she walks almost has me hard again, so I get up to wash my face and calm the raging hormones inside me. At this rate, I will not make it out of this hotel, and neither will she.

The mirror reflects back a man that looks content but most of all relieved. The worry on my face is barely visible and the fine lines of stress have smoothed out. I really thought I was going to lose my opportunity to have a mate. Smiling at myself, I rinse my mouth with the generic mouthwash the hotel provides, feeling ready to conquer the world.

***

We head over to my favorite diner and sit in my usual booth. Jodi nearly trips when she spots Iris with me, and I can already see her mind working as she approaches. This woman is just as bad as my mother when she gets an idea in her head.

"Oh, my goodness, tell me this is the reason you have been coming in here with sad puppy eyes." Jodi beams at Iris. I choke on my spit at how straight forward that is and gawk at Iris for giggling. Her choice of words doesn't help either.

"Jodi, I told you about my mother, not her or is age catching up to you?" I snap at Jodi and boy does she not like that.

"First of all, mind your manners, young man. I have known you since you were a snot-nosed tot soiling your diapers. Besides, you think I can't see through you. I knew there was more than your mother's story. No one mopes the way you did unless it's a broken heart." Jodi slaps my head with her notepad. "I'm glad you made up with her though." Jodi winks at Iris and smiles.

"Oh, I like her," Iris whispers to me. Jodi chuckles and walks away without taking our orders.

"Well, that's my therapist I told you about", I laugh and pull up the menu trying to hide my face from everyone. We place our orders, and Jodi brings coffee to tie us over while we wait.

The air is filled with bacon and coffee. The colors on the walls look bright and the food floating to the tables all look delicious. They must have changed the light bulbs or something. I don't remember everything looking so… vibrant.

I shrug away the thought and go on to tell Iris about what happened before her being attacked and what my mom discovered. Iris' eyes lose focus a bit as if rummaging through her thoughts.

Our food arrives just then, and Iris goes on to tell me about her friend and the spell book she bought at random. Then the little ritual they did and what came of it. By the time she finishes, we are almost done with our food.

"Wait, so is she a real witch?"

"I'm inclined to think so. How would the spell have worked otherwise? However real a spell may be, if you don't carry magic in your blood then the spells are still useless." Iris sighs and shrugs her shoulders.

"Do you think Jesika will lend us the book? Since it must be the real deal, and if I'm right, the handwriting might match the writing in my dad's ledger." Iris agrees that it is worth a shot and wastes no time texting Jesika.

"Okay, I told her to meet us at your house. Let's finish and head home." Iris finishes her plate and responds to a chime on her phone. "Okay she said she is on her way. Let's go". I swear this is the only person that can order me around like this. I still have some home fries left on my plate, but I grab the two pieces of bacon instead and follow Iris. It's freaking sexy as hell how bossy she is, and I'd give up my potatoes any day for her.

It really is, Zeus adds his seal of approval.

***

Arriving home, I change into a clean set of clothes in my room while Iris waits in the living room. The feeling of having her with me is so comfortable and natural that I can only smile to myself thinking how it's just the beginning.

Laughter erupts from the kitchen when I step out of my room and I follow the delightful sound to find my mate, face deep in a photo album. Definitely not where I left her. Tears roll down her cheeks as she tries to catch her breath.

"Oh my god, why is he naked covered in white stuff?" Another laugh fills the room. Iris points at a picture and shows my mom waiting for an answer.

"He was potty training and decided he was a big boy and took off his diaper. Since it was summer, he had seen his father powder himself and wanted to do the same." My mother joins in with her cackle.

"Mom! You waste no time, do you?" I sit on the opposite side and watch my mate flip through my childhood.

Goddess, I love this woman.

Iris' eyes shoot up at me wide and almost in shock. "What?" I reply snapping out of my thoughts.

"You realize I just heard what you said, right?" Iris grins.

"Oh!.... w-well it's true." I realize it's extremely fast. Maybe it's from inexperience but it's how I feel. I can't help it.

I know. I can feel it from you every second we spend together. Iris links to me and returns to the pictures, continuing to flip through it.

My mother's phone rings, startling her since the phone was already in her hand. She gets up to answer it and walks away for privacy. My nerves unravel and get the best of me. I can't believe I projected my thoughts to her.

Unable to hide the redness in my cheeks, I go to the kitchen to get a cold drink. I might as well have said those words out loud and now my heart is racing to the point of rattling my ribs.

I pace the kitchen floor before opening the fridge, "dammit Lenny, he ate my damn pudding". That man will wipe the house clean if left to his own devices. How his parents aren't bankrupt is beyond me.

The only other option is a bottle of water since it's too early to chug the beer sitting next to it. I grab the water instead and chug half the bottle when the doorbell rings. It must be Jesika and with that thought,

I mad dash out of the kitchen and open the door almost tripping on the runner in the hallway.

Of course, I give it the evil eye as I continue to the door more calmly. By the smell of it, I can confirm it is Jesika unless a giant bundle of sage has come to life and is waiting at my door.

"Assuming your Jesika?" I raise a brow but smile.

"Yes, and your definitely mister hunky Kristofer." A proud grin slaps her face.

Iris obviously gave her a good enough description of me for her friend to know who I am. I chuckle nodding my head at the term hunky and step aside to let her in. My mother then comes speeding out of my office and into the kitchen.

"Let's head over to Atlas. I think I got an address." My mother tells Iris as I walk in with Jesika.

"Munchkin head!" Iris jumps out of her seat and runs to her friend.

"Oompa loompa cheeks" Jesika squeals back. For the next two minutes, they jump around in circles. *What kind of pet names are those? I* wonder but smile at the odd expression on my mother's face reflecting my thoughts.

"Okay, now that they stopped squealing, let's go." I push both the girls out of the house and into my truck. Mom follows and sits in the front seat.

"Hey, let me see your wrist. Still there?" In the mirror I see Iris showing her wrist to Jesika. "It's gone!" Her voice is a little too high-pitched for my liking.

"Yeah, it went away after a few days but it's odd cuz it feels like it's still there. Like underneath." Iris rubs her wrist and arm in thought.

I pull into the pack house and guide the chatty girls through the door. Atlas is notified of our arrival by the young wolf that answered the door but since he is in a meeting we wait in the living room for him to finish.

"Iris?" A tall but skinny wolf walks in and beams at my mate. He runs to her and hugs her before I can stop him. I growl and let my canines come down.

"Hi Finn. Okay let go, you're squeezing too tight". She shoots a look at me apologizing for Finn, but I wasn't having it. What bothers me more, oddly enough, is how uncomfortable she looks from being held. Clearly, she is panicking. I growl louder towards the man hugging my girl.

"I believe she said to get off." I scoff at the rudeness of this so-called Finn. He breaks away and glares at me only adding fuel to the fire.

"You are not my Alpha, so watch your mouth," Finn approaches me which is a grave mistake on his part.

I stand up from the armchair and tower over the pathetic thing of a wolf. "I may not be your Alpha, but I am HER mate. Touch her again and you're losing your arms for starters." Finn looks over at Iris in disbelief. She nods and stands next to me to hold my hand.

"We're mates", Iris squeezes me. Finn, however, does not accept it. That is his second mistake.

He throws a punch my way and I dodge it with ease, landing my own in his ribs with a quick hook. The sound of them cracking is loud, but it appeases my anger. I forgot to hold back a bit considering his frame, but I regret nothing. He backs away pathetically, slowly catching his breath as he heals. He lunges again and I push Iris out of the way. I grab Flynn or whatever his name is by the throat and squeeze, watching him squirm under my grip.

"WHAT IS GOING ON HERE?" Atlas demands from the entrance, his voice booming into the room. I let go of Fisk or whatever and he drops to his knees in a coughing fit.

"He attacked my mate", Iris answers her brother and locks her hand into mine.

Fern, *what the hell is his stupid name?* His name annoys me so much. *I don't know or care*, Zeus replies just as annoyed as I am. Anyways, Floyd turns to Iris with tears in his eyes. Already producing a sob story.

"You would choose this filth over me?" Felix snaps at Iris but gestures to me.

"He is not filth and yes, I will choose him over and over again because he is the most amazing soul I've ever witnessed. I can't say the same for you Finn." Iris spits back, anger evident in her face. *Finn that's his name.*

Atlas grabs Felipe by his collar and leads him outside to separate us.

How are you instantly forgetting the name? Zeus barks at me annoyed yet laughing.

Ain't my fault his name is stupid, I retort but it is not one of my best comebacks.

"Thanks for sticking up for me. I will never let Franco touch you again." I caress her cheek.

"Franco? It's Finn." Iris chuckles.

"Whatever..." I kiss her nose and sigh with happiness.

Chapter 12

Kristofer

IRIS SITS IN ATLS' office with Jesika and me, waiting for Atlas to return from setting Fabio or whatever his name is, straight. That damn wolf dared touch Iris without her permission, yet I admire the strength she showed in not letting it break her down.

I know she feels me staring at her with how she pauses from talking with Jesika to steal glances my way, but I can't stop admiring my beautiful mate. I also can't forget the image of how she initially tensed up when that wolf, Fabien hugged her. A whisper of a sigh escapes my lips, and I shift in my seat with impatience. I know her confidence is growing to what I am sure must be its former glory, and it brings me much joy to know that I can be beside her as she self-discovers her strength.

Iris has come such a long way in a short amount of time just to have him touch her unwarranted and unravel her a bit. *Honestly, I am just glad he didn't hold her for too long,* I think to myself as she giggles at whatever Jesika is telling her. I'm surprised I kept my cool as well as I did but I don't know if I'll be successful a second time.

Atlas walks in with a scowl and heaves a sigh of what must be frustration. His golden eyes have a bit of a flare to them which could only suggest he had to use his Alpha tone.

Flanagan probably is giving him a hard time over failing to be Iris' mate. Alpha Atlas takes a seat at his desk and leans onto his elbows rubbing his temples to attempt some form of relief from the stress building between his brows. His lips are pursed together tightly reflecting the same tension in his shoulders. The air is thick with anxiety.

Iris sneezes, causing Atlas to look up at us for the first time since he sat down. His questioning gaze slowly shifts from the girls to me and back again in wait for an explanation. His muscles flex and tenses up ever so slightly and what little patience I have left, holds me back as I look him straight in the eye waiting for him to speak first. I know I am in my right but being in his home I know better than to ignore whatever he may have to say. I am the guest here.

"Leave him alone. He did nothing wrong. Kris could have torn him off me, punched him, clawed him, anything but he didn't. I had told Finn to get off me and he didn't. Kris reminded him of what I said, and Finn lost it, challenging Kristofer instead. Would you have backed down if someone was latched on to Luna as if he were theirs and then challenges you, as an Alpha no less?" Atlas eyes his sister, softening his expression at the mention of his Luna.

"I hate when you make a point. Still, this is my house, and I should have been called to handle it instead." The last bit of anger fades from his voice but he eyes me in a final reprimand that tells me I should know better. "Okay, so show me the book." Jesika gives it to him as Cecile walks in with Martha.

"Damn, it's the same crest from the hit order on your heads." Atlas runs his fingers over the leather noticing the darkened edges and patches. I follow his movements maybe even following the same train of thought, *burns*.

"Hit order?" Martha and Iris say in unison. They weren't made privy to that piece of information when they were first briefed on the situation.

"Open it and compare the writing to Jude's ledger." Cecile hands it over and Atlas places the items side by side.

"Don't ignore me! What hit order? On whom?" Iris says to Atlas while snapping her fingers.

"We found a hit order on both you and Kristofer's heads, it's how we found the crest." Atlas continues examining the book and ledger, looking for similarities between the strokes of the letters. His fingers trace the writing simultaneously and continue down the page with his expression matching what I already know to be true.

Iris snaps her head at me angrily and I swiftly look away admiring the ceiling and the fine carving on the crown molding I never realized existed until this moment. It's fine work and adds an elegant touch to the history around the office. It's unique and a perfect distraction to the glare burning my way.

"The lettering is the same. The S and the L have the same cursive loops. The P and Q as well. I'd say it's most certainly his. So, if that's the case, maybe the symbol is a family crest?" Atlas questions Martha and Iris.

"Impossible!" Iris stands up from the chair slamming her hand on the desk. "If that is a family crest then how do you explain the mark appearing on my wrist a few days ago? It only had one arrow, not three." Tears fall from her eyes.

"What do you mean, on your wrist?" Atlas looks at his sister's wrist expecting to see the crest and so do I. Although I am sure I would have seen something like that sooner. Back at the hotel.

"The day I left the cabin I went to Jesika's apartment; we did a spell from that book to reveal the truth. I had too many questions and not enough answers. The stupid crest then appeared on my skin but with only one arrow and after a few days it disappeared." Iris turns to her mother and so does Atlas.

Martha twitches in place. She looks nervous and I can only guess there is something she isn't telling us. A missing piece to this puzzle.

"Mom, explain." Atlas uses his Alpha tone. He knows he should never do so towards his parents but at this point, she has too many skeletons in her closet that are now biting us in the ass.

"Let me start by saying I love you both very much and I want you to keep that in mind as you listen." Atlas nods but Iris doesn't. The steam rolling off her is every indication that she is ready to walk out of this office.

Iris looks at her wrist and rubs it looking uncomfortable. I hate seeing her like this and reach for her, but she flinches. Something she hasn't done in a while with me. My chest tightens but I retrieve my hand and watch her rock side to side on her feet waiting for Martha to speak.

She is anxious, Zeus chimes in.

I know Zeus, but I can't do anything if she doesn't let me.

"When Iris was about 3 years old the crest mark from my dream and the one you see there appeared on her wrist. It was so small that she thought nothing of it, but it terrified me. The same day it appeared, so did Liber de Beur. He wanted to take her and raise her as a high elf, in other words, a healer. At least that's what he wanted me to believe. I found out quickly he is in fact a dark elf and has a bad reputation and history with the rest of his kind.

"He is one of the rare few born with an immense amount of power. He can wield fire and water, perform summoning's, and intricate spell magic. Most elves only have an affinity to one element. Luckily, we were in a public area, so I called Raven to come get us through the link." Martha sighs heavily, her eyes glossing in tears.

Iris goes pale standing against the wall. I did not even notice when she managed to back herself up into it. Subconsciously she is running away. I am sure Iris would collapse or leave this room if not for the wall holding her up. Martha continues her story pulling me back to her.

"I stayed with her close, waiting for her father and when Liber sensed my husband arriving, he sneered and left. He was still settling in because his first home had burned down due to a rogue wolf just before Iris was born. He also lacked a following at the time. He knew if he were to plan a kidnapping of any kind, he would need manpower. Now that I think about it, he probably didn't act because he lost his book in the fire, and maybe even the medium he used to channel his magic." Martha sits down sobbing softly.

"Wait, so the book I brought over is…is that why it's a bit burned?" Jesika gasps. Martha nods in agreement and continues.

"Raven asked me what was wrong, and I told him that I was simply tired because I didn't eat well that day. He drove us home and that was that. I then took Iris to a doctor outside our pack and had her blood tested. It came back not a match with Raven. He wasn't her biological father.

"At that point, it was obvious who was, and I got scared. That nightmare I had wasn't a nightmare but a magical conception. So, I asked them if they knew of a witch who could bind her blood. I got the information and left." I look over to Iris who is crying silently and slowly sliding down the wall from what should be a shock.

Without a second of hesitation, I get up and go to her, opening my arms. She comes to me sobbing against my chest as my shirt happily collects her tears. Gently I lift her in my arms and sit back down with her on my lap. It took more than effort to not run away with her and hide her from the pain she is currently feeling. Seeing her hurt is the last thing I would ever want, so I hug her tightly in hopes that I can pour my strength and love into her.

Martha looks my way, sad, but I give her a look of contempt. I couldn't begin to understand the hurt Iris is battling. Nevertheless, Martha finishes her story.

"One day I had everything ready, and I told Raven that me and Iris were having a mother-daughter weekend. I drove up the mountains and found the witch. She bound her blood preventing the elf traits from presenting itself. The witch, however, warned me that the binding would weaken as she got older and could unbind on its own. If it were ever to fully break, then her power could go out of control. I waved it off and left. I never heard from Liber again either.

"I can only think that binding the blood hid her from him somehow and he is back now because the binding weakened enough. He wants her for something, but I don't think he knows that she manifested her active powers. Although her crest appearing could make things worse. She is practically a beacon for him no matter where she is."

We just can't catch a break. Martha's lip quivers as her face floods with tears. She has been keeping such a large secret for over two decades. We sit there in silence taking in all the information, all but Iris. She stops hiding her face in my chest and faces her mother.

"So, I am half FUCKING ELF? This is bullshit." Iris jumps off my lap and closes the distance between her and her mother.

"Sweety, I'm sorry, I-." Martha pleads but Iris cuts her off not listening. At this point, I don't know if I should intervene or not. It is not my place. These are family affairs that I can't fully meddle with, despite it somehow involving me.

"No, you don't get to just apologize. Yeah, being a swinger is one thing and I backed you on it. You loving Cecile, I support you on that too. Those are secrets you keep and hold to your heart if you wish. But not telling your own daughter that she is a hybrid?! A damn were-elf! And one that could magically explode outta nowhere!! That is not something you get to say like it's nothing! This is why I never fit in. Why I was always slower, colder, more tired, just a cheap version of what a wolf is supposed to be." Iris storms out of the office with tears full of rage.

"Damn, mom. She has a point." Atlas doesn't even have the strength to seem angry.

"I just wanted to protect her and have her live a normal life." Martha sobs uncontrollably while Cecile hugs her.

"And how is that turning out for her mother? Yes, do your part and protect her but at some point, you should have come clean with her." Atlas opens the old leather book completely ignoring the presence of anyone else in the room. His word is final.

***

I walk out of the house to find Iris sitting in the car's back seat. She is crying into her hands loud enough for me to hear through the car doors without so much as using my heightened hearing. I knock on the window although I see the lock on the other doors are open.

Iris peeks at me through her fingers and opens the door before pulling me in. I sit with her on my lap, letting her cry until the anger subsides enough to allow her to breathe normally. Even so, it's hard to tell when the right time is to speak. I don't know how to comfort or soothe someone, but I pray that at least my warmth is enough to comfort her.

Flowery words or gentle voices are not my strong suit. Never have been and now I wish I was more in touch with my feminine side. With a soft breath against her neck, I run my fingers through her hair hoping I can relate what I want to say through my touch.

"Can you drive us back to your place?" Iris whispers into the crook of my neck.

Without a second thought, I put her down on the seat and get out from the back of the car to drive us home. If she wants to be away from everyone to get herself together then that's what I will do for her. And with a desperation, that is brewing within me, I speed off, kicking up dirt behind us, revealing a trail of our escape. I adjust my rear-view mirror and crumble at the sight of my mate's reddened eyes and watery cheeks.

Nora, are you okay? Did you know? Zeus reaches out to Iris' wolf.

No, I didn't. This happened before I showed myself to her.

I listen in on the conversation between my wolf Zeus and Nora and wonder if Iris can hear them too.

I know what you're thinking Kris and no, she can't hear us. Nora is blocking her out. Zeus clarifies right on cue. It's creepy sometimes how well he knows me. While we can communicate with our wolves telepathically, it doesn't mean we can always hear each other's thoughts. We do safeguard our minds most of the time. We fall silent the rest of the ride home.

Arriving at home is quick and I rush to open the door for Iris and scoop her up into my arms, giving her the freedom to hide her face into my body if she pleases. Walking into the pack house, I pass by a few wolves that are lounging around. The looks on their faces say they want to ask what is going on, but they don't dare ask since the look on my face screams 'don't'.

With my foot, I push open the door to my room and freeze. Books lay spewed across my desk, clothes on the floor, and a couple of candy bonbons sit on my nightstand. Not a total disaster but messy and not a great first impression.

"I'm going to lay you down and then draw you a bath,

okay?" I whisper to Iris while I nuzzle into her hair. She smells wonderful but I also smell her anger and sadness. Hopefully a warm soak will do her some good and help her clear her thoughts and sort her heart.

"No, don't let go." She clings to me tighter.

Keep her in your arms and run the bath. Our mate is trembling. Zeus is right.

She is scared and hurting, letting go of her now is the last thing she wants. She is seeking comfort and warmth, and I almost robbed her of it. Albeit, unintentionally, but still.

"Okay, I won't let go," I reassure her and give her a gentle squeeze.

Her weight almost seems like nothing to me and feels at home in my arms. It's where she is meant to be, at least, it's what my heart is yelling from the rooftops the more we spend time with one another.

Carefully, I shift her weight and sit on the edge of the tub while I run the bath. I make note of how plain the bathroom seems. It can use a bit of a feminine touch, that way she has options when she bathes. I Candles and bath bombs like the ones my mom uses would be a great addition and maybe I can add a little caddy for a pillow and other things to relax.

Nothing Stays Buried

The bathroom steams up from the hot water and that alone has Iris relaxing a bit in my lap. The way her body feels less tense has me smiling but this isn't the time to talk to her about these sudden changes I want to make. Nor about how much my heart is swelling with emotions for her. Right now, is the time for her and her alone.

The tub is full, and I want to place her in the water, but I can't with my promise of not letting go. I don't have the heart to do it even though I am taking her words a bit too literal. So, with no other option, I remove her shoes and socks before removing my own. I shift her weight to one side and lift her so I can step into the tub with her. If I didn't have such a large tub, this would not be possible.

My tub is custom-made due to my large size and now I am grateful I had it redone. I lower myself with her slowly, fully clothed, and yet she doesn't flinch or question my actions. A soft sigh escapes her lips instead and in the warmth of the surrounding water, she lulls into a deep slumber against my chest. The erratic beating in my chest drumming her a lullaby to sleep.

For the first few minutes I listen to the soft breaths echo in the bathroom, whispering back to me her sorrows. My breaths are now heavier and deeper, bouncing back against the tiled walls to brush away the sadness of her whispered cries. The sound of her heart beating against my chest, beats against my ears and plays the sweetest melody.

"Half-elf or not, I'll always love you Iris", I add to the whispers mixing in the steamed room. My eyes grow heavy and soon I find myself joining her in dreamland.

Chapter 13

Iris

A SOFT COOL LIGHT wakes me from my sleep. I stir a bit on the hard bed beneath me that's... breathing? I blink a few times at that thought and open my eyes to find the moon shining through my window. No, those aren't my curtains and it's not my window. It's not even my room. Nothing in this room is remotely close to being mine and the hard bed I'm sleeping on is Kristofer's chest.

I lay my head back down and listen to his heart calling my name in rhythm while mine quietly responds. He submerged us both making sure to keep his promise and not let go and that thought chips away a chunk of my heart and stores it away just for him.

I sit up and touch my body to feel what I have on. It's light and soft but most importantly, it is oversized. At some point, Kristofer must have undressed me and slipped on one of his shirts. With the light of the moon shining through I can see that Kristofer has on just his underwear.

I lift the shirt to my face and inhale his scent. My lungs fill with the aroma of freshly ground coffee and cinnamon, making my chest tighten. The sobs roll out of me as if a seal holding back the dam, broke. Arms wrap around me hushing my cries in futile attempts. Kristofer hugs me tighter whispering something to me, but I can't hear him.

I can't hear his voice. Instead, I hear my mother and the things she said in front of everyone. The story that unfolded. The truth that had been buried beneath the lies of who I am. I hated myself growing up because I am different. I am weaker, get colder, I don't shift as big as the other wolves, and my senses lack the depth and perception that all others have. For the longest, I accepted I was simply born with a weak Lycan gland. Yet, I am not all these things because I am defective like I thought but instead a hybrid out of a forced pregnancy.

I have nothing against elves of course, especially with our kind adopting Ithil, goddess bless Alpha Robert. But this kind of truth, a truth that defines my very being and answers so much of what's happening to me, to only be revealed after the fact...hurts. It hurts more than being told I was inadequate.

Liber de Beur. Elf. NOT your biological father. Binding. The words of my mother stir like a chant in ridicule. Mocking my naivety. All I ask is for acceptance, love, and a peace of mind. All I want is for this pain inside to go away and the darkness that is plaguing me since the day Rick robbed me of everything, to turn into light. Rescue me goddess, rescue from this hurt. I scream into my mind as I spiral in my chaos. The turmoil and tornado of all my self-doubt and worth swirling in a raging storm that breaks my heart.

"…is" Kristofer calls out to me in a faraway panic. The sound of his voice is distant but it's getting closer as my name on his lips start to take over the storm in my chest and the clear the clouds in my mind.

"IRIS!" He calls me again and I open my eyes to find random objects floating in his room, surrounding us like the hurricane forming in my soul, waiting for direction. I blink in shock, and they drop causing loud thuds to bang throughout the house.

"No, I didn't mean, I-" the words won't form. How am I doing this? Why am I the cause of everything so violent?

"Shhh…it's okay. It's okay, nothing happened." Kristofer caresses me and rocks side to side in comfort with me in his arms.

I take deep breaths of his scent to calm down and focus on matching my breathing with his. I can't believe I manifested my feelings.

"Better?" He whispers in my ear when my breathing evens out.

"Yes, a bit," I whisper back with my eyes closed. I don't want to see the mess. The proof of my blood is scattered on the floor, and I refuse to acknowledge it.

"Come, let's go back to sleep. I'll make you breakfast in the morning."

Kristofer lays me down and covers me with a blanket while he sleeps on top of it. The warmth of his bare chest sends me to sleep quickly.

Well, maybe a bit too quickly, or rather not at all, maybe? I open my eyes and find that I am no longer in the room with Kristofer but by a lodge by a lake. There isn't a soul in sight. Nothing but silent trees swaying ever so slightly in the wind. The moon is hiding behind the clouds and a dense fog is rolling off the lake and over the grass to greet me at my feet.

"Thank you for coming." A voice calls out from the shadows.

"Who's there?" I call out but nothing is moving. No one is there. None of which I can see.

"Only one of the strongest Elves to live." The voice laughs as if it were common knowledge to know who he speaks of.

"I don't know anyone who carries such a self-proclaimed title." As brave as my words may sound, I'm scared out of my mind. My feet are glued to where they are while my knees threaten to give out as they shake in fear.

Out from the shadows, a tall man with dark blonde hair and eyes black as night, emerges. His grin expresses all ill intent, but I cannot deny that this man is indeed my father. The shape of his eyes, the curve of his lips, and even something in the way he smiles is just like mine.

"Liber de Beur," I announce while I shudder at the bitter taste it leaves in my mouth.

His smile grows wider and in less than a blink of an eye, he is nothing more than an inch before me. I do everything to keep myself from screaming. The way his presence frightens me triggers my fight or flight, but I am frozen in place. Literally unable to physically move.

He smells strong, like sulfur, as if he crawled out from the depths of hell. Goddess knows if this man is best friends with the king of hell himself. And I wouldn't put it pass him if he is. My stomach churns and the groan forming in my throat almost gives away my displeasure of everything that makes up this man.

His hand, as quickly as his appearance, wraps around my throat as he chants. My eyes roll back, and my body turns cold. Ice runs through my veins from where his touch burns me. All my senses are on overdrive, but I push through it to fight against it. I lift my arms struggling and clawing away at the strong man before me. I scream at my father, but my voice is silent.

The cold crawling through my veins reaches my wrist where the crest now appears with a slight glow. It changes and now has two arrows over the moon. Whatever he is doing is forcing the blood binding that my mother placed to weaken further. He is forcing my awakening.

Losing my ability to breathe while Liber chants in a tongue unbeknownst to me, I claw furiously at him ripping his shirt as I do. My wrist is on fire but before I can faint from my pain, my veins blacken beneath my skin. His chants grow louder almost commanding the darkness to spread. Across my skin the black veins race and engulf me in its hold.

My body goes rigid. The power is all consuming. Relentless and foreboding, as it inches higher up my neck. And just as I gasp for breath, the darkness that invades my veins pool into my eyes in finality. Screaming, I wake up as the vividness of the dream has me digging at my skin to relieve the burning underneath.

Kristofer jumps out of the bed, bearing his fangs and extending his claws. His reaction to my distress is in a half daze but even so, he scans the room for the threat. My body trembles in a cold sweat and I realize that my veins don't truly burn but the fresh scratches I inflicted on my skin, do. I'm panting, and wince when the crest forms back on my skin with the two arrows just as I saw in what I now know was a dream of sorts.

"Iris, are you okay?" Kristofer retracts his fangs and releases his fist upon further examining the state I am in.

The realization of how I looked in my dream settles in, and I jump off the bed to run to the bathroom for the mirror. Without a word, I stare at my reflection and while my eyes are bloodshot, I swear I see a faint bit of black leaving my eyes. Retracting. Blinking several times to verify I am not hallucinating, my eyes water from the bathroom's bright light.

"It was a dream," I whisper to myself. Just as I turn to leave, I spot in the mirror from my peripheral, Liber behind me smiling in a cloud of dark smoke.

Quickly, I turn back around, but he isn't there or anywhere in the bathroom. Looking back to the mirror, it's back to empty with nothing but a scared girl looking back.

"What the hell is happening?"

***

After a brief shower and calling Jesika over, I go downstairs to manage a pot of coffee. That isn't an ordinary dream I had. Something is happening and I need to know what.

"Hey," I wave at Kristofer who is sitting at the table with two place settings and a worried look. He stands up letting go of the tension in his shoulders.

"Hey," he replies in a shy whisper. "I made breakfast and coffee." Kristofer points to the plates with food. It makes me wonder if Nora told him I was craving coffee.

"Just what I needed," I take my seat and sip the coffee that is still relatively warm. The liquid fuel gives me the temporary boost I need to make it through the day. I'd dare say that he might have made it a bit too strong but maybe that is a good thing.

"Do you want to talk about it?" Kristofer manages after an awkward silence as we eat the spread that he made for us. Scrambled eggs with cheese, toast with jam, bacon, and a bowl of fruit topped off with whipped cream. I don't realize how hungry I am until I take in the first bite of food.

"No." I quickly spit out. It sounds harsh but I truly don't want to talk about anything at the moment. I wouldn't even know where to start. Kristofer nods and picks at his food with his fork. Clearly unsure of what else to say when a sudden ding sounds off in the kitchen. I yelp in my seat and watch Kristofer get up and return with waffles he had in the toaster.

Kristofer sets the small plate with the waffles for me to grab and sits down with a sigh. He pushes around his eggs and pokes the half-eaten bacon. It is annoying to watch and makes me feel a new type of anger. I ignore the rising feeling because Kristofer has done nothing but cater to my every need. He may be sulking, but he is staying quiet and giving me my space.

He sips his coffee but the sound of him doing so grates my ears. Everything is irritating me because, well because it all seems selfish. Fuck it, I'll admit to myself what this is. He is being, selfish. He isn't helping me because of me, he is doing it out of his own self-serving virgin need. Because we are mates. He is only putting up with me so that he doesn't die alone. He is doing it for himself, "selfish fucking prick". I mumble to myself.

"What?" Kristofer stops drinking the coffee with his brows furrowed and a bit hurt.

Shit, did I say that out loud?

What the hell Iris? Nora scolds me.

    I don't know. I didn't mean it, Nora. I just… I felt so angry all of a sudden. I reply and look up to Kristofer who is still waiting for an answer, hurt spread across his face.

    "Sorry." I suck my teeth and leave the table dropping my fork. Tears threaten to break free, but I don't stop. Instead, I speed walk out of the house passing Jesika who is just arriving.

    "Hey. Iris I-" Jesika tries to stop me, but I keep walking. I drown out everyone and disappear into the tree line.

***

Kristofer

    "What the hell was that?" Jesika walks into the kitchen to find Lenny sitting in my seat finishing off my breakfast while I put away Iris' just in case she is hungry later.

    "I don't know. She just needs time to process," I reply, not believing my own words and slamming the refrigerator closed. Something is wrong, I can feel it, or rather, our bond feels it. Ever since the nightmare, something is off.

    "Shouldn't we go after her?" Jesika sits across from Lenny who is also finishing my coffee.

    "No, she will return when she calms down." I leave the kitchen and walk up to my room where I can be alone and look out my window. "Goddess please keep my Luna safe," I whisper against the window watching my fogged breath slowly disappear from the cold glass.

***

Iris

The naked trees of the winter morning do little to hide the morning sun. I lean against the thin black ash tree and carefully remove my clothes.

Want to go for a run Nora?

Are you sure? Iris, why not go back and talk to Kris?

Not right now. Let's run. I am not ready to talk to Kris.

I shift into Nora and take a seat in the back of her mind. This will always be my favorite place to be. As I look through her eyes, I settled into the corner of her mind. She pushes my clothes to the side as if it makes a difference and chuckle because either way it will get wet with the snow. Then she goes off in a sprint.

The joy she feels as she sprints freely surrounds me and I swim in it, allowing it to chase away the darkness and anger from earlier. I love how free she feels when she takes over. It's a little secret of mine, how much I enjoy watching the world through her eyes. It's calming in every sense. Sometimes it's the only way I can sort out my thoughts.

Nora finds a small cliff overlooking the river. A bit of Luna Cassius and my brother's scent is lingering here. This must be a date spot for them. A gross thought but it's too beautiful of a spot to leave.

Nora sits down finding comfort in the familiar scents and I watch the semi-frozen water below rush by.

Iris, you need to talk to your mom. You can't ignore her forever. Or anyone else for that matter.

I can't forgive what she did, Nora. I huff in the depths of her mind.

Are you a mother?

I… Her question startles me, and I have no idea how to respond.

Exactly, you can't begin to know what she felt or the position she was in. She did nothing TO you. She did something FOR you. Nora scolds me as if it were my mother herself telling me this.

Are you taking her side?

I am not taking anyone's side. Both of you have every right to feel as you do. But giving her the cold shoulder doesn't solve anything. Talk with her. You already lost one parent; you don't need to lose the other. Stop hiding. Nora huffs and I can see the puff of cold air disappear through her eyes. She makes sense and being angry isn't the answer. I just feel so useless and the anxiety from the dream doesn't help.

Nora, I'm not hiding. I just need to think.

Yes, you are and think about what? All you need to do is be the one to start the conversation. Think of it this way. You had a whole support group with you that understood what happened with Rick and a mate that has been taking your lead so that you can heal. What did Martha have? She was violated by an elf and when she told her husband, he shrugged it off. She lived with it for over 20 years. Only to then mourn her husband's death by murder. Do you think she had the chance to heal? Nora huffs again and I know she is angry with me. This is the first time she has ever reprimanded me to this extent, and I can't blame her in the least.

... I guess I didn't see it that way. I admit.

Anger does that. So now that you see it, go to her. I'll take you.

Okay.

Nora shakes her fur out and sprints into the snow-covered trees. I wish I could feel the way the wind blows through her fur. I can only feel her emotions but it's enough to tell me it feels wonderful. It isn't long before we reach home. Nora walks around back and scratches the door with a soft bark. Atlas opens up with a slight smile.

"Come in Nora. Is my sister hiding again?" He chuckles.

"WOOF."

Don't agree with that idiot. I'm not hiding.

Uh-huh.

Atlas chuckles again, "Okay let me open her bedroom for you to change. Mom is in her room with Cecile. She refuses to eat anything; just thought I'd mention it."

Nora's claws click on the stairs like mini stilettos against the wood. I am sure my brother is cringing at the thought of the scratches on the floor but that's what he gets for teasing. He opens my bedroom door and Nora barks her thanks.

Kiss ass.

Shut up, whiney pants. I shift back into myself the second the door closes behind us.

Kris?

Yes, Iris? Is everything okay?

I'm fine. I'm home. Just wanted to let you know, I'm safe.

Okay, let me know if you need me to pick you up.

I will. I'm gonna talk to mom.

That's my good girl. I'll be here when you need me.

I pause at him calling me a good girl and make a note to explore that later.

Okay. I reply and my cheeks fill with warmth. *My good girl, okay maybe I like how that sounds,* I smile in thought. With a quick change of clothes, I head over to mom's room, but I can't bring myself to knock. My heart is racing with anger again and it wants to take wings over my mind. These last few weeks have been hell and it's mostly because of her secrets.

Is it though? Would things have happened differently with Liber had you known the truth? Nora asks, making it obvious that she is listening to my thoughts.

I don't know.

Exactly. Stop persecuting your mother before giving her a chance. Nora chimes in before closing herself off. I sigh and raise my fist to knock but hesitate.

"Come in, Iris." My mother calls out behind the door with a trembling tone. She already knows I'm standing here contemplating the situation. I shouldn't be surprised though. It could have been my smell that gave me away. The door creaks open and Cecile stands up from the bed to leave us alone. I try to smile at her as she walks out of the room, but I think I'm making an awkward smirk instead.

"Iris..." Mom calls out to me with her hand extended, beckoning me over to her. I take the spot Cecile left warm on the bed and hold my mother's hand. Now that I am closer to her, I can see how much she has been crying. The red in her eyes, the puffiness underneath, and the crazy bed head most likely from tossing and turning all night. She hasn't slept.

My silence did that.

"Mom, I-"

"No honey, let me say something first." She cuts me off but the plea in her eyes to let her speak first breaks my heart into shattered pieces. I nod. "I had never been more terrified in my life than when I had that dream. Deep down in my heart, I knew what happened but with my dream being dismissed so easily I truly had no choice but to move forward without looking back. I love you more than anything in this world and if you were born anything like me, I knew that everything would be just fine. When the crest first appeared on your wrist as a toddler, I was terrified. Then you did something that I never expected.

"We were on a play date with other pups. I was with the parents while you and the others played in a park. Then a scream caught our attention, and we all ran to you kids and I found you staring at one of the pups who was frozen in place. He was holding your toy. The mother of the child couldn't snap him out of it. She couldn't move him either. It wasn't until I grabbed your attention that the boy then collapsed. You told me he took your toy from you and was sad.

"No one understood what happened, but I knew you were the one controlling him. That was what made me find a way to bind your powers. You are the first elf that I know of that can effectively control magic without a medium." Mom cries all over again but this time I hug her. I hate myself for not seeing how much she is enduring on her own. The only one truly being selfish is me.

"I'm so sorry mom," I apologize over and over.

"It's okay honey, you have every right to be upset as well."

"No mom. No matter how upset I am, that was no way to treat you. Yes, I'm still angry and I hate that I am not my father's daughters but that is no fault of your own. I love you and you did everything you could to protect me. I still think you should have told me when I got a bit older though." I turn to my mother to face her.

"Yes, dear. You're right. I was just scared of what might happen if I did. I'm sorry. But there is one more thing you should know. Before I bound your blood, the witch used a stone to see what kind of magic you were born with. Know that Liber is a dark elf, we expected you to have just as much power as he, if not more. However, the stone that detects the magic of elves, kept changing colors. It wouldn't stay as one. Then it became a swirl of white, blue, and red which eventually turned light shade of purple. This was unheard of.

"Usually, it's either white for summoning magic, blue for elemental magic, or red for the rare few that are born overpowered and have the ability for both summoning and elemental. Yours showed all three colors before combining into purple, a color that has never been expressed before according to elven history."

I lay down next to mom and looked up to the ceiling, "so what does that mean?"

"I don't know but it scared me even more, so we quickly bound your blood, and I prayed to the goddess that the binding never weakened."

"Do you think that's why Liber wants me? You think he knew this would happen?"

Mom turned on her side to face me, "No, he might have gambled on it, but I don't think he is strong enough to divine the future." Mom caressed my cheek. "I truly am sorry I hurt you. I wish that man wasn't your father."

I hug her again, hating myself for not giving her the chance to speak. The chance to say her peace and pave the space for her to heal as Kris did for me.

"Don't apologize, mom. I am the one who is sorry. You did nothing wrong and did it all to protect me from him. I have the best mother a girl could ask for." I mumble the words in the embrace we are squeezing each other in.

You did well, Nora compliments me.

I feel like crap though. I would have done the same now that I know everything.

That's why you shouldn't persecute before a fair trial.

Okay, judge Nora, I get it. I chuckle inside.

Chapter 14

Iris

IT IS A WEEK LATER since showing up with the book. I made up with my mom and am trying to maintain an open mind about the situation with my new bloodline. If I ever am to be a mother, I can only imagine how overprotective I will be with my child. I would also kill Kristofer if he were to ever ignore me when I tell him about any weird dreams.

With a slight nod to myself in the mirror after tying my hair, I grab the spell book from my nightstand. Jesika, who is visiting every day after work is here again and we are going to read out a few spells for me to try.

The thought of the book belonging to my biological father makes the leather of the book feel like acid against my fingers. It's all in my head but the ill feeling that rises within me makes the bile linger in my throat. Sighing, I push the thought aside and open the ancient words of my father.

The book creaks a soft sound of distress as the leather bends around the spine. With my thumb, I flip the pages allowing my eyes to scan them. A simple spell catches my eye, and it is perfect to try and see if I'm capable of practicing. If it is true that my blood has awakened, and my powers are those of elven descent then I should be able to use my powers at will and control them on command.

"Jesika, can you hold up the book so I can read it while I make the hand gestures?" I hand her the book and step back to give us space.

"Sure, just don't turn my hair a weird color." Jesika giggles. She always knows how to lighten the mood and I'm grateful for that. Her friendship has been the light to so many of my dark days.

Jesika holds the book open on the spell and I begin to mimic the hand pictographs.

"From the sky you strike

and with light you fall

Generate with might

Form into a ball"

A crackling sound erupts, and an odd haze takes form into the shape of a ball. It is almost like a Tesla coil without the glass to enclose it. The intensity of it grows the longer I stare at it unsure of how I can create such a thing on my first try.

"Um, Iris? I think you should stop." Jesika warns but her voice is far in my mind. The feeling of the electricity against my hands does more than electrify me ever so gently. It calls to something within me. It beckons something deep, and I want to know what it is.

"I'm fine," I reply but I think I whisper it more to myself than to her. A reassurance to myself that I can keep going and be okay. But I am not sure about something else. Something deep down in the depths of my soul drawing forward. It is reaching out and answering the call that this ball of energy in my hands is bringing forth.

"No, seriously. Stop!" Jesika sounds frantic but even further away than before. The ball of electricity crackles louder in my hand, sending a buzz throughout my body. My hair is standing on end and has me transfixed. "IRIS!"

The shriek that leaves Jesika's throat brings me back to the moment. It drags me out of the tunnel that I found myself walking towards and I snap my head over to her. But in that split second that my attention moves away from my hands, the ball shoots out from between my fingers in a loud clap, and light flashes throughout the entire house.

The windows shatter and the walls shake, leaving me and Jesika screaming in shock. My mother runs into the kitchen in a panic only to die laughing when she sees the state my best friend and I are in.

"What in the world happened for you two to look like that?" Mom holds her stomach while she laughs at our appearance. We turn to one another, and I take in how her hair is standing straight up, her eyes wide open, and her shirt burnt with her sleeves slightly smoking. I can only assume that I look the same or worse.

We keel over laughing at one another and mom walks away without an answer. We are too far gone in our laughter and the ridiculousness of it all.

I straighten my hair back into my ponytail and let the facts sink in. Something is calling out to me and the magic amplifies whatever that something is. With a deep breath and achy sides from laughing too much, I acknowledge that my powers are more than I can handle at the moment. We decide to flip through the book and find a spell that teaches how to manipulate inanimate objects instead. After a few tries of making a pencil levitate, and then writing my name on the wall, I make an origami bird and try and make it fly.

"Oh my god you did…it?" Jesika's excitement falls as the origami bird goes up in flames. Her lips pout at the failed attempt but what I don't tell her is that I feel the lure of whatever beckons me getting stronger. Atlas walks into the room just in time to see the hovering ball of fire and lifts a brow in question when it vanishes.

"Don't ask." I glare at my brother and try to do another spell. With a relaxed hand and soft shoulders, I weave my hands in the air to conjure water. A small droplet forms and eventually a ball of water the size of a baseball floats in the air. Excited to see its working, I break my focus and accidentally send it flying toward Atlas.

Unamused by what I just did, Atlas turns around and leaves while Jesika and I snicker until he leaves the room before we laugh out loud at my brother looking like a wet mop.

"I don't get it." I slump my shoulders in defeat. Whenever I try to do something small, it just goes haywire. Thankfully this time it is water so there isn't any damage unless you take into consideration my brother's hair.

"Try to move that vase to the table." Jesika, who is sitting in one of the chairs, asks giddily.

"Okay, but I don't think I can." I shrug and wave my hand towards the flower vase. The water and flower rise but the vase stays in place, so I let the water down to refill the porcelain decor before I end up having to mop again.

"Okay, um how can I make the vase lift with it?" I try again with the same result.

"Try using the water to tilt the vase over. Essentially you want the vase to be upside down so the water can carry the vase instead of moving it all as a unit. Technically you're manipulating the water and not the vase." Cassius walks in and sits next to Jesika as if watching Houdini with anticipation.

"Carry the vase? hmmm...", I lift the water out of the vase and move it underneath it while swirling it like a disc. I then attempt to lift the vase and to my surprise, it works. However, the concentration to maintain what I am doing is making me break a sweat. The vase is almost at the table when Lenny walks in.

"Anyone made lunch?" Lenny doesn't wait for a response and opens the pantry. The distraction however is enough to have me look away and drop the vase and water by Cassius.

"Oh, my goddess. I am so sorry." I run over to Cassius and grab the vase he manages to catch before it breaks on the table.

"Sure, he gets an apology, but I get a fit of laughter when I was your victim." Atlas walks back in with a new set of dry clothes and his hair slicked back.

"Damn right," I smirk at my brother. He rolls his eyes and then smacks Lenny in the back of the head because he dares to finish off the last of the donuts. The fact that Lenny is already comfortable enough to come in here and eat our food is hilarious to me. Our packs have only been hanging out with one another for a few months since Luna and my brother got together.

"Iris, Kris is here!" Mom calls out at the same time I hear the front door open and close. My heart races a mile a minute making me extremely aware of how I look and if he will still find me attractive.

"Calm down horn dog," Atlas looks at me wiggling his brows.

"Eww, don't ever do that again." We all laugh as Kristofer walks in.

"Who's a horn dog? Cassius or Atlas?" Kristofer asks with a straight face.

I laugh ridiculously hard because it's the first time I see my brother and his mate look so flustered. There has to be more to that story, and I need to know.

Then it dawns on me. I'm laughing. I've been laughing all day. It can't be that I'm fine because I know I'm far from it but being surrounded by so many people that I love may be allowing me to find momentary solace. That must be the reason.

"Did I miss something?" Kristofer hugs me in greeting not missing a beat when he sniffs the smoke off my clothes.

"Hi," I whisper, pulling his attention down to me. I miss his scent invading me the way that it does. He whispers back, and for a second, I forget there are others in the room.

Kristofer

I look around for Finn, hate his name. Last, I hear, he is on cleaning duty for the month and isn't allowed to speak to anyone. Not as severe a punishment as I hoped but as he said, *i'M nOt HiS AlPhA*. Zeus laughs at my inner mocking and agrees that the punishment is light.

"Hey, help me practice." Iris calls out to me, and I gladly oblige. I didn't even notice that I let go of her at some point. We walk out back into the cold of the setting sun.

"How can I help?"

"Well, I want to try something. I figured if I could control water then I should in turn be able to control people. Mom did say that I had an instance as a child when I controlled a kid. So, I want you to stand there while I try to move your arms and legs." Iris smiled as if she is offering me ice cream and not requesting to pull my strings.

"Uh, you want to be a puppet master and me your puppet. Uh, no thank you. I like my limbs where they are," I turn to walk back into the house.

"Oh, come on. Please? I won't hurt you. Don't you trust me?" Iris pouts her lips, and my heart is immediately tugged by the strings she already attached.

"Okay, fine. A little bit," I walk back. "But you need to stop when I ask. Okay?" I can't believe I am agreeing to this but Iris nods in agreement.

Iris

I close my eyes and take a deep breath. *I can do this. I've practiced...a bit,* I think to myself nervousness on overdrive. My fingers twitch as I gather my mental composure. Most of what I read in the book, I can recall, and the small portion written on blood bending gives just enough instruction to attempt.

If I did it before then I can do it again and that thought is the only thing motivating me. I lift my hand and point a finger as I set my eyes on my mate. A rush flows through my body in tingles and an odd sensation builds in my right arm before flowing through to my fingertip. The magic coursing my veins is heavy and a wave of nausea knocks at my throat. With a deep breath, I will the blood in his arm to move on my command.

"This feels weird." Kristofer chuckles but it sounds faint to me. Like distant laughter from a child in their room playing with their toys. Ah. There goes that feeling again. The calling.

"I bet. No one likes to lose control of their body." The words drip off my tongue with more malice than I expected to give. A dark shadow looms over me while dread and despair fill my stomach. I feel sick to my core but most of all, I feel...

Kristofer's arm bends slightly in an odd manner when I cock my head to the side. I look up to his face and smile as his is contorting in pain.

"Iris what are you doing?" He cries as my lips curl to what I assume is a grin. I don't feel like my usual self, and I do. *Now this, this is power.* I think with gratification as I watch my powers control this man with ease.

Iris, snap out of it. Someone inside of me begs. Who is that again? Why can't I remember her name? Oh yea, a wolf.

Stupid dog, mind your business. I reply to the animal inside me trying to stop me.

Iris this isn't you talking. It's consuming you. She nags.

I SAID QUIET! I shut out the mutt from my mind.

Kristofer lets out a howl as his arm snaps back and breaks.

"Iris!" He calls out in pain but it's music to my ears. With the flick of my finger, his other arm snaps as well. "Stop! Please!" His words continue to fall on deaf ears because mine only recognizes the pure delight in his agony. "Iris, please!"

There it goes again. His pain. His begging for me to stop, a symphony made for me. "Doesn't feel too good now, does it?" I smile.

Iris, he is not Rick. Let him go. You'll kill him.

Ah, Nora. That is her name. I thought I shut her out but there she goes butting in again. I ignore Nora's words and lift Kristofer off the ground. Not as high as I hoped but enough. Enough that if he fell, he could hurt himself. I snap one leg and then the other.

"Let me go," Kristofer bellows so loud I almost falter. His whimpers fill the night with a sweet melody.

"Okay, okay, let me see what else I can do." I wipe a tear from my eye and release my hold on Kristofer's blood.

"Iris!" Atlas yells out my name from inside the house.

"Atlas, hel-," Kristofer tries to call for my brother but it's too late. With my other hand, I gesture in circular motions and begin to pull the blood out from within him through his pores. As if to siphon his very life force.

"Oh my goddess, Kris!" Atlas runs out and tries to pull down my dying mate. Tears of blood bleed from his eyes and gurgles form in his throat as he chokes. *What is this feeling? I've never felt this...free!*

"Shit." Atlas tackles me to the ground with the full weight of his body, Alpha tone, and pheromones, suffocating me to force me to stop what I am doing.

"Who are you?" I laugh at the stupid question but Atlas releases more of his pheromones covering me in a thick clouded scent. A wave of nausea strangles my throat, and I snap out of it as something drips from my nose. *Blood?* A thud breaks the silence but neither I nor Atlas look back. I can tell he is mind-linking with someone and most likely it's to get Kristofer some help.

He must be the one who just fell. My heart beats erratically in my chest matching the rhythm of my breathing. I can see everything happening, but I am unable to understand why it is happening. The feeling is like the full moon shift when I am inside Nora, no longer in control.

"I..I.." I stare at my brother unable to explain what is happening and worst of all why. But I remember it all vividly. "Iris. I'm Iris." I fumble, ready to cry.

"Iris wouldn't do this to anyone, especially not her mate, and my sister's eyes were never completely blacked out. But you…" Atlas huffs and grabs my shoulders lifting me and slamming me back down to the ground. "Who are you?" He yells as light flashes before my eyes from the impact on the back of my head.

His voice cracks and I can see the tears beginning to form.

"Atlas, it's me…I-"

"STOP LYING!" Atlas cries and the shock of it makes me gasp as if a veil is lifting from me. My vision clears more so than before, and my mind is once again clear of the dark fog. The calling is gone.

"Iris?" Atlas' tears drip down my cheek. "Are you back?" his voice is so gentle that I barely here the words off his tongue.

"I-I think so."

"Your eyes, they're normal again. They're hazel." Atlas sighs with relief and hugs me tighter than I care for, but I don't feel the same relief he does.

"Kristofer...I... I couldn't stop. It just...and I just watched...I-I..." I break down in his arms. The darkness. It is relentless and it may have cost me my mate.

"Before Kris, we need to talk about what just happened. You looked like a completely different person." Atlas helps me up. I must face what I have done. But I don't want to.

"It's hard to say for sure if it is me or something else. It was like, the second I began to control his blood, darkness took over. All my anger, fear, and hate turned into power. It drove my actions, my words, and my thoughts. I felt like I was sitting in the back seat while I watched my body enjoy the pain it was inflicting. Or rather I was inflicting. There was a darkness that called out to me and then took over." My hands tremble, remembering how Kristofer cried. *How did I find joy in that?*

"Then what if that's what Liber is banking on?" Atlas paces back and forth. "Iris I can't just let this slide", he avoids my eyes but as Alpha, he is right. I shouldn't get special treatment just because I am his sister. What I did is wrong and most importantly it makes me dangerous.

"I'll take whatever punishment you deem fit but first, I want to see Kris." I'm doing everything to not break. But I am there. I am at that point. One slight wind will cause me to topple over the edge that I am standing on.

"Iris-"

"I'm scared, Atty", I cry into my hands cutting him off.

"You only called me that when you were a kid. What are you scared of? The punishment or-"

"My powers!" I cut him off again. "How angry I felt, the way I enjoyed it, everything. What if I'm a monster now? What if I always was a monster? I wasn't in control back there, my anger was. It's like everything I've been feeling since Rick, came gushing out and I liked it. I didn't mean for any of that to happen and I don't want it to happen again, but I liked it the feeling." Tears drain from my face.

"Well, I can tell you with certainty that you're not a monster. I think you have been dealing with a lot on your own. You need to talk to someone. A therapist. Don't bottle things up. I know what holding something inside you for a long time feels like. It's torture. One I don't wish for you to endure. " Atlas strokes my arm trying his best to comfort me.

"But...I hurt Kris. How is that not proof that I'm evil?"

"Because Raven is your father. Our father. Not that bastard. You are a good person, one who used to cry for me when I fell or when mom would punish me by kneeling over rice. You would say that if you cried for me instead, it would make my pain go away faster. How is a person like that, evil?" He opens his arms, and I hug my brother while crying harder than before, "Come, let's see Kris."

***

The house is buzzing but when my smell hits their noses the whispers die down making it obvious, that it is me they are buzzing about. I walk into the infirmary and find blood everywhere. Kristofer's face is lacerated, bruises cover his neck, he is being placed in a brace because his spine broke in four places, and his limbs seem to need casts as well.

I can't stomach this. How can I do this to my mate, my partner? "Atlas, I don't think..." I back up slowly, but Atlas stops me from leaving.

"Iris?" A strained voice calls out for me. The one eye that isn't swollen shut looks at me. "Come."

My feet carry me to my mate, but I don't know how I am still standing with how my legs shake beneath me.

Nora, I can't do this. I can't see him.

You can and you will. YOU did this, Iris. Nora reminds me but that is the exact reason why I can't.

Nora, I didn't mean to. I falter in my step towards my mate.

It doesn't change the fact you still did it, now does it? All you can do is make sure it doesn't happen again.

"Iris, please *cough* don't cry." Kristofer tries to speak but his weak voice is hoarse and grainy.

"I'm so sorry Kris. I told you to trust me and... all I did was..." I look down at his body where Sylvie and another wolf are placing the second cast on his legs.

"Iris, did you plan to do this to me?" Kristofer manages to ask and the hurt in his voice is deep. Emotional. Raw.

"NO! Never. I-"

"Then don't blame yourself. It's not like you forced me to stay and help you. I chose to do so." Kristofer starts a coughing fit and it chips away at me. I hand him a glass of water with, trembling, only to realize he can't hold it nor lift himself to drink it.

"I'll get him a straw." Atlas steps out of the room quickly before returning with one in hand.

"Here you go," I place the straw in the cup and bend it towards Kristofer.

"Thank you," he sighs. "You couldn't have known you'd lose your control to magic. If anything, we learned that controlling blood shouldn't be taken lightly and maybe it isn't something you should do." Kristofer coughs again and I quickly give him more water.

"Yeah, I don't think I ever want to try it again. I don't know what I was thinking." My voice breaks and I feel another round of tears coming. He says I couldn't have known but that feeling that I had. That dark energy that coursed through me was something I felt before.

Ever since that dream with my father, that feeling has lingered.

Kristofer screams when Sylvie begins the cast on his arm, and it scares me out of my thoughts. I give his body a once over again. His strong capable body and I broke it. The arms that held me and comforted me are in tatters because of my darkness.

I run out of the room not wanting to face it. I can't. I don't want to have this power, nor do I deserve Kristofer's love.

Chapter 15

Iris

THE BRIGHT MOON SHINES through the window inside my cell in my brother's basement. Before he could think of a proper punishment for me, I asked him to put me here. I am scared to lose control again. The feeling of enjoying the power scares me more than the power itself. There is no way that I will allow myself to ever be that person again. Yet, it explains so much about my father. If he felt even a fraction of what I do, then I get it. The only difference is, he gives into it while I abhor it.

Chills run down my spine. The amount of silver in this cell is uncomfortable. The silver on the bars prevents me from touching them and the silver-filled chains on my wrist that were modified just for me, somehow prevent me from using my magic. I am not sure how but the simple fact of having something hollow and filled with silver, isn't allowing me to produce anything.

After the first three days of being here in solitude, I tried using my powers. The need to practice good magic is great. I thought that maybe if I can practice enough good, it can counter the bad feelings. Simple ones that I learned should be enough that I can fine-tune my abilities. But nothing happens when I try. My power is there within me, but it is buried behind a veil of sorts.

After a week of crying every day and screaming in anger, I bang my fists against the wall until they bleed and then fall asleep from exhaustion. There is no doubt in my mind that it is the elf in me that is dark, and I hate that it wants to get out. There is nothing else that can explain where all this is coming from.

A cool draft seeps in from the window. The night is young, and I know bathing in the moonlight will do me some good, but I am scared to remove the chains.

"I wish it were me instead," I mumble to myself.

"You think Kristofer would enjoy hearing that?" Cassius walks down the stairs into the basement.

"If it was me who was hurt, I wouldn't feel this miserable." I cry again surprised that I still have tears left to cry.

"Don't say that. You will learn in time how to wield what you have been given. I trust you to use your abilities wisely now that you know how powerful your magic can be." Cassius puts on gloves.

"What are you doing?" I snap.

"Getting you out so we can practice."

"NO!" I yell and the bars shake a little. I guess I can still use some magic after all. "I don't want to hurt anyone else. Just leave me alone."

"So, you plan on hiding down here forever? What about Kris?"

"What about him? He's better off without me. I can't...I don't want to hurt him again." I turn around and face the wall.

"Stop it, Iris. You know that is not true. He is miserable right now because he hasn't seen you. You think he doesn't feel the mind fuck you are experiencing?" Cassius proceeds to remove the chains around the lock and open the cell.

"Cassius, please. I don't think I can do it. And why are you even wearing gloves. Silver doesn't hurt you." I beg and back away until I am against the wall.

Cassius walks in shrugging off what I said and sits on the bed next to me, "did you know that I slept on this very bed once before?"

"Huh?"

"I guess Atlas didn't tell you how they found me unconscious in a cave and then treated my wounds before locking me in here?" Cassius chuckles.

"No. He never did." I turn to him and then sit where he is patting the bed.

"It was love at first sight with your brother. I can't imagine a life without him and trust me there were times when I thought he was better off without me too because of my father." Cassius sighs and twiddles his thumbs.

"He doesn't know this but, when my father came into the picture, I thought this was it. I thought I was going to die a young man. I had no faith in myself, nor did I understand my powers. Deep down I truly think I won against him out of sheer luck and a pinch of stupid bravado."

"I can't imagine what it must have been like for you. Didn't your father want you dead?" I scoot closer to Cassius. I never realized how similar our situations are.

"Yea. He wanted me probably for the same reason your father wants you. Our blood holds great power. Yet that doesn't make us evil. It's how we use it that defines us. I think you are simply not ready to use that level of magic yet. You need to build endurance to it and heal the heart before attempting anything on that scale." My brother-in-law ruffles my hair with the giant glove he has on.

"I'm scared Cass," I look up at him teary-eyed.

"I know but that's why you can't stay in here. Let me help you find your strength." Cassius hugs me and I cry just a little into his chest. "It's okay, let it all out." He strokes my head until I stop. He pulls me away and a long snot stretches from my nose to his hair, "You're disgusting." His face makes me chuckle just a little and I use the blanket to wipe his hair and my nose. "That's more disgusting."

"Don't worry, I'll throw it in the wash."

"Okay, well let's get those chains off you. Go sleep in your room and tomorrow morning we begin." Cassius proceeds to remove my cuffs and escort me to my room. It is going to be a long night.

***

I follow a trail on the floor being careful with my step. Wet earth and incense fill my lungs. Something is wrong. The path I follow widens and, in the clearing, I can see mountains. I walk further but the closer I get the more those mountains don't seem to be as high nor were they mountains at all. Piles of bodies lay lifeless on the ground while holes filled the earth far and wide.

Flies cover the dead and, in the center, I see a lion...*a shifter?*

Yes, I'm a lion shifter.

What's happening? I ask, hoping I am just seeing things.

Help us...

Huh? I look around to see who else he is referring to.

Help us! The shifter screams and suddenly like a ghost, he flies towards me and through me.

I scream, waking up in a cold sweat. It feels like I haven't slept at all but evidently, I did, given that the sun is up and invading my room.

A knock raps on my door, "Come eat so we can train."

"Okay," I yell back at Mr. Bushy Tail Cassius.

I bathe to rid my body of the sweat and shrug off the dream that most likely is from stress. After I am done and dressed, I sit down in the kitchen for a light breakfast and push around the eggs not feeling my appetite anymore.

"Hey, it's okay."

I look at my brother-in-law, "I didn't say anything".

"I can feel Nora stirring inside you." Cassius gives an apologetic smile.

"Oh, I'm just nervous is all." I lie, I'm terrified, especially after that dream but I won't say it out loud.

"Okay, I think that is far enough."

"I don't feel like eating. Can we just go train?" I push the plate to the side and sip the coffee instead.

"Okay fine. Let's go. We are burning daylight anyways." Cassius gets up and I am on his tail.

"The first thing we need to learn is control. One thing I learned to be the foundation of it all, is controlling my breathing and then my emotions."

I nod and mimic what he does. But my mind isn't fully present. It wanders with each given moment. I take a deep breath doing my best to clear my mind and slow my breathing. *Ugh, my dream.* My heart thumps a bit slower but I can't seem to keep it steady.

"Now as if you have been doing this all your life, control the water in that well by the shed and fill the bucket next to it. Feel it. Envision it."

I nod and roll my arms towards myself. Flashes of Kristofer's body writhing in pain flash before me. The piles of bodies from my dream. I twitch as the water emerges from the well in an eruption, sending water everywhere but the bucket.

"Try to focus, you well until you feel the control of the water. Try again"

I bite my lip and try again doing the same motion with my arms. The water comes up again and I sway my hands slowly to drop the water into the bucket. At least that's what I want to happen. Instead, the water crashes down so hard, that the bucket cracks and breaks apart.

"That was good. In the end, I think you got a little excited. Try to maintain control the entire time. Don't let your mind wander. Again." Cassius crosses his arms in wait.

"But I don't have a bucket now."

"Oh, yeah. Um...gimme a sec." Cassius runs into the shed and pushes out our wheelbarrow. "Put the water in here."

"Are you crazy? What if I break that too? Atlas will kill me and then you." I look back to see if my brother is already making his way toward me.

"Bah, leave your brother to me." He chuckles.

He's right. Who am I kidding? My brother would kill me but only slap Cassius' wrist before he kisses it and apologizes for tapping it too hard.

I lift the water the same way as before from the well and maneuver it over the wheelbarrow. Slowly this time, I lower my hands and fill my new target. The excitement of filling my target is overwhelming. Even with this being a small victory, it is a victory, nonetheless. I jump for joy without thinking and add an extra bit of pressure in the last bit of the water before fully releasing it.

"Shit!" Cassius curses as the water crashes down and forcing the weight of the water to pop off the front wheel. The tire bounces once before rolling for a bit and resting on the grass. "Uh, so I'm going to hide this under a tarp." Cassius tips it over the barrel to drain the water and runs inside the shed to hide the damage. *So much for handling my brother,* I smirk at the thought, but an odd sensation tickles the back of my neck. The unease of my dream lingers again.

"Okay, let's pause on the water and move to the next lesson, which is fire, and this, I know well. Earlier you said you made an origami go up in flames, right?"

"Yeah."

"Okay now let's control conjuring a small flame first." Cassius starts to shift into Shoneah. The tattoos spread across his body in a way that seems familiar. *This is like my dream. It's like the veins,* I push the thought aside.

It's not exactly the same, but now the image of it won't go away. Cassius opens his hands and a tiny blue light forms in the center. It grows until a ball is formed and then spreads outward like a glove over his hand.

"It's all about envisioning what you want to produce. I always picture a specific spot inside my body that stores my fire. Whether that's really how it is, I doubt it, but it helps me accurately use what I need and control the force. I picture that storage area in my body open and pulling out however much power I need and then that energy traveling down my arm and into my hand. Once I physically start to see the fire, I then picture the shape I want it to be." Cassius stands behind me and places both his arms under mine.

"What are you doing?" I ask, curious about the odd position we are standing in.

"I want you to feel how my magic travels and then use that feeling to produce your own."

"Uh, won't I burn?" the skepticism evident in my voice.

"No, I control the fire which in turn controls what damage I want to inflict. I can even heal with my fire if I wish it to do so." Cassius sounds proud of himself, as he should be. If ever I can become as calm and confident as him with my abilities, I'd be proud too.

"Okay, I trust you."

Cassius lifts my arms with his and places his palms against the back of my hands. It's weird but I can understand why he does this the second our skin touches. His magic courses down his arms against my skin from his shoulders to the tips of his fingers.

Again, my dream rears its ugly head. It trails like a soft tingle with a bit of sparks that travels against my skin and morphs into black veins. As the magic reaches our hands, I gasp at the little ball of flames in my palm when he flips our hands over. But that too changes into darkness.

A black ball of fire takes shape, swirling like a void ready to suck me in. My chest tightens and my throat constricts, making it hard to breathe. The power feeding from his hand flowing into mine send a surge through me, suffocating. It is entrapping me in the same kind of pull it had that night. This evil that lurks within me is pulling free as it grabs hold of this magic that Cassius is releasing, and I pay the price of admission by fading into the black hole of its vortex. I shrivel into the nothingness.

"Iris, are you okay?" A distant voice calls out to me.

My eyes are heavy, but I lift them enough to see Cassius hovering over me, still in his shaman mode, "what happened?"

I wince trying to lift my head. The weight of my body lends to the idea that I am drugged. Like a heavy sedation barely wearing off.

"You blacked out before we could even start. You scared me there for a second." Shoneah's appearance disperses, and Cassius is back to his original form.

"What do you mean? I saw you make the fireball." I sit up with Cassius' help and squeeze his hands when everything spins.

"No, I stood behind you and asked if you were ready to start but instead of a response, you collapsed." He picks a leaf off my arm.

"How is that possible? I can still feel your energy in my hand."

"Nope. If you're not up for it. We can go back inside for now. Maybe you need some rest." Cassius smiles sympathetically.

"I'm fine. Show me what to do." I wave off his worry but there is no denying that I am a bit scared of what just happened.

Cassius nods and repositions behind me exactly like before. He releases his magic, and it travels down the length of my arms but this time, I do not feel the darkness. The flame that forms in our hands is a gentle vivid blue.

"This is so cool and you're right, it doesn't burn!" I know I sound like a child in awe of her big brother-in-law, but it is magnificent to experience up close what is now so normal to him. Especially now that it doesn't feel like the air is being pulled out from my lungs. This is the opposite, in fact. It is calming and soothing with a light that fills me up and chases away the remaining shadows hiding within me.

Cassius laughs, "Now try and use that same feeling. Imagine where your storage box would be and pull out the amount of magic you need."

I inhale deeply and close my eyes, picturing a small box close to my shoulder. It is small and intricate, like a treasure box made of wood and gold trim. The key is in the lock waiting for me to twist it open and lift the lid.

Reaching in, I pull out a bit of fire magic from inside and close the lid. My right shoulder warms up, but I continue to envision it rolling down my arm as I lift it before me. The tingles and sparks race down my arm along with the magic which feels rather ticklish. Almost playful.

Then another similar box appears, a dark red one with black burnt carvings engraved all around it. My instincts tell me I shouldn't touch it, but it opens on its own regardless. A dark cloud spills out like a miasma of death. I shake my head and refocus. I won't let the contents of that box have its way again.

The box pulls back the dark cloud and shuts itself closed before it disappears. The knot forming in my stomach settles and I no longer feel the dread from before. A bit of heat builds in the center of my hand from the original wooden box in almost a swirling motion. It feels nice against my skin.

"Iris, open your eyes," Cassius whispers into my ear but I keep them closed. What if the flames are black or red?

"Iris, open!" He says louder this time and the excitement in his voice has me curious. I slowly part my eyes to witness purple flames circling in my hands. Tears well up and I close my fists extinguishing the flames in relief.

I'm not...evil. I'm good...

Kristofer

I flip the pages of the book Atlas lent me, feeling better than I did a week ago. My arms are healed, and my left leg is back in shape but my right leg and back are still on the mend. My right leg unfortunately didn't set right, and the healing process was excruciating. Sylvie knocked me out with painkillers and an anesthetic before she broke my bone again to reset it. This is the first time I have been hurt to this extent and I now know that wolves heal slower when they have extensive injuries.

I simply thought that we healed quickly no matter what, but that is no longer the case. It makes sense the more I think about it. If the body is forced to spread its resources so thinly to help heal itself, then it makes sense for it to take longer to accomplish the task.

Now, my back is another story. Two parts of it have mended but the third place it broke is still not quite there. I have movement but it's stiff and I don't have full range of it just yet. I put the book down wishing for Iris' warmth instead of this lonely recovery.

"I miss your smile," I whisper to myself. Nothing could have prepared me for this but even though I am on the mend I can't say that I am not scared. Not for me but for my mate. She has this power in her that she can't control. It is being fueled by her anger and the more she gives into it, the darker it may likely become. The way the cabin is destroyed is enough proof that she is formidable but with the way she is now, she is dangerous.

Iris is a raw ball of power that is struggling to stay contained. Had it been anyone else, a child, her mother, her brother, anyone, what would be of her mind then?

I sigh, placing the book on my chest and groan when I twist slightly to cover myself better with the blanket. My pain and condition are prime examples of the danger she poses not just to others but to herself. The only thing I can do now is pray to the goddess that she learns to wield her magic and gain the strength to be confident even if just a little. I love her more with each passing day and only wish for her happiness, even with her being a nuke and her father hovering his finger over the detonator.

I don't know if she knows that I am not mad at her, but I guess that's why she isn't visiting me. Her guilt must be overriding every thought. The link between us is shut off and the only thing keeping me at ease is that I can smell her in the house and at times I am sure she is standing behind the bedroom door. Every night I am graced with the smell of brownies and marshmallows seeping from under the door.

Like now, it wraps me tight and holds me there like a hug made for me alone and yet in that sweet embrace I feel her sadness.

"Iris..." I whisper and a whispered gasp carries the scent away.

Chapter 16

Kristofer

A WEEK AND A HALF of loneliness keeps me company as I've yet to see Iris in person. I can't speak with her either through our link since she refuses to open up to me. The only thing that I have to give me comfort is the nightly visit at my door.

Iris stays there for a while before retreating to bed and it gives me comfort that she still thinks to come near even through her pain. I won't lie and say that I have not been tempted to open the door when I know she is standing there.

My back is fully healed, and I can walk again without assistance. I am back to normal and yet I can't get my feet to go to her myself. I look out the window as I have been doing the last couple of mornings and catch Iris practicing her magic outside. She looks beautiful wielding her flames and glistening beneath the water she commands.

She dances with the fire and water twirling simultaneously with a smile on her face. Iris has mastered her ability to control them with how elegantly they take shape and interlock with one another. How I wish to hold her and tell her it is not her fault and that I have erased the memory. Iris looks my way spotting me at the window. My breath hitches and in a childish attempt I say,

Hi, I know the link is closed but a fool can dream.

Hi, she replies and my heart skips a beat at the sound of her voice.

You're doing great out there. *Ugh, what the hell am I saying?*

I don't know about that, but you sound like a creep. Zeus chimes in and laughs at his remark.

Shut up, Zeus!

I'm doing my best. I don't want to be the monster I was in front of you. The smile drops from her lips.

Iris, you were never a-

Kris, stop. I know what I did, and I am truly sorry. I can never make up for it, but I can learn so that it won't happen again. I just need time. A tear rolls down her cheek and the pain gathering in my chest swells with my own.

Babe, you're not or ever was a monster. You are Iris Ellwood. A badass woman I am honored to call my mate. You don't have to do this alone. I am here for you, no matter what. Iris stares at me for a bit as if trying to find a way to refute my plea.

Do you want some hot chocolate? Iris cleverly redirects the conversation and twiddles her thumbs.

Hmm, will it have roasted marshmallows? I ask while relishing in how adorable she looks.

Of course, a very handsome man showed me how to make it. And there it is, her smile. I let go of a breath and fill my lungs with relief.

Looks like I have competition then. I reply with a smile and watch as she makes her way inside the house.

***

"What's wrong?" I ask Iris who is downing her second cup of hot chocolate.

"So, I had another dream...err vision."

"Vision?" I ask and finish the rest in my mug.

"While Cass was helping me train, I saw lion shifters and piled bodies everywhere. The shifter asked for my help before he disappeared."

Her sorrowed expression flickers with the memory of the vision and my heart breaks at how deep her sadness goes, "Iris, what do you think it means?"

"I don't know but I'm scared. My head is a mess trying to figure out what it means. I can't tell up from down anymore. I thought I was making progress but after I hurt you, I..." She takes a deep breath trying to calm herself, but I scoop her into my arms and hold her against me. The chair falls to the floor from the sudden movement.

"Iris, I am here. Feel my strength. I know you're scared but we will get through this together. I am just as terrified about all of this, but I have faith in us getting through it. I have faith in you and your strength.

I will not go anywhere. Even if you had broken every bone in my body, I would have found a way to quickly heal and hold you as I do now." I squeeze her tighter trying to pour of all my love to fill the parts of her that is sad and afraid.

"Kristofer, don't say things like that." She sniffles.

"But it's true. What happened was a mistake but one that can be learned from, and I love you no less for it. Please have as much faith in me as I do in you." I pull away from Iris to look her in her watery hazel eyes.

"I do have faith in you. It's me I lack faith in." Iris pulls out of my arms and walks away, leaving me once again alone.

***

I can't say what time it is but sitting here for so long has my mind in circles. The frustration of not knowing what to do to help Iris is weighing on me in a way I didn't expect. All I want to do is help but she is so lost in figuring it out on her own while she beats herself up over it that it's difficult to get through to her. Yet, I also understand this is something she needs to do for herself.

"Maybe I should go for a run?" I mumble to myself. Going back to sleep is not an option. It's still a little dark out and the sun won't be up until another hour or so. The dark morning is chilly, and the air smells of a possible snowfall. This winter has been colder than most, but I welcome it against my skin. I prefer it over the hot summer days.

Skittering from the trees reminds me of the impending sunrise. The sky is progressively getting brighter welcoming the new day. I do some light stretching of my legs and make my way to the back of the house. Maybe clearing my senses will help refresh my mind.

The bite from the cold nips at me trying to stiffen my muscles but it fails to do so as they warm up in the light jog. My breath leaves trails behind me with every huff taking my stress along with it. *This feels nice,* I haven't had time to myself like this in a while. When before it was all, I had and hated it, I now appreciate the small moments of solitude.

My jogging picks up into a run and the warmth in my bones energizes me like a fresh pair of batteries placed in a new toy. My movements are becoming more fluid and the bits of me that were still needing repair fade away into a memory better left forgotten.

After a while of running, my feet find their way home. It wasn't my intent, but I am so lost in thought, that my inner compass brought me here. I go in through the back door without so much as a sound. Alex must have finally oiled the screen door like I asked him to as it didn't squeak as if it were being murdered.

I don't want to wake anyone who might still be asleep so I carefully close the door behind me before the wind can slam it shut. I wonder if Iris is doing okay because my mind naturally wanders to her if my thoughts are idle for too long. Then again, even when they are not, she is all I think of. This run made me realize that smothering her could be just as crippling. She needs to come to me on her own terms without me pressuring her.

Gently, I take one step at a time to prevent the floor from creaking too loudly, when voices and laughter make me pause mid step. *Who's up at this hour?*

More giggling ensues, "Stop making me laugh. Everyone is going to wake up."

A soft low growl vibrates through the air, "Not my fault you're ticklish." More giggles.

"I swear Demi, stop." The whispers sound all too much like Alex and his smell only confirms it. *Alex and...no way, really?* I recognize that other scent anywhere.

"Then kiss me and I'll stop." The deep husky voice from my Beta replies. *What the hell did he just say?*

"Demi, I told you. I don't want to start anything. You know your mate is out there. I'm not going to get in the way-" Alex is suddenly cut off, but I can't tell why. I tip-toe closer and stop when they start to moan in unison.

"Demi... please." A breathy voice whispers from Alex. *Oh my goddess, what am I listening to?!?!*

THEY FUCKING?! Zeus with his vulgar mouth shouts in my head the obvious.

I turn around and begin to tip-toe back towards the door, so I can make a louder entrance to alert them.

"Shhh, baby. Just focus on me right now."

Baby? What the hell? I cannot process what's happening. Another moan reaches my ears. Alex is most definitely enjoying whatever my Beta is doing a bit too much.

I know you're there Kris. My Beta pops in my head. That dirty geezer. He knew and didn't stop.

What the hell Demetrius? Or should I say, Demi!

He's, my mate. My Beta responds quickly. Frozen mid-step, I stare at the wall in front of me. How does that make sense? Alex thinks Demetrius has a different mate.

If that's true, why did he say that? This guy either thinks I'm stupid or deaf.

For some reason, he doesn't know. The bond hasn't affected him for some reason, but I've known since his eighteenth birthday.

Then stop talking to me about it, you idiot, tell him instead. I reach for the door.

I'm scared.

Ugh, let's talk about this later big guy, not while you guys are sucking faces or... other things. I shut off the link and leave to make my way back to Atlas' pack house instead.

That is the last thing I expected. I guess it makes sense why they were always together. I did notice how Alex is no longer hung up on Cassius and how his eyes always follow my Beta but to think he did so without realizing they are mates. He must truly like him and when he does discover the truth, I fear they will be worse than rabbits.

Man, that pup is lucky. He found his mate right away whether he knows it or not. *I wonder if the ten-year gap bothers them.* Well, I guess not since they were just going at it. Didn't seem like the first-time playing hanky-panky either.

I close the door behind me softly and greet the cold once more. The air is crisp filling my lungs as I take a step off the porch. A scream echoes through the area making my hairs stand on end. I look around before realizing the screaming is in my head.

Kris help! Iris comes blaring into my mind louder this time and I run in her direction.

What's wrong?

Liber is here!

Chapter 17

Kristofer

MY BREATHING GROWS heavy as I run into the woods. With as much as I can muster, I hammer out my legs into a sprint but with the exertion from earlier, I lose my footing. The fire burning in my legs has me tripping and down I go like a felled tree.

This is more exercise than I intended but life never goes as planned. Disregarding the advice of the doctor I shift into Zeus. If it hinders my healing, then so be it. I do my best to stay calm but the thought of Liber doing something to Iris is making me imagine the worst-case scenario. Zeus sends a mind-link to the pack to prepare to fight and to call our allied packs.

This can't be happening. Not now when none of us are ready. But that could be precisely what Liber is banking and I won't give him the satisfaction of being right.

While Zeus is making good time with his run, he is still struggling with his hind legs. I send a prayer to the goddess to keep my mate safe and to give me and

Zeus the strength we need to make it on time. It is all I can do at the moment.

I've alerted Alpha Robert, Alpha Vinny, and Luna Melody. They will be here soon. Demetrius links with Zeus which fills me with a bit of relief knowing that reinforcements will arrive.

Thank you. Zeus replies.

The cold air and glaring snow make it more difficult for Zeus to navigate. The snow isn't fluffy anymore but instead a melting sludge that is slowing down our steps. Light from the morning sun dances between the trees the higher it rises, aiding in turning the sludge into puddles. Clumps of snow plop from branches frightening Zeus the first couple of times. It doesn't help that I am on edge as well and am adding to him being jumpy. But Zeus is our best bet in making it on time for whatever may happen.

Now that the sun is high enough, the woods resemble a world of mirrors. Each step is more difficult than the last with his legs going numb. Blinded by the reflection, the grueling run finally nears its end.

Zeus and I see the house, so he picks up his speed ignoring the tears forming from the glare or the painful burn in his muscles. He can smell Iris and the others along with a very unfamiliar stench. A mixture of rotting wood and sulfur clinging the hairs of his snout.

A tall slender man with long dark blond hair comes into view and he is holding Atlas by the throat. The owner of such an offending smell according to Zeus, stands overlooking the others with their leader in hand. Zeus snarls and carefully walks over to Iris' side, limping. Seeing her safe lessens the tension I have but not enough to make me feel any better.

Cassius runs out from around the back of the pack house and shifts into Shoneah. Tattoos trail down his body with blue flames forming like gloves around his fist. This is something that Zeus, I, and the others can't get used to. It's an experience that exhilarates anyone who bears witness and fear to those on the receiving end. Shoneah lifts his hands as if holding something. A stance meant for those wielding a sword. Zeus stands in front of Iris and wraps his tail around her leg.

Cassius as Shoneah

Liber flinches at the sight of me. I can only hope my appearance is enough to deter him and for a moment Liber falters in keeping his poker face. His eyes flicker over my arms, taking in how I look but more importantly, trying to assess how much of a threat I may be. He tosses my mate aside after regaining his composure and steps towards me. A hint of recognition flashing for a second behind his dark eyes.

"I wouldn't take another step if I were you." I snap angrily at how he manhandled my mate and right before me no less. My fists hurt from how hard I am clenching them, but I increase the size of my flames to assert myself.

"Funny. Now, who might you be?" Liber de Beur chuckles mockingly. *Does he not find me threatening enough?* My confidence wavers ever so slightly but I can't show that to him. I can't give him the upper hand. He has already done too much damage to this family. My family. And it stops here.

"My name is Shoneah."

Liber stops and stares as if looking at a ghost, but I doubt he was alive the last time a shaman reincarnated. For a moment, fear fills his dark dead-like eyes but just as quickly, it's gone. The black coal of his irises softens into a cool collected gaze, examining me as he would a spell book. A smile curves the corners of his lips, replacing any idea that I stand a chance, with doubt.

"I've heard of you. You're something like a reincarnated bitch, right?" Liber's words are acid to my ears. How can he say something like that so easily? I shudder with his words hitting every nerve in my body. But I steady my feet; I know better than to feed into the dark elf and his empty words. That could be a second mistake with the first being me underestimating him.

"Nice to know you've heard of me, although I have no idea who you are," I smirk. I have no idea if this will work. It's the only card I have to buy us time.

You idiot, why are you taunting him? Wolfie snaps at me.

Because if I can separate him from the others, there will be fewer casualties.

Oh, okay. Carry on. Wolfie knows I'm right. Even if I am the only casualty, it is better than all of us dying.

"You talk a lot for a mutt. Why not mind your business while I have a chat with my daughter." Liber turns his back to face Iris. The way she steps back means I need to stall longer. She is terrified and needs a moment to find her courage. I just hope she finds it quickly.

"Oh, will you look at this? He's scared." I try to laugh menacingly but it comes out more like nervous laughter. I'm not good at playing mister tough guy but I must do something to distract him. One last attempt to force Liber into a fight with me alone, works.

Liber turns around swinging, sending a blade of water through the air in my direction. The water hardens into ice midair and narrowly misses my cheek as I bend backward attempting to dodge. "You dare speak down to me, dog!" Another blade of ice flies towards me but I manage to dodge that as well. Libers movements are becoming quicker and looking away from him could prove my downfall.

I will distract Liber. Everyone, try and get out of here. I mind link with all the wolves that had been out and about. They aren't warriors and I need them safely out of the way if an all-out fight were to break out with more than just me and this elf.

"Is that all you've got?" My mouth is on a roll but why stop now? I continue my taunts while backing away in the opposite direction from everyone else. From the corner of my eye, I can see Atlas regaining consciousness on the ground and my heart does a slight somersault. I can breathe a bit better and refocus on the bastard of an elven father before me.

Liber yells in anger, clasps his hands together, and pulls them apart to form a ball of red fire. Like a pitcher from a baseball game out of hell, he throws the fire hard and fast. However, with the speed it flies toward me, I can't dodge it fully. It hits my shoulder making me stumble back. The pain from his flames is nothing I have ever felt. It burns hotter than regular fire and burns more than just my flesh. It is eating away at something inside as if consuming my essence.

I scream with the smell of my burnt flesh choking me. "You son of a-" I bite my tongue and take my stance once more. If he throws another fireball, I'll be ready. Pulling a healthy dose of magic from within me, I engulf my arms in my flames to heal myself and prepare for his next attack. Fighting fire with fire is a game I can play but he won't see mine coming.

"What are you doing? You hold nothing," Liber laughs at the stance I take and throws another fireball at me.

This is my chance. The fireball spins rapidly as it hurls my way in fury. The heat of it makes it hard to see the closer it gets but I swing. Twisting my body and using the momentum to drive my arms at full throttle, I swing. A sword made of my blue flames rises from my fist and connects with the red fireball. "Catch," I spit out as I send it back hurling to Liber with double the speed from before. The red ball of fire swirls as it hurls towards Liber mixed with my blue flames in a spiral of destruction.

The heaving ball of fire hits Liber in the stomach, sending him flying a few feet and landing on his back. The fire burned through his clothes, exposing the burnt flesh of his abdomen. Liber struggles to catch his breath and stays down for a bit to regain his composure. I look around to make sure everyone is gone and contemplate my next move.

Something is wrong, Wolfie sounds worried.

What do you mean?

The last to make a run for it is being held back by lion shifters.

What?! He had backup?!

I need to do something, but I don't know what. The ache in my ribs, threaten to break with my trembling heart. I can't protect everyone at once. Even I don't have mastery of my powers, but this man is going out of his way to get Iris without caring as to who crosses him. He fights me as if we are lifelong enemies and for what? To talk with his daughter? How is it that, even as a shaman, I can't find the right thing to do?

This man is ruthless with his means. So much of my father is in this man and then it hits me. The real reason I am choking up with this fight and it's terrifying. I am facing my father all over again.

"You tricked me." Liber groans. He rolls over onto his side and stands up clenching his stomach. "You're stronger than you let on, aren't you?" Flashes of him and my father begin to melt into one another.

The person I am fighting no longer looks like an elf but like a hybrid of the worst fathers in history.

He drops his hand and the skin on his abdomen looks healed and untouched. Nausea fills my throat and chokes the air out of my lungs as flashes of him and my father continue to blur into one another, but I can't falter, not now.

"You talk too much." I mock but I know it's useless if I don't know what to do next. Libers face fills with rage and one by one he launches fireballs at me. Each one that comes towards me, I deflect with my flame sword. But all I see at this point is how much Liber is like Honovi. *What have we done as children to deserve such heartless fathers?* I think to myself as I deflect with tears obstructing my vision.

This dark elf is playing with me. Another flash of my father pulls my attention, and I tremble. How is it that after everything I went through, my father is still tormenting me? I watch as Liber takes a deep breath and claps his hands, sending a wave of wind toward me. My feet barely move, holding me in place to take on the impact directly.

Something inside me flickers and the Shoneah's spirit itself wants to come out and take control. An act of self-preservation due to my internal conflict. I stumble back with unsteady feet. Wave after wave, they grow stronger. Each clap pushing me back until I eventually pin against a tree.

Is this my punishment for what I did to Honovi? Tears fall as I squirm.

Stop it. This is not a punishment. HE is not your father. Snap out of it. Wolfie scolds me but it's too late. The barrage of wind isn't allowing me to light my flames long enough to use them.

Liber waves his arms and then does a lifting motion. A giant wall of dirt surrounds me like a cocoon, almost fully encasing me. The walls are solid and nothing, but a small hole is left above me. Now that the wind isn't hitting me, I light my flames and press my hands to harden the wet dirt so I can shatter it from within. But I don't have enough time, water pours in through the hole, filling it until I am completely submerged.

I can't breathe...

Atlas

"Wait, something is wrong. I'm going back." I call out to the others that have made it into Kristofer's home.

Alpha, they have us trapped. They won't let us leave. Finn calls out to me in the mind link.

Who does?

Lion shifters. He answers. I curse myself for not being more careful. Letting myself focus only on getting Iris to safety after regaining consciousness, left me neglecting the rest of the wolves. *This is not the wolf my father raised.*

I curse myself and shift to run towards Finn. The group before me is huddled together in a small group hugging one another. Finn points into the tree line and I manage to see something that resembles lion shifters leave.

"What happened?" I shift back.

"I don't know. One minute they were stopping us from going anywhere and the next minute, they turned around and leave without a word." Finn explains while trembling.

"That doesn't make any sense."

"They weren't right, Alpha. They were mostly bones and others looked like their skin was dried up clinging to its skeleton. They smelled horrendously and their eye sockets were like black shadows. I think they were reanimated somehow." Finn turns pale at his words. He clenches his mouth and turns around to let out the bile he held.

"Great. That means more magic is involved and a strong one at that. Where's Shoneah?" I look around the group. Then my throat begins to close. I can't breathe. My heart is racing, and the panic is sending my head into a spin. But it isn't me that's having trouble breathing. It's my mate.

I shift back into Leo and run faster than I ever thought possible. I whisper to myself for my Luna's well-being, but I can feel something is wrong. I urge Leo to run faster, wanting to scream and tear away at the bastard who hurt my Luna.

Leo spots something odd and heads straight towards it. I can feel Cassius and he is no longer in Shoneah form with how weak our bond is now. He is in there. I am sure of it, so I shift back into myself and bang on the tomb-like dome. Repeatedly I hit the same spot over and over. I punch and claw and punch again, crying and yelling at the goddess for not keeping him safe like I asked. My fist is bloody, and I curse myself again for failing as the Alpha. As his mate. There is no way I am losing him.

I punch one more time through the pain in my knuckles and water sprouts from the hole I make. Furiously I dig with my hands where the water is leaking from and like a dam that's been set free, the structure breaks open and out spills my Luna.

"Cassius wake up!" His tattoos are gone, and his hair is back to normal as I suspected and for once I am not relieved to see him as himself. If his transformation faded, then it can only mean one thing.

I put my head to his chest. "Shit, you're not breathing." His lips are growing a deep shade of purple by the second and water is spilling from the corners of his mouth. My mate is drowning

The wheels in my mind are turning as I flip him over to drain the water in his mouth and start chest compressions. If I remember correctly, I count thirty repetitions then fill his lungs with as much life as I can give. With each compression I hate myself for not being by his side. I cry out into the world as I count with my hands on his sternum. My arms are locked straight and with my weight I pour my heart and soul into bringing him back. "Wake up! Please wake..." I fill his lungs again. One breath. Two breaths. Then I lock my hands and begin again. The force of my compressions cracks a couple of ribs, but I keep going.

"Don't leave me Cass. I can't do this life without you." As selfish as I sound, I can't. Or rather, I don't want to live this life without him. There is no one else that can fill this emptiness I have inside. He is my only one. The only person that completes me. My love.

Tears riddle my face as I continue the compressions. The cries that leave my throat boom through the acres that surround us, but I continue. I won't stop until I see life back in his eyes.

"Alpha!" Finn and a couple of others run towards me, but I ignore them and finish my count, "twenty-nine, thirty."

I pinch his nose and press my mouth to his, filling Cassius' chest again for two large breaths and begin another set of compressions. I will do this for as long as it takes. I need...I, "...Cass", I whisper to myself when my mate begins to cough up water. It pours out of him like a hose.

"BABE!" I turn him over and wait for him to take a deep breath on his own. The smallest hint of life flickers in his eyes before they roll back, and he faints.

Chapter 18

Atlas

CASSIUS IS RESTING in the infirmary over at Kristofer's and all I want to do is sit in there and watch over him. No one feels safe at the pack house but with the allies already beginning to trickle in, it's our safest bet to remain together so we are never left alone. I can't thank Kristofer enough for calling in reinforcements. My heart still hurts from all the crying I did but I will do it again if it means saving the one that I love. The thought of losing Cassius is not something I want to feel again. I don't wish that on anyone.

Cassius stirs in his sleep in a groan, but he is breathing better than before. His breaths are not as shallow, and his coughing has subsided. The doctor told me that I fractured a couple of his ribs with my compressions but that I did the right thing acting so quickly. I knew I broke something when I felt it under my weight, but I didn't care.

"Hey, the others are here. Come greet everyone and let Luna sleep." Mom calls out to me from the door.

The last thing I want to do is to leave him here alone. If he wakes up, then I want to be the first person he sees. Yet, my duties as an Alpha take priority right now.

"Okay..." I kiss Cassius on the forehead and tuck him in before leaving him alone to rest.

***

"There ya are, my boy. Looking more like ya father each time I see ya." Alpha Robert opens his big hairy arms to hug me.

"Hi, Uncle Robert." I hug him and chuckle at how big he has gotten. The man does not know how to put down his fork. However, I won't joke like that out loud or he will be tackling me to the floor to teach me a lesson in respecting my elders.

"Wow, ya haven't called me that in years." Alpha Robert smiles as he pulls away. Although not my uncle by blood, I always saw him as such. He was always the cool one during the get togethers my dad had. I look up to the guy because he always had my dad's back, whether it was, disputes between packs or my father cheating in a poker game.

In fact, they were both runners-up for the choice of Alpha for my pack before I was born. In the end, my father was voted in, and luckily enough another pack had an Alpha stepping down from old age and accepted Uncle Robert to be their leader.

"You know you love it," I reply with a light punch to the man's fluffy gut.

"Hey Alpha Atlas, long time!" Ithil walks in with a dorky smile.

"Wow, letting your hair grow?" I yank at the long ponytail Ithil is sporting. Now he definitely looks like an elf.

"Ow, you boob. Don't yank it. It's still attached to my head you know."

"Boob?" I repeat lifting a brow his way.

"Yeah, boob!" We hug each other while laughing. It has been too long since I have seen so many of these faces. I will make sure to do gatherings again.

"Hey, Alpha Kristofer, where's Iris?" I can smell her, so I know she is somewhere in the house.

"…Sleeping," Kristofer fidgets. He probably doesn't want to really say what's going on.

Is she really sleeping?

No, she is hiding inside Nora in Cassius' old room. She doesn't want to see anyone.

Oh, okay. I'll check on her later then.

"Okay. Anyways, how do you know Uncle Robert?" I ask remembering that Kristofer is the one that gathered everyone.

"He is really good friends with my parents. Wait did you say Uncle Robert?" Kristofer pauses and gives me a look I understand too well.

"Okay, not gonna go there. I don't need another swinger's story." I reply and the two of us start laughing at the very real possibility.

I leave Kristofer to tend to the guest still walking in and head into the kitchen to make something light for when Cassius wakes up.

The fridge is already open, and someone is wiggling their butt while digging for food. I have a funny feeling I know exactly who it is.

"Hey Lenny," I pass him by and go to the pantry. He is the only one who is ever that excited when looking inside a refrigerator. I can practically see a tail wagging. His relationship with food is stronger than any mate bond I have seen.

A bang and then a curse emanates from the fridge at the sound of my voice, "Hey Alpha Atlas." Lenny rubs his head.

"How are you not fat?" I ask while pushing him aside to grab some leftover chicken that Cecile had mentioned for me to eat. According to mom, Cecile's chicken is second to none. The anticipation for this meal has me salivating from the hype.

"Lenny, did you eat the chicken?"

"No. There was chicken in here?! Ugh, Cecile makes some mean chicken." He huffs seeming genuinely annoyed and opens the container in his hand and drools over the lasagna inside. For once I don't think he is lying.

"Great, I was looking forward to using it for Cass. Now
what?!" I slump my shoulders and begin to rummage the fridge for other leftovers that might have survived Lenny's stomach or the chicken culprit.

"Oh, hey cousin!" a chipper but muffled voice walks in behind me.

I pop out of the fridge with some stir-fried pepper steak in hand, "hey Rory. When did... is that chicken?!" I glare at the half-eaten drumstick in his hand wrapped in a napkin by the bone.

"...uh", Rory hesitates and looks at Lenny.

"Run!" Lenny commands him and off Rory goes with the drumstick in his mouth in a fit of giggles.

"I hate you right now." I proceed to make steak fajitas for Cassius while Lenny devours the lasagna unphased by my words. If I didn't know any better, I'd say he is making love to the dam food. I don't think he even bothered to heat it and is simply going to town on the thing. "Savage", I mutter under my breath. Might as well get a room at this point.

Happy with how the fajitas turned out, I collect the tray of food and drinks to bring over to the infirmary. Cassius has been sleeping half a day and all I want to see is his beautiful deep black eyes smiling at me. Weaving in and out of the crowd accumulating in the house I go into the infirmary to find my mate stretching with sleepy eyes and a little yawn.

"Finally," I whisper.

***

Kristofer

"We need to form a plan. The way he toyed with us and Cassius just shows the lengths he will go without breaking a sweat." I look around at the Alphas in the room. "What do we know so far?"

Atlas opens a map of the surrounding territories, "first off, he came in from this direction. For now, we can assume he came from somewhere northwest of here." Atlas places a chess piece on the map. "This rook will represent Liber."

"Okay, we also know he has forces on his side." I place two knights around the rook to represent the lion shifters. "We can safely assume he has more lion shifters as a backup.

"Lion shifters? What are lion shifters doing way out here?" Alpha Robert questions me and Atlas.

"Well, Flint made an interesting observation."

"Who?" Luna Melody interrupts me.

"He means Finn. He specifically has amnesia when it comes to his name." Atlas replies on my behalf while the others in the room snicker. "Anyways, what he was going to say is that Finn noticed the lion shifters were dead. They smelled of death and rot and most were purely bones. Their eyes were also just black shadows."

"Necromancy?!" Alpha Vinny gasps.

"Our thoughts exactly. And if that's the case, then his army could come in great numbers. We also established he has found a new medium. He was wielding magic pretty well against Shoneah." I look around at the concerned faces in the room.

"Does he know we have his book?" Luna Melody takes the spell book that sits on my desk.

"I don't think so. He also doesn't know we might have a witch of our own either. Could come in handy." Atlas smirks. "Iris' best friend, Jesika, is loyal to her."

"We also need to find a way to find his medium and destroy it. If we can't beat him with numbers then we should at least render him useless or at least weak. That is the only thing we can do on short notice." I knock over the rook on the map with the flick of a finger taking down the knights with it.

****

Iris

"Nora, I'm coming in," Cassius calls out to Nora. "Hey, can I talk to Iris?" He stands by the door and Nora nods after I agree with her to shift.

"Need me?" I ask while reaching for the blanket on his bed to wrap myself in.

"Want to talk about it?" Cassius sits on his next to me.

I sigh, "I froze Cass. I saw my father and froze while you fought and got hurt. I'm useless. All I do is get the people around me injured."

"Listen, Iris, because of me being a reincarnate, I am a bit more resilient than other wolves which is why I stood up to him first but also don't forget, I am this pack soon to be Luna. It is my duty now to protect both my families. I would have stepped up regardless of who Liber is." Cassius places his hand on my back, rubbing soothingly.

"It doesn't change the fact that I froze. I hurt the man I love and froze before the one that deserves my anger. How does that make sense?" I lay my head on his shoulder.

"It's normal to be afraid. That just shows how much you value life, that you can't just take it so easily from another. You are the strongest person I know; did I ever tell you that?"

"Oh please, I'm not." I roll my eyes even though he can't see it. This brother-in-law of mine really know all the right things to say.

"I'm serious. You endure so much and still try to fight. You push through and keep going. So what, if sometimes you stumble and falter, what is important is that you get back up." His strokes my hair.

"I just wish I would stop stumbling then. I don't want to falter anymore. Why can't I be more like you?" A sigh heavier than intended escapes my lips.

"Oh sis, I have faltered, stumbled, and fainted, more times than I can count. I was terrified while facing Liber as well, but I have also burned down barns, trees, and mailboxes to try and hone my powers."

"Mailboxes?" I chuckle slightly at the random object. I'm going to have to ask my brother about it.

"Long story, point is, I didn't get these powers and have command right away. I practiced just like you, faced my father on more than one occasion, and was beaten every time. I managed in the end because I had your brother and Kristofer with me." Cassius draws my chin up to look at him.

"As my little sister, I refuse to let you fail in the battles you face. Your battles are our battles. Let us in, allow us to help. You don't need to do this alone."

"Now you sound like Kristofer." I give him a straight look.

"Then he is a wise man and like me, he loves you dearly." He smiles, "Get dressed and come down to say hi to the other packs arriving."

"Wait, were you really scared of Liber" I grab Cassius' hand as he stands up.

"Yes, he reminds me too much of my father." He sighs, "Come, I'm sure your mate is worried about you."

My brother truly found the perfect Luna. He knows all the right things to say and the love he has is embedded in every word he shares. I can't let him down or anyone else. We can do this. Together.

"Okay."

Chapter 19

Iris

"YOU THINK A BIT of magic display and I will run? Liber de Buer runs from no one." He squeezes an already unconscious Atlas even tighter, threatening to snuff out the bit of life that is left within him. The way his body is limp makes me want to scream in hopes that I can do the same thing I did last time in the cabin. Liber snaps Atlas' neck and drops him towards me like a rag doll. He lays by my feet lifeless with his head bent in an awkward angle. The light in his eyes gone.

"STOP!" I wake up screaming in a cold sweat making Kristofer jolt awake from his sleep. We nodded off in the living room with me on his lap, which I am now finding more comfortable than my bed. His warmth lulls me to sleep easier than any medicine. Uncle Robert runs into the room.

"What's wrong deary, ya alright?" Uncle Robert walks over to the sofa.

"Sorry, I guess I had a nightmare."

"About what?" Kristofer wipes the damp hair that's clinging to my forehead and tucks it behind my ear.

"About what just happened with Liber but different. This time." I look up with my eyes watering at the image of my brother dying before me. Kristofer stares at me with so much love and sadness.

"Oh deary, don't worry, we are all here for ya. We will stay until this is settled." Uncle Robert squeezes my knee in reassurance and gets up. "Want some coffee?"

"No, it's okay. Thanks for the offer. " I give a half-hearted smile.

"Want some hot chocolate instead?" Kristofer whispers and strokes my hair.

"Yes, please," I whisper back.

"So that's how it is, huh." Uncle Robert chuckles, "Come say hi to Pearson, he arrived shortly after you fell asleep." He calls out as he leaves the living room.

"Who's Pearson?" Kristofer lifts me off his lap.

"His son. We grew up like cousins, but I haven't seen him since my father's funeral. We were all so close back then. I thought you knew Uncle Robert?" I reply and melt against Kristofer's comforting hand on my cheek.

"I do but I don't remember him having another son named Pearson." Kristofer ponders a bit but shakes his head no.

"Do you remember little Roberto?" I smile.

"Yeah, we played a lot together."

"Same guy. He changed his name when he turned 18 because he hated the name. Now he's Pearson." I chuckle at the shock strewn on his face.

"How did I not know this? I really am out of touch with everyone, aren't I?" Kristofer scratches the gruff growing on his face and lifts me off his lap to go make the hot chocolate.

***

Kristofer

The house is oddly quiet despite the number of bodies currently occupying it. It is my first time meeting most the of the wolves here but I am grateful for the new connections. They all seem like nice allies and Atlas seems to view them more like family. Luna Melody is definitely a character I hadn't met before now. I simply knew the name.

"How long do you plan on staring son?" Luna Melody lifts a brow with a smirk.

"Oh, sorry. I didn't realize I was staring." I avert my eyes to my sandwich. Her aura is so much like my mother that I instinctively looked away.

"I can tell. You seemed lost in thought." She walks over and sits across from me. "Want to talk about it? I'm all ears." Luna Melody flicks her ears at me.

"It's nothing really. Just thinking on all that's happened over the last few months and now this maniac showing up." I shrug my shoulders and take a bite from my sandwich.

"Mom, this is bullshit." A young wolf walks into the kitchen in a huff.

"Watch your mouth. This isn't your home." Luna Melody snaps. "Sorry, Alpha Kristofer." The wolf gives a slight bow. So slight it was barely noticeable. Cheeky little wolf. I like her.

She looks strong, more so than most female wolves. Her light caramel skin expresses the chisel in her muscles. Defining them beautifully as if sun kissed. Long black curls dance with every movement she makes. One part is braided underneath adorned with golden cuffs and intertwined with a white leather thread. All of it frames her beautifully soft features with one green eye and the other hazel. *Still, Iris is be-*

"What's the problem?" Luna Melody breaks my train of thought, so I take another bite of my sandwich.

"Veronica broke up with me because she said she wants someone who she can go steady with."

"Maeve, hunny, not everyone wants a friend with benefits or a relationship that's pleasure and nothing else."

"Yeah well, she knew what it was from the beginning. It's not like it's anything new. Ugh, it's hard enough to find a human that doesn't get suspicious but now I gotta worry about other wolves." Maeve crosses her arms annoyed.

"It's only natural. Besides what if you find your mate?" Luna Melody gives her the same brow she gave me.

"This is annoying." Maeve walks out of the kitchen in a stomp. You would think she was a teen and not a young adult. "Rory, let's watch a movie," Maeve calls out from the hallway.

"Wait until you have kids." Luna sucks her teeth still looking in the direction her daughter went.

I choke on my sandwich, "kids?" Iris and I haven't even gone that far yet. We haven't had sex let alone think of children.

"What's with that response? Isn't Iris your mate?"

"...Yes." I take a sip of water. Truly it hadn't crossed my mind yet. But now that I have a moment, I'd love to have little ones running around. It's most definitely a thought. It makes me wonder if she ever considered kids before. To see a little Iris running around or a little me chasing after a little brother or sister will bring me more joy than I can imagine. I think having two kiddos running around would be perfect.

***

The night is growing late and the overstimulation of having so many wolves in the house is tiring me out. I look for Iris who I am told is in my room reading a book. I'm sure she probably feels the same way to be hiding in here reading a book. I close the door and strip down to my underwear before crawling into bed and posing seductively or at least what

I think is seductive. I could very well look like an old pervy man.

Iris doesn't even notice me as she sits at my desk with her nose in the book. I clear my throat, but it does nothing to get her to look my way. She giggles at whatever it is she is reading, and I close my eyes to the sound of her. I drift in and out of sleep and the last thing I hear is Iris gasping and mumbling something about a golden dragon and a fae. Her voice is soothing and off I go into dreamland.

****

Iris

I tip-toe out of the room making sure not to wake up Kristofer who is sleeping so soundly. If only I looked his way when he first came to bed because he is looking like a tall glass of deliciousness, and I am thirsty. He did make an effort to grab my attention, but I ignored him to finish the chapter I was in. By the time I looked his way, he was fast asleep. After reading such a juicy book, I worked up an even bigger appetite, but I'll let him rest and get actual food for now.

Making my way through the hall and into the kitchen, I grab a large bowl and mix two cereals into a sugary combo. I fill the bowl with milk and then grab a large spoon.

"Mmmmm," I hum as the sugar filled cereal hits my stomach.

"What are you eating that has you looking so happy?" A guy walks into the kitchen and sits across from me.

"Uh, cereal. Who are you?" I ask while shoving another spoonful of cereal in my mouth.

"I'm Manny, I am with Alpha Vinny. I joined his pack not too long ago." He smirks and brushes his hair back flexing his muscles in a poor attempt to impress me. A fool to think he looks anything better than my man. A smile tugs at my lips at thought of referring to Kristofer as my man.

"What are you doing?" A voice calls out from the kitchen door and Manny sits up straight. "She is off limits; you touch my cousin and you're gonna have bigger problems." Pearson walks in and sits next to me.

"I wasn't doing anything, jeez." Manny pouts and I snort which isn't smart considering it sent milk up my nose. I choke on the cereal I'm chewing, and Pearson has to hit my back to help me out.

"Dear goddess woman, swallow your food properly." Pearson laughs.

"No, I'm hungry. Chewing takes too long." I smirk and continue eating.

"You guys really do seem close. You sure she is just a cousin?" Manny gets up and sits to the other side of me putting his arm around my shoulders. I sigh because I know if Kristofer wakes up, he will throw a fit.

"Manny, stop it. I'm not interested, and I am already spoken for." I brush his arm off.

"Manny, you are going to regret being stupid. When a woman says no, it's no. No exception." Pearson reaches over and slaps the back of Manny's head.

"I'm just teasing. Sheesh." Manny rubs his head before attempting to place his arm back around me.

"Boy you better think twice about where you're putting that arm if you'd like for it remain attached." Kristofer's voice is deeper than normal since he just woke up. He probably noticed my presence gone from the room.

Manny freezes with his arm midair. "Alpha Kristofer, didn't see you there. Hi." Pearson chuckles and a grin spring to my lips.

"I am sure she told you she isn't interested." Alpha Kristofer walks to the cabinet. The air grows thick with tension between them. Manny trembles a bit with both hands in his lap looking red as a tomato.

"Are you by any chance her mate, Alpha Kristofer?" Manny looks up to him in an attempt to seem calm, but I know Kristofer is purposely using his pheromones to intimidate the poor wolf.

"Would you look at that Pearson, he isn't as stupid as you said." Kristofer fills his cup with water and walks out of the kitchen. Pearson straightens in his seat, wide-eyed.

"What?" Manny snaps at Pearson.

"I swear, I didn't say anything to him about you!" Pearson tries to defend himself but runs out of the kitchen with Manny chasing after him.

Enjoy your cereal babe. Kristofer links with me and the chuckles that escape my lips are plentiful.

Thanks babe, see you in a few. I continue eating in silence.

Chapter 20

Atlas

TWO DAYS LATER Alpha Robert and Alpha Vinny set out to the woods to set up traps. This would help us learn ahead of time if someone is closing in on the property. Similar to the bear traps the hunters use and so generously lay out for us. However, ours also sends a signal of the location that the trap triggered.

Jesika is with Iris and Cassius practicing magic spells, while Alpha Kristofer is with the others forming a plan, should Liber attack first again.

I grab most of the food I just bought from the truck and walk into the pack house. It is the least I can do considering that I am crashing in someone else's home and eating all of their food. Well, if I am honest, Lenny is eating all the food, but I should still chip in.

Mom grabs the bags from me and begins to cook up a frenzy. Within the pack house and the ones staying in the cabins around the property, there are at least a little over a hundred of us. Things finally feel like they are in our control again, but the Lion shifters still provide a wild card that we haven't figured out how to deal with yet.

My head is pulled back by my hair and my mouth is covered with the softest lips. I allow the tongue to invade my mouth as I inhale the scent that I love so much.

"What has you thinking so hard?" Cassius breaks the kiss, and I whimper from the loss.

"Everything but right now my mind is blank thanks to you," I respond staring at his lips.

"Then let me offer you a bit more of a distraction," Cassius smirks in his little dirty way.

I chuckle, "Stop, we have too many wolves here. Kissing is enough." I cover his lips with mine and let myself melt into him. This man truly is my everything.

***

Kristofer

"Babe, are you in here?" I open the door to my room, but Iris is nowhere to be found.

Looking for me? Iris' voice echoes in my mind.

Yes, where are you?

Meet me out front. She replies and I eagerly make my way to her. The smile plastered on my face as I make my way through the house is probably comical. Anyone would think I am about to get laid. Grabbing my coat by the door only to find my mate outside by my truck with the keys in hand, I begin to think that maybe that assumption may be right.

"What's going on?" I walk over to her but all she does is open the door and sit in the passenger seat. I follow her and get in the driver's side, "where to my love?"

"The cabin." Is all she says and then puts on her seat belt.

We arrive not too long after and I take off my coat and shoes. Iris winks at me and walks away into the room without a word. My vision adjusts enough to make out flower petals on the floor and tea-light candles lighting a bit of the pathway.

With gentle steps to the room, my eyes follow the lit candles on the floor. They trail all the way to the nightstand with a bucket of champagne on ice. More petals are scattered across the room and bed filling the air with the scent of roses. The reality of my joke sets in, and I am getting nervous at the thought.

"Babe, what's all this?" I look up to find myself alone in the room when the bathroom door opens.

"I had Jesika set this up", Iris steps out in a long T-shirt and no bra. But not just any T-shirt either, she is wearing mine. The points of her nipples pebble against the shirt and the color of her areolas are a soft shadow against the thin white material.

"Uh..." My mouth drops. She looks incredible and the ache I am developing in my jeans is proof. I drop the car keys not sure of what to do as she walks over to me in a sultry manner swaying her hips with a wicked smile I want to kiss.

"I need to unwind. I need to clear my mind, and I think this will be a perfect way to accomplish that." Iris strips off my clothes without a word while I stand there frozen against her touch. She must think I am such a fool for just standing here but I can't seem to move.

A naughty hand runs over my bulge making me hyper aware I have nothing on but my boxer briefs. She guides me to the bed and pushes me over making me chuckle nervously as I bounce on the springy mattress. Iris climbs on top of me sliding her hands up my legs to my thighs. I quiver from the anticipation. She trails her fingers higher followed by her kisses to my chest.

"Are you sure about this?" I barely manage to say between panting breaths. I want her to keep going but I need to make sure. She flicks her tongue, and I shudder. The sensation is wild, and I never thought that I'd like someone playing with my nipples.

"Very", Iris drags her tongue down to my twitching erection. A distraction as she pulls down my briefs tossing them aside as I spring free. But for one reason or another, I blush into oblivion. A small drip falls from my tip onto my stomach and Iris licks it clean.

This vixen is extremely sexy but dangerously arousing. With a firm hand, she grips my length and slowly strokes it. A moan escapes the depths of soul. Her touch alone sends fireworks through my body and straight toward my ever-hardening dick. *I have never felt more like a virgin than I do right now*, I think as I do my best to not come from her strokes alone.

Iris smiles wickedly as she closes her lips around my shaft. Her warm mouth takes me in, and I find myself rocking against her face gently. I am chasing every sensation she is providing. Like a hungry rabid animal that was just given an opportunity to feast.

"Goddess this feels amazing," I whisper, mentally trying to keep myself from ejaculating too early. *Has her tongue always been this skilled?* My question slips away with the slight tug of my balls as she massages them. How do partners last so long during sex? I want to burst in her mouth already and we haven't spent that much time doing this. A few minutes maybe but I don't want it to end so quickly.

Her warm tongue swirls around my dick and slurps up to the tip before going back down its length. I shudder once more as I struggle to contain myself. Iris bobs her head, sucking me hard and I can only imagine the sound it will make if she pops off my crown again. The wet sound of her lips elicits another moan. It rolls out of my chest as the feeling rises from the depths of my balls.

Iris works her hands and her mouth in sync with one another, but I eagerly thrust into her impatiently with none of the gentleness from earlier. I hit the back of her throat making her gagging sounds fill the room to keep my moans company. The tightness grabs hold of me again. I am close.

I pant and grunt louder in the hollow walls feeling my release closer. **Come for me, baby.** Iris' voice enters my mind sending me into a frenzy of faster thrusts into her mouth. With a twist of her drenched hands, my balls tighten all the way against me, and I send all my warm seed into her mouth.

Her throat closes around me swallowing before taking more of what I am spilling. I catch my breath and watch Iris sit up and wipe her bottom lip with her thumb, suggesting a delicious meal was had. *Damn, that's sexy.*

"Fuck babe." I pant slightly catching my breath.

"It's only the beginning."

Iris straddles me and lifts off her shirt. Whipping it around until it rolls up, she uses the shirt to tie my hands above my head. She leans over me, and the position is just as seductive as the sound of her voice.

"Ready to lose your V-card?" She grinds herself against my newly growing erection while her breasts hover over my face. If only I could reach with my tongue, but she pulls back just enough to deny me access. Holding me in place, she moves her hips again and I am sent back to the edge of orgasm. Her hips whine in a circle allowing her silky underwear to slip to the side. The wetness from her arousal lubricates my erection and all I can think of is how bad I want to be inside her. But my growing orgasm is threatening to erupt and shout to the world my inexperience.

I blush at the thought but do my best to focus on her movements. Every time she is with Jesika, she comes back more daring, and I love it. My mind wonders what that might mean but her grinding against me pulls me from my thoughts. I need to be inside her. I want her to wrap me with her body and drive me over the edge in a way that only she knows how.

I groan at the feel of her wet warmth on me, but man is that nipple swaying in front of me tempting. She leans a bit forward with her eyes closed and I flick her hardened nub with my tongue. She jerks with a slight yelp.

"I'm ready." I moan again wanting to shove myself inside her. The animalistic urge to plunge into her is getting the best of me but I need her to do it. She needs to be the one to say she is ready and place me at her entrance.

"Hmm, not yet actually. Let me feed you first." I furrow my brows only to slowly realize her meaning when she scoots herself up and sits on my face, straddling my mouth between her thighs. The smell of her arousal makes my nostrils flare. "Eat baby", she demands, and, in that moment, I am sure my eyes burst green with the way hers reflect in response.

I work my tongue remembering all the places she liked before. I suck on her swollen clit and elicit a moan so feral it makes my dick vibrate with need. Her excitement almost has me forgetting how timid she could sometimes be. Iris sucks in a breath while I flick her swollen clit rapidly and then latch on to it, sucking hard as if to pull her love potion out of her.

My beautiful mate rocks her hips smothering my face with her core, dripping her excitement down my chin. "Yes, right there," she whispers.

I suck again and another moan screams out of her as I flick the alphabet like I had read on the internet to do. She is close with how her thighs squeeze my head and how her legs vibrate. She screams when I follow the pattern of the letter M. I repeat the pattern over and over with varying speed.

Iris grabs my head pressing me harder against her and rocks her hips faster. "Don't stop, Alpha, fuck me with that tongue". Zeus wants to take over and begs for me to have Nora come out, but I push him aside because this is my moment. He can fuck Nora another day.

I want my hands free so I can grab her lips and spread them for better access. The urge to devour her has me leaking with the urge to spill myself. I jerk myself off as Iris makes a mess of my face unable to contain myself anymore. I come all over her back and the grunt I release against her swollen pussy makes her shatter against me.

My mission to have her clit swollen from the pleasures I give her throbs as evidence against my tongue. I taste her. All of her and growl with satisfaction. Without a second thought, I return to my meal and lick off all the sweet nectar. That coats her lips. This has me high as I switch up my pace with my tongue and I find new spots. I lick, I nip, I suck, everywhere.

Everything tastes sweet on my taste buds. But most importantly, I want to learn her. Perfect the art of satisfying her arousal with my lips. She is creating a thirst in me that only she can quench. So, I rub my face into her core and lick up through her wet slit. She squeezes her thighs again in response.

Folding my tongue, I plunge into her and fuck her the best I could. She moans my name. Just for me, because of me, she moans her ecstasy. I continue to ravish her and lavish every inch of her center that pulsates in response. Iris looks down in shock. "How are you this good?"

"I'm hungry," I mumble into her nether lips and lock eyes with her. It's the truth. I can't say that I am skilled or good at what I am doing because it is all new to me. But I am hungry for her, and I yearned to be this intimate with her so much that I dreamt of how I'd pleasure her too many times to count.

"Your eyes are practically glowing. Do I excite you that much?" She giggles and rocks herself against me more.

"Yes, now squirt for me as you did before," I command, and Iris bites her lip making my boner twitch back to life for a third time.

"You got it."

Iris releases my hands from her shirt, and I put them to work. I grab onto her ass with one and with the other I plunge two fingers inside her trembling walls. My tongue roams in circles while my fingers continue to plunge into her wet cave. All of her is soaking my face again. The best facial anyone could ask for.

Clamping down on her clit, I suck hard making her scream my name to the goddess. This is it. Curving my fingers like she taught me; I work her g-spot. Her release showers me once more as she pulls away and starts rubbing her clit aggressively. She squirts all over my chest, bed, and face. It is glorious to see. All her juice and excitement cover me in a shower of compliments. And I happily drown in it.

"Fuck, that was hot," I growl at my mate.

She pants hard and uses the shirt she tied me with to wipe my face. "That felt so good, babe." Iris' breathing steadies a bit as she stares into my green eyes. The emotions I see within them light me on fire. I nod my head in agreement, but my boner is now harder than it ever should be. It's almost too painful to bear. She slips down and positions herself over my dick.

"Do with me what you wish," I tell her as I poke her core with my member. Iris lowers herself onto my body. Her warm walls close around me griping every inch of my length in a chokehold. "Fuck!" I yell. This feeling, the sensations, everything is overwhelming. This is sex. *I am finally having sex!* I mentally scream in virgin.

This is what it feels like to be in your mate. No wonder mates go at it like rabbits all the time. She fills herself up with me completely.

"Guess you're not a virgin anymore. Now, would you like to have your way with *me* instead? I'm a big girl. I can take it some clumsy dick." She nibbles her lip, and it is all the invitation I need despite calling my dick clumsy.

I flip on top of her and thrust into her warmth. My breath hitches as the assault to my senses go on overdrive. Iris gasps as I stretch her out or at least I hope that is the reason why.

I thrust my hips against her slowly until the initial sensation subsides because the last thing I need is to come again. My hips find a rhythm and I increase my speed, slapping my balls against her ass in the process. An applause to our performance.

Iris bites her lip with a grin so wicked, it spurs one onto my lips as well. Harder, I thrust my cock into her and watch as her breast bounce with joy. They invite me for a taste, and I delightfully oblige. I pull her down towards me so I can greedily take in the nipple that is begging me for attention. Iris arches her back in response and grabs my hair to hold me in place. I suck on her tender breast thrusting harder within her, happily suffocating against her chest.

"Alpha..." She moans and I bite her hard nub, growling at the title. *This woman is going to be the death of me.* I sit up again and lift her onto me in a sitting position. My hips grind up into her, pulling her close to my chest and holding her in place. My arms wrap around her waist and back.

She fits in my arms like a glove. Iris was made for me. My lips take in her neglected breast, and I suck it as if I need her milk to survive. The day she carries my children, I will gladly feed from her and live of her sweet nourishment.

I bury my face into her chest and start pounding away. "Babe, your so fucking tight right now," I grunt between her breasts. I lose myself in the passion between her legs.

She is like a drug, and I am completely addicted. And her moans are songs to my heart that only I can orchestrate the symphony for. The way she moves puts me in a trance I don't want to get out of. She is the master of everything that is me and I welcome it. I am completely under her spell and that's okay. I want to be. I crave the need to be. I am her tool to use as she pleases, and I will gladly provide my services until my last breath if it means she could have another.

"Give me more baby," Iris pleads and who am I to deny her needs? I do my best to carry her off the bed without removing myself from her core. My left leg unfortunately is asleep and struggling to get us scooted to the edge of the bed so we can stand. I awkwardly scoot to the edge in a rocking motion.

Finally, I stand up with her in my arms and slam her against the wall. "Ow", Iris winces. I thump her head on the wall a little too hard.

"Sorry," I blush under her smile. She must find it funny how little I know but I will wipe that smile off her face if it's the last thing I do.

Sensing my hesitation, Iris' hands roam my back up to my hair. She pulls my hair and bites my bottom lip. Her eyes are wild with a fire that matches my own.

All my need, all of my thirty years of waiting for her, my mate, I am releasing it now. It is all the encouragement I need so I slam my mouth against hers once more. Maybe a bit too hard since Iris yelps a bit and I am almost certain shit bit her tongue. The need to get off is so great I am indeed as she predicted, a clumsy dick.

We kiss feverishly as I thrust into her pool, forcing her lips to part from mine in moans and screams of pleasure. "Fuck me harder Alpha", she bellows throwing her head back and hitting the wall of her own accord. "More baby...more," she screams again as she pants.

Her chest is heaving and gasping for breath. I continue to hit the spot that is driving her mad, but the position is at a weird angle. I can't hold it much longer. Unfortunately, the visual is all too much, and I thrust recklessly causing my dick to slip out of her and poke her in the ass. Iris yelps so loud I almost drop her, but I manage to keep her pinned against the wall.

"Shit, that hurt!" Iris' eyes grow watery. Goddess help me not mess this up any further. I am succeeding in making myself seem a fool every step of the way.

"I'm sorry. Are you okay?" I ask and wipe the tear that broke free of her. She nods at me and tells me to continue. I use this opportunity to straighten up and get comfortable.

I dig my face into her neck and suck on her between kisses. Her scent gives me such a sense of calm and yet such euphoria it's more than intoxicating. It is doing well to remove this embarrassment that plagues me with every slip up.

Scared to make the same mistake, I decide to put her down and bend her over the bed before reinserting myself, pounding away and slapping her ass as I go. Moans ripple out of her replacing any other word that may come to mind. They are the sexiest sounds on earth, and I play with them as I hit different angles within her and change her tune. The sounds she produces vary in pitch, tone, and length and it speaks my language.

My eyes droop down admiring the plump thickness of her behind with a red hue claiming her skin in the shape of my hand. It is beautiful to see her cheeks bounce against me. I slap her red bottom again and again until she screams so loud, I slow down to keep from releasing again.

Her hot pussy squeezes and threatens to drain me dry every time she screams my name. But then I think, what if I hurt her? I pump into her more slowly, worried that I may be going overboard.

Her body tenses and I must be right if she is no longer moving against me. I knew that I would be a disaster at this, and I will have to make it up to her later in some other way but before I could say anything, Iris squirts in a gush all over the bed and our feet.

"Oh my god", she yells into the sheets as she buries her face in the bed. Her legs and walls are violently shaking against me, and it pushes me over the edge before I am ready. I hammer away at her forcing a high-pitched vocal opera from her throat as I begin my orgasm.

"Babe, I'm cumming," I yell, pulling out of her and pumping all of me on her back once more. "Shit".

Her knees give out and she slumps to the floor splashing a bit of her wetness onto my legs. She is covered in a beautiful mess of our love. I hold out my hand and help her stand up in my arms only for both of us to slip and luckily land on the bed. I thought I ruined our moment but somehow, I made this gorgeous woman come apart in more ways than one. Iris is laughing in a fit of giggles, and I can't help but join her. My first time did not pan out how I expected but she is satisfied and so am I.

Alpha Kristofer, where are you? Hurry home.

What's wrong Alpha Atlas?

Liber!

Chapter 21

Iris

"YOU THINK A BIT of magic display and I will run? Liber de Buer runs from no one". He squeezes an already unconscious Atlas even tighter, threatening to snuff out the last bit of life that is left within him. The sound of his heart beating slowly stirs all of us with panic.

Even with Kristofer and I running all the stop lights, we arrive late. Now this man is holding my brother's limp body, and I am too scared to move, afraid it'll cause my brother's death. "Don't let this be it." I whisper to myself as I watch the scene before me play out perfectly.

My knuckles turn white while I squeeze my fist to keep myself from screaming, digging my nails deep into my skin. This is happening too quickly. I am not ready to face this man. Taking in a deep inhale, my nerves settle a bit.

Zeus's pack is already waiting with our allies. All they need is the signal to be given. They are all in position as planned. The scent of every single one of them waiting for the right time to reveal themselves steady's my nerves further. "We do this together" I remind myself. We wait for the right time to turn the odds in our favor. And that time is the moment Liber lets go of my brother. I shift into my wolf.

"Let him go and I'll let you live", Shoneah's voice booms through the air despite still being mostly in Cassius's normal form. Only his hair has changed color which is the first time I have seen him this way in a partial shift of sorts. His voice cracks through the wind making everyone shudder. All but Liber. He remains stoic. The exact opposite of the turmoil raging inside Nora and I's my body.

Nora looks back at Shoneah, who is visibly showing unease and the trickle of fear building underneath his skin. Something you rarely see because of how well he hides his emotions when facing an enemy. But not this time. His emotions are slipping with my brother's life hanging in the balance of his fingers.

Liber's face shifts with anger, his stance ready to pounce, and the flames emerging from his fist, crackle with rage. The last time he must have spoken with this much fervor has to be against his father, at least from the stories I've heard.

Liber drops Atlas, laughing at what I can only assume is the thud my brother's body makes. "I'm surprised you're still alive and yet you still want to take me on." Liber licks his lips.

"I won't be killed off that easily!" Shoneah shouts as the tattoos race up his arms and his long hair turns to a silver-white hue that is brighter than before, erasing all traces of my brother-in-law's appearance. With his hair loose, the wind picks up around him from his transformation, making his hair flow upwards. Like snakes off Medusa's head, his hair dances around him waiting for a command.

"ATTACK!" Liber shouts lifting his arms signaling a swarm of goblins and shapeshifters spill out from the trees behind him. Never had the woods held so many creatures so skillfully hidden. Some even seem to appear out of thin air. Then again, they look just like how Finn described the lion shifters. It shouldn't be of surprise that their presences weren't felt.

The goblins race out of hiding in variations of decomposition states. Some are made fully of bones, aged, and withered. The legs of some show the previous breaks or deformities that must have made it difficult for them in their mortal life. Others still have pieces of flesh rotting on their bones which could only suggest that the time of their passing isn't too long ago. Not a long enough moment of peace. Their clothes hang loosely with holes doing little to hold them together.

As if the volume is turning up around Nora and me, the clanging of swords, bones rattling, and howls commence the fight of our worlds clashing. Each wolf is taking on one to two creatures in what seems like a one-sided fight, with us being on the losing end.

There are too many that are well-armed while not enough of us have weapons for close combat. As wolves, we tend to rely on our physical abilities while we have others hiding to snipe from a distance.

Nora looks down at her trembling legs. Unable to move. Her feet have rooted in the witness of such chaos. It's terrifying to see death running around like pawns of a psychopath's game. An unnatural reanimation of those who should be resting.

The undead creatures fighting on behalf of Liber, all have a dark aura like smoke that surrounds their bodies. It is as if the Grim Reaper himself is pulling the strings of the remains. Like a puppet master of war. Then again, I guess my father can now be considered as such.

The only reprieve is that most of the enemies are goblins. Taking them down might be easy due to their small stature but their weapons are a problem. Nora jumps out of the way as a goblin comes at us. His lower jaw is missing and so is his left arm, but his right holds a large thick branch. He swings but Nora doesn't move fast enough to dodge the blow to her face. A pool of blood fills her mouth.

She turns to the goblin who is already swinging for his next hit and ducks just in time. The force is something unnatural. Nora jumps back to create distance but bumps into another shifter instead. He turns to us with just his torso. It cracks and the bones grind against each other as the shifter forces his body into an unnatural position and with his canine's lurches toward us.

Nora

Stuck between the two I yelp as the goblin aims for my legs swiping and the other shifter for my head. I snap my jaw, but it remains completely unphased by me biting him and continues to try to expose my throat. I clamp down as hard as I can but the bone only cracks under my weak jaw.

I kick the goblin off with my hind leg while he tries to climb my body. Everything is happening too quickly, and I may have to resign to letting one have its way while I handle the other. In that moment a shadow flies over me and knocks the shifter off.

Pearson's wolf fights the shifter and bites off his head. When the body stops moving, I get up as quickly as I can because now, I know how to stop them.

Pearson's wolf barks my way, and I return the call to let him know I am fine. With blood in my eye, I do my best to take out the goblins but even with their size, they are no less formidable than the shifters. I run towards one of our warriors, Scott, who is struggling with two shifters on him. I pounce on one but with an ease I did not expect, it flings me off him. These shifters may even be stronger than when they were alive.

The variety of cat-shifters and bear-shifters in human form is daunting. Each shifting back and forth taking advantage of the coverage the trees offer. It's a sight I never thought I'd witness. Watching bones shift unbound by the skin is something out of a horror story.

With a small whine, I get up from the tree I am slammed against. Pain shoots up from my leg and I am sure it is fractured, and I may have also cracked a rib evident by the pain when I breathe. My unsteady footing falters as I am rushed by what seems like a beast from hell. A large shadow barrels through me, landing on my back again. I look to where the shadow went and gasp.

MANNY! I call out but it is too late. The bear shifter rams through everyone and pins Manny against a tree. I can hear his struggle to breathe but before he can make an effort to fight, the bear swipes Manny's head clean off. I barely Just learned his name and he is already gone beyond repair.

Zeus runs towards me to see if I am alright, and I nod but it's a lie. There's too much bloodshed and I'm in pain as each piece of my rib heals in place. Both physically and mentally, I struggle. My strength is escaping me, but I stand up again and with a deep breath, I yip at Zeus.

I need to be strong for Iris. Zeus and I charge back into the fight. This time I will wield her magic. A very fortunate realization through Iris' training is my ability to use some of her powers even in wolf form. This proves for a good strategy. Any magic used can be explained by Shoneah and Liber will not be the wiser until it is too late.

Yet with this barrage of attacks from the undead, I can't catch my breath long enough to focus. The pain in my leg worsens and my limping is keeping me from fighting properly.

Something needs to be done about the bear-shifters. I link to Kristofer.

You read my mind. He replies. **Everyone, we need to separate the bear-shifters. Snipers, they are the top priority, take them out. Alex, I'm counting on you buddy.**

The wolves howl in unison and we begin to move in ways to control the fight.

Cassius as Shoneah

"Okay, you have me to yourself. Ready to die?" I taunt Liber still holding up my hands in stance.

"You are a lot of talk for a person that was already beaten once," Liber retorts and swings an arm around before directing his aim to me. I barrel roll out of the way narrowly escaping the blades of fire. His attacks seem faster than before. *Was he toying with me last time?*

I grit my teeth and charge, swinging my arms with brute force. A sword manifests itself from my hands, forming a hilt up into a blade made of flames both blue and yellow. It catches Liber off guard even though he has seen this move before. The flame sword slices into Liber's shoulder in a single blow. He screams in pain bellowing into the air with a voice so hoarse it almost mimics a rabid beast going mad. A vocal scream, both tonal and crippling.

Blood drips down his arm and chest from the gash that holds the flames of the sword within it. Quickly I step back and with each step, I unleash an arrow. In quick short bursts, I bury my flame arrows into his torso.

Scott, grab Alpha Atlas, I call out through the link at the wolf closest to me. Nine, ten, eleven arrows in already, and Liber is on his knees bellowing in pain.

Yes, Luna, Scott replies. With Atlas in the clear, I begin to double my arrows.

Liber shouts something in an elvish tongue and the bones that are fighting others beside me, turn and attack me instead. They swarm me, unphased by my flames, and pin me down. The strength in their bones weigh me down like a ton against my limbs preventing me from struggling against them. My vision blurs as a knot ties in my stomach. It makes a vile taste sit in my throat. My heart is beating beyond control, and I can barely see through the tunnel vision that my tattoos are fading from my arms.

Liber weaves a hand sign swiftly like a ritual rehearsed repeatedly and chants a spell. His words sound familiar, like one Iris might have said but his pronunciation is different. Water appears around him lifting him off the ground to his feet in swirls. I try to get a grip on myself and force my transformation again. *I can't let fear take me.*

He chants the spell louder. It's a spell Iris had tried a few times but couldn't master. The words are the same but the way he pronounces them is different. The flames in his shoulder disperse and the wound begins to heal. This man will not be easy to overcome if his magic affords him the ability to heal.

I finally understand that if we are to win against this man, we can't give our opponent the chance to mend himself. A barrage of attacks may be the best hope we have at a chance at victory.

"Now, let's keep you busy." Liber smirks at me but before I can ask what he means, the ground beneath me shakes. A feeling I know all too well. "Why don't you get comfortable, hm?" Liber raises his arms and from the ground a wall of mud rises around me and like a mummy, I am trapped in what seems like a sarcophagus. I am once again in a tomb.

I can't breathe! I gasp for air as this time my grave is completely sealed shut. No water. No air. Just muffled war beyond my tomb and an old friend, darkness, as company. My mind slips in and out of conscious's and I find myself as that little boy covered in his mother's blood hiding in the dark of a cave.

Help...me...

***

Zeus

I'm clearing off the dead slowly. We only manage to take down three of the bear-shifters but there are still too many of them doing damage. Each one is expending more energy from us than I thought possible.

Alpha Robert, triangle formation and go for the legs.

Alpha Robert howls and orders his wolves. Ithil pairs up with Alpha Robert and Robert's son, Pearson. I order my men to do the same and begin tackling the undead. Some of their movement is awkward and unpredictable which makes it hard to effectively take them down. Their inability to feel pain makes them continuously attack without regard to themselves. What worries me even more is the fact that the lion shifters haven't appeared. We are well into the fight and yet the most formidable of them all have yet to appear.

With Demetrius's wolf, Alcide, and Spike's wolf, Adriel, we work to take down the shifters. One distracts, the other takes out the limbs, and the third decapitates. This new plan is finally making the difference we need to turn the odd in our favor.

Alcide bites the spine of a cat-shifter and snaps it off, essentially decapitating it in one fell swoop. The shifter falls into a pile of its own bones. Unsettling but satisfying. I call out to Nora who is fighting alongside Lenny and Rory. Exhaustion kicking in.

We will wear ourselves out at this rate. My mind syncs with theirs in conversation.

I agree but this is the most progress we have made so far. Lenny replies as he continues to swiftly evade attacks. Nora on the other hand is slowing down.

She looks to be in pain, but I can't seem to make out why.

Just use your magic. I tell Nora directly. It's not like Liber will know where the magic is coming from. Nora nods and with a flick of her snout, the goblins fly in all directions. Like flies, most of them drop unable to reanimate. Others had their heads come off while some stand back up running around without arms or using their arms to walk if they lost their legs.

"So, I see my little dog of a daughter learned some tricks," Liber shouts in her direction with venom dripping off each word. My heart clenches when the bond between Nora and I grip at Liber calling my mate his little dog. But I need to stay strong and give her strength in return. The road ahead is treacherous and a moment of weakness is enough to equal an unfortunate end. The goblins surrounding Liber all stop what they are doing and in unison gang up on Nora.

They groan in odd tonal voices and speak incoherently amongst one another. Zooming left and right, she is fighting and clawing while snapping the necks off the goblins with her magic using wind as her source. Experiencing her fight in perfect sync with me feels amazing but the number of enemies keeps increasing and closing in on her.

Two goblins go for my leg, while another jumps on my back. Distracted from watching Nora, I let myself get caught. Uneven teeth bite through my fur and into my back, forcing a howl to rip through me with a chunk of my flesh pulling away from my torso. White searing pain grips my body as I desperately try to breathe through it.

Alcide and Adriel come to my aid and finish off the ones attacking me. The pain drumming in me along with my exhaustion is pulling my senses away.

ZEUS! I hear Nora's voice in my head but even so, it seems far away. My vision tunnels into a small dot of light.

"There's too much blood," is the last thing I hear Spike shout after shifting in front of me.

***

Atlas

After the treatment from Scott, I am able to fight with him and Mavis by my side. We tear the heads off the shifters after realizing this breaks whatever spell they are under. But doing so is leaving us with fewer wolves. The cat-shifters are picking us clean, and our numbers are dwindling. As agile as cats are naturally, with this dark smoke-like aura they are faster than shadows chased in the dark.

Everyone needs to stay in formation. Do not let them separate you. I call out to everyone through the link. But as I do, one of the cat-shifters is about to attack one of my men. I shift and give it chase.

Leo

Mavis and Scott are close behind me in their wolf forms, but the cat-shifter is too agile between the trees. It maneuvers itself through the fight as if it were being led instead. My breathing is heavy and labored, and I know that I do not have the speed to catch up to it.

Ivar, go around. I will keep chasing. Elu, I need you to run the side and direct him towards Ivar. I link with Scott and Mavis before I spring to action hoping it'll work.

The fire in my legs from pushing my limits builds at an incredible speed. The trees are now a blur as they swish past us. The blood pumping in my ears drowns out the noise of everything around me. But it seems the plan is working. The cat is going straight to Ivar, Mavis' wolf. In a perfectly timed pounce, Ivar tackles the shifter and Elu jumps in for the kill. Panting from the exertion, we yip and then return to the others.

Seeing so many bones on the floor blending with the snow makes it a scene from a horror movie to say the least. While the blood is only that from our own bodies losing a limb or gushing from wounds, the sound of crushed bones and tortured screams, mixed with the howls echoing among them is the only song sung through the chaos. A lullaby that will haunt us every night coming forth.

Ivar looks around with a bit of hope seeing they are getting the upper hand. He dodges the blow of a goblin but as I manage to pull it away from Ivar, he is stabbed. A bone sticks out of his side with blood dripping from the wound. The goblin thought to use the bone of another to attack Ivar and before I can do anything to the creature, Elu takes him down. I rip the head off the goblin while Elu protects Ivar to make sure he isn't injured further.

I need someone to take Ivar out of here. I call out to the pack. Nora limps towards me but I shake my head. She looks ready to fall over but she should do what she is here to do.

Not you. Get Liber instead. I insist on her and she nods in understanding. She limps as best she can over to the man who shares her DNA. If she is going to face the man that's been haunting her then this is her chance to do so. Now or never.

Nora

"Oh, you came to me willingly. How kind of you." Liber mocks me as I bare my teeth and growl my hatred for the man. "Nora, my little puppy. If you show daddy a trick, I will give you a treat." Liber laughs hysterically but I stand in front of him growling. Everyone is exhausted and the fighting is never ending but this is our moment. I focus all my energy and look right into Liber's eyes. Panting heavily and wobbling on my paws, I grit my teeth. Being in wolf form and using Iris' elf abilities is draining and I haven't had the chance to build the stamina that I need for it.

You got this Nora. Atlas pops into my mind and I refocus. Liber becomes motionless under my gaze. The shock in his face when realizing he can't move is satisfying to no end, but it doesn't last long. Liber struggles against it and slowly regains control. So, I shift back to human form to finish the job.

Iris

I bend him backward eliciting cries from my father, Liber. He fights back with his increasing resistance, forcing me to exert more energy and lose my strength. *I can't do it. I'm not strong enough. I...I can't do it.*

Iris, keep trying! Pearson comes blaring into my mind. **You've go-** His voice cuts off and I look back to find he is separated from his father.

"Is this how you treat your dear old dad?" Liber pulls my attention back to him. He has control again and surrounds me with his flames. The heat encasing my bare skin threatens to melt it off. "Bad child", he whispers as he closes in on me. "Now tell me, how did you control me like that?"

I spit in his face, refusing the tell him a thing.

"Very well. As you wish." Liber increases the heat of the flames now making it hard to breathe. I scream from the depths of my soul. Everything is swirling in my mind, everything is failing, and I am too weak to do anything. I scream louder and as I do a familiar sensation surrounds me. A gust of wind wraps around me. My skin cools and through my screams, I hear an odd silence.

I open my eyes to find a similar scene to that of the cabin. All the bones that had piled up are thrashed around surrounding me. Most of the undead are rendered useless and gives me a temporary sense of relief. That's when I spot an odd mound on the ground the length of a body located by Liber. He stands before me with bones protruding from his body in shock with blood dripping from his lips.

"That power...I must have.... that power." Liber sways with the color draining from his face. His knees give out and he is caught by the lion-shifters before he can hit the ground. They lift Liber with ease and one of them roars at the remaining others.

"NO!" Uncle Robert screams as the lion-shifters quickly sprint towards him and Pearson. Robert drops to his knees covered in blood.

"Oh, my goddess", I run to Uncle Robert, but I know before I even reach him.

The other two lion-shifters attack Ithil and Maeve. Just as quickly as the first, Maeve falls like a rag doll. Gurgles sound from her throat filling the air. Ithil skillfully fights with his sword but even then, he lasts all of a minute longer than Maeve before he falls into a bloody mess as well.

"My precious boy. Why, my precious boy?" Uncle Robert cries uncontrollably as the wolf in his arms shifts into his human form and takes his last breath. His only son, Pearson, is gone. My cousin is gone. I cry letting out another deafening scream but the lions retreat taking Liber with them.

***

Alex

In the distance, Demetrius and Spike are handling two shifters at once. He pins one down trying to rip the head off his skeletal opponent while another is on his back. He snaps the neck off the one on the floor and flips over the one on top of him. Just as he does so, a third shifter and goblin run towards Demetrius. My nerves have been shot for a while now and I am running low on ammo.

I pan the scope between the approaching shifters and the last of the two bear shifters destroying Luna Melody's wolves. With a deep breath, I focus on the bear and as I exhale, I pull the trigger and take my shot. The bear jolts but he doesn't fall. I steady myself, readjust, and take another shot. The bear-shifter falls. Nice. I turn back to Demetrius, and he is bleeding while struggling with the two that ran after him. Spike is nowhere to be seen.

I curse him for leaving Demetrius behind and steady my rifle. It is up to me to make sure he makes it out alive. With a slow breath, I put my finger on the trigger. A sudden pang and a burst of senses come to life within me, taking over my body in a convulsion as I pull the trigger. *Huh?* My mind goes blank. The shot misses the enemy and hits my Beta instead. It's the last thing I see before a white light takes over.

Chapter 22

Atlas

THIS DAY IS BEYOND my wildest nightmares. A day where the living and the dead collide in a battle for dominion over the other. Never have I knocked on death's door this much. I am honestly grateful that death never answers, although that time may come sooner than I think. Ever since the great war of Gaea Cry 500 years ago, there has not been a need for war amongst any of our kind. So much blood was shed between the different species that our numbers dwindled immensely back then. All of our numbers did, but it achieved a peace that kept us all from repeating history ever since. Yet now we can add fighting with the dead to the new tide that is turning. *How did it come to this?*

I stand in the piles of bones from the beheaded dead-walkers, naked and covered in wounds. Some are healing while others remain fresh. I'm worn out from head to toe and the thought of this not being over tires me more. But I pull whatever I can from the depths within me and look around for the wounded while removing the dead. Few of the men I am finding are okay, but the injuries will be hard to heal from. Seeing how long it took for Kristofer to heal is enough for me to know that some of these men will be out of commission for a bit.

Too many of our men have lost their lives or are barely hanging on to it and all I can do is push on and prepare for the next attack. My aching feet drag through the mess on the ground and toward the group assisting some of the injured wolves that can't transform back to their human state. Kristofer's Beta and the Beta of the others are taking care of most of our fallen and my heart grows heavy. My brothers are tired and battered but it is a price that grows bigger still as I walk through trees that are scarred from our claws. It's not over and more will fall.

A chill runs down my spine and it's the first time I feel a bit of the cold from winter's breath. Either that or it's the chill from the souls we lost leaving the Earth to meet our goddess.

My knees grow weak at the sight of what I find next to me. Down to the ground, I fall next to the head of a young wolf. I had only just met him and spoke with him about how great he would be as a teacher. His wish was to work with children and couldn't wait to find his mate so he could start his own family. As I look into the lifeless eyes of the detached head that rests on the ground beside me, I weep the grief of the sudden loss of a man I barely knew.

"Manny, you meet our goddess too soon." I sob my words and close his graying eyes with my fingertips. I gather some dirt in my hand and hold it up in the air, "welcome him into your shimmering light. Help his wolf find another. Let his soul find peace with you goddess. From this life and on to the next, he travels forth." I dab my thumb into the dirt in my palm and paint a crescent on Manny's forehead. "Be safe in your travels." My heavy heart sobs again as I carry his head back to his body that sits slumped by a tree not too far away.

"Scott..." I call out but my exhaustion is taking over. I can barely move a muscle nor take in a breath deep enough. I lean on a tree that is graciously supporting me a few feet from where I left Manny.

"Alpha Atlas, are you okay?" Scott limps towards me.

"I see you're hurt too but can you help me walk around? I need to assess the rest of the area." I hold out my arm and Scott kindly nods and puts it over his shoulder.

Together we continue walking through the horror of the fallen. The sound of the fight still echoes in the hollow of the trees as I walk past. These trees will never provide the same peace they used to. Out in the distance, Spike limps carrying someone familiar. "Is that.... Ithil?" I look at Scott who shrugs.

"I think it is. I hope he is okay, but they are too far away to tell." Scott tries to help me pick up the pace, but I can't move any faster.

"I'm sure he is, or they would have called to you by now with the bad news." Scott tries to reassure me, and it works...a little. He's right. Had Ithil died, I would have been alerted right away.

"Alpha Atlas, isn't that Beta Mavis?" Scott nods in the direction he is looking, and I follow with already watery eyes expecting my Beta to be dead.

"Mavis!" I let go of Scott and stumble my way over to him, falling to my knees just before I reach him. No one bothered to remove the bone he was stabbed with. The amount of blood staining his shirt is alarming and most likely fatal. I call out to him once more, but he doesn't move. If he were to die, I am not sure how this will break me apart. What would I tell Donna? Scott touches his skin and pauses for a moment. The lines on his face fill with worry as he shakes his head no.

"He feels cold," Scott whispers barely loud enough for me to hear.

This won't be how his story ends. While it is a noble that his life was giving so that others may live. I do not accept his death. He needs to live. I pull out the bone in anger knowing he wouldn't be able to heal if the bone stayed lodged within him. "Didn't I leave him with you? Why didn't you help him as I continued fighting?" I scream in anger to Scott.

"I...I... have no excuse. I was fighting as well and got carried away. I have no words Alpha Atlas, I am sorry." Scott's eyes water in fear and hurt and I realize it's wrong for me to blame him. I was there too protecting Mavis. These men are my responsibility, not Scott's.

I scoff at myself and return to Mavis who doesn't seem to feel as cold anymore. I place an ear on his chest and a small heartbeat register. There's hope yet. He just needs the chance to heal.

"Take him to my home to be examined, please. I'm sorry Scott, it's not your fault." I pat Scott on the shoulder and steady myself before I walk off to check on others.

***

After gathering our fallen brothers and sisters, we march in silence towards the river. With so many traveling to the afterlife, we carry the bodies on wagons, in our arms, and some on gurneys we made from broken sturdy branches. In silence, the woods joined our march of departure. My eyes can barely stay open from the last bit of adrenaline having left my body. But I must continue and properly depart our loved ones. The last time I did this march was for my father. The tears I shed now are both old and new, and they both share my sorrow.

The river rushing in the distance grows near and as the view of the cold water grows closer to our feet, I stop and wait for the rest to gather. I ask for a member of each of our packs to step forward to help with the cleansing of the bodies.

Quietly, five people along with their Alpha and Luna step forward to assist with cleansing our fallen wolves by the water. The river stains in red as it washes away the dirt from wounds. Soft sobs echo within the silence, but Maeve interrupts the whispered cries and steps forward to sing our song of purification.

"Through light, our souls, begin to change

A beau—ty soooo profo-und.

In time, we pass

Our wolves, at last

Find our moon goddess pro–ud.

Let the waters clean the vessels we loved.

Let the moon, touch their skin...."

Her voice carries through the air while the others hum her tune. The group sways holding hands with tear-stained cheeks. As we finish with the cleanse and wrap them in white linen, the men and women singing build a pyre. One by one we lay the fallen and form a circle around them. As everyone lifts their hands to the sky, the Alphas, Luna Melody, and I step forward.

"Bless this knife dear moon goddess and as I cut my hand and accept the release of my men and women that were under my care. I hand them over to be a part of your family." I slice my hand and drip blood on the pyre. The others do the same to release their former pack members.

"Goddess take them home," I call out, and in unison we all shout, "You are free." I light the pyre and step back with the others as it catches fire and spreads to free our beloved.

Most of us watch in silence while some let out their first cry. I do my best to watch on and pay my respects but the trauma of having to watch my father in the same manner yanks my heart to pieces. This is too difficult to do but for those who look up to me, I must bear not just my privilege but also my burden as their chosen leader.

The heat of the pyre grows as large as the fire itself. We step back unable to handle being too close.

The clouds move to uncover the moon, revealing herself over our hurting hearts, and flurries of white light ascend from the fire drifting up into the night sky. They are traveling, no longer bound to this realm. Now we let the bodies burn completely before we can bury the bones in the morning. With heavy feet and even heavier hearts, we march back to the house in silence.

"Iris," I call out to her, but she doesn't move. She wasn't with us by the river for the march of departure and I thought that maybe she was with her mate. Now that I think about it, I don't see her mate either.

With long strides, I run over to my sister who is crying, whispering Pearson's name as if afraid to say his name too loud. Her hands are stained red from helping Uncle Robert carry his son. That much I remember from when I helped gather the other bodies.

Uncle Robert wanted to do his own private march with his pack. Iris seems to not even register my presence as I carry her to the steps of our home if only to remove her from where she stood. The last time I held her like this wasn't on a happy occasion either but as her big brother, I'm grateful I can at least do this much, "hey where's Kris?", I whisper, afraid to further burden her tears.

Iris slowly looks up and scans the area before her and then me. The emptiness in her eyes fills with despair as they trail behind me in an attempt to find her mate. The way her face changes from confusion to concern and then fear, only tells me, she forgot to look for her mate. "I don't know where he is. I feel him but...very faint." She gets up almost losing her balance, but I sit her back down with a tug of her arm and leave her there with Maeve who arrived shortly afraid I set Iris down.

"I'll look for him. I also need to find Cass. Who knows, they may be together." I give Iris my big-brother-look to make sure she stays put and run off to find Kristofer.

Quietly, Mavis, Robert, Vinny, and Melody gather the bones from Liber's undead army. They fill large black bags with the remains to figure out what to do with them later. Now that the bones are all unanimated, it doesn't seem scary. If anything, it seems sad. I nod as I run past them and continue to search but with how far the fight spread out, Kristofer can be anywhere at this point. I pick up my pace until I see a figure slumped over that looks like Kristofer, my friend, propped against a tree. Someone must have moved him there. His head is hanging low, and his arms are sitting in his lap, limp.

"Hey, wake up." I give Kristofer a few slaps.

"IRIS!" Kristofer screams out and takes a swing at me. His heavy hook catches my chin and knocks me over.

"What in the world?!" I rub my sore jaw contemplating if I should just leave him there.

"Atlas! Sorry. What happened?" Kristofer's eyes are bloodshot.

"It looks like you passed out. Are you hurt anywhere?" I answer and look around for my mate hoping he is near. It has been a while since I have seen him as well.

Kristofer looks at me for a moment, "Actually yeah. I was bit on my back by one of the undead walkers." He leans forward so I can see. A chunk of flesh is still mending itself on his back, but the bleeding is much less than a wound that size should have.

"Looks like you'll be fine. You're healing nicely.

Alpha Kristofer, Alpha Atlas!

I turn to see one of Kristofer's wolves running towards us.

"What is it?" Kristofer groans in pain.

"It's Alex and Beta. Somehow, Alex shot Demetrius and they're unconscious." He huffs as he tries to catch his breath.

"How the hell?!" Kristofer bellows but then groans in pain again. "We need to go."

"Wait, I'll help you. You can't walk in that condition. Give me a sec." I pat Kristofer's shoulder and run off to Iris.

"Hey, sis. I found Kris and he is doing alright but we are going back to his house. It's his Beta and Alex. Somethings wrong."

She nods half dazed then tilts her head at me, "You could have just linked and told me. What about Luna?"

I stiffen at those words. I have yet to find him, and I am helping everyone else but my own mate. How can I be so daft as to not realize that I have stopped feeling him? *Why can't I feel him?!*

I race off to where I last remember Liber and him fighting. Adrenaline drains into my ears blocking out every sound around me, but the one of my racing heart. Nothing. There's nothing to be found anywhere. Luna is gone. This can't be happening again. My knees give out and I fall to the ground caving to the tears that have been welling up. *Think Atlas, think. Where is he? Where could he have gone? Was he taken? Killed?* I pound on the ground with my fist then stop to look at what I hit that made a hollow sound. The sound the ground makes is unnatural as I hit it again and take note that the shape of the mound next to me is unusual.

The ground beside me is raised in a mound and the length of a body. A small whole is visible, and I hit it again. Like before it sounds hollow, and the hole widens. With another hit, it clicks that this is the same thing Liber did to Cassius before up against the tree....*no!* I stand up and begin stomping on it with the heel of my foot.

Atlas? Where are you?

Iris calls for me. Kristofer must have asked her to find me because I left him there waiting but I can't go. Not now. Cassius is in there. I know it. I keep stomping using all my weight. On the third try, the heel of my foot goes through.

"You! I'm sorry, I don't know your name but come help me." I call out to a wolf that is near me cleaning up some of the bones and weapons.

"Yes, Alpha." The older man leaves the bones he is stacking up and comes over to help me break open the rest of the dome.

Quickly we work on freeing the body inside. Unlike the first time, there isn't water to drown him, but this must have been sealed tight, depriving his lungs of oxygen. My poor mate must have clawed enough to create the small hole I found but it probably wasn't enough. I try to push away the thought that he might have suffocated and work faster in clearing the last bits covering him. Pulling him out and brushing away the dirt from his face, under the moonlight his skin is pale a blue.

"Cass, baby, wake up." I tap his cheek a few times but no response. "Shit, I might have to do CPR again." A tear rolls down my cheek as I get in position.

"Wait, look at his chest. It's moving slightly. I think he is breathing, just very shallow." The wolf points at Cassius' chest and he is right. It is moving slightly but not enough to fill his lungs. I hold my own breath to not rob him of his and put a finger under his nose to feel the air moving in and out of him.

The guilt of forgetting him grips me and it is taking everything I have to not break down. While I understand that I was doing my part as an Alpha to pack, I am also his mate and should have looked for him the second I realized I had not seen him. Lifting him into my arms, I carry him home. Kristofer will have to attend to his Beta on his own after he heals enough to do so. For now, my attention is on my mate.

Chapter 23

Kristofer

ATLAS ISN'T COMING, KRIS. Iris flows into my mind. Something must have happened for him to leave me like here after telling me to wait. I groan against the tree but the wound on my back is becoming bearable enough, allowing me to move a bit more as time passes. I exhale the death I have been breathing for the last thirty minutes or so as my eyes wander around the scene before me.

The strong scent of putrid blood from within the shattered bones of the raised dead lingers in the air mixed with the fresh blood spilled of our own falling brethren. The mixture churns my stomach like sour soup looking for an exit. The ground is stained red in random places, marking the locations where each hit imprinted itself the history of our war cries. "Was the Gaea Cry not enough?" I whisper into the night.

The men slowly rise as their wounds heal enough to permit them mobility, limping from exhaustion and pain. Had we not called in our allies, this could have ended very differently but I am sure we have not seen the last of Liber. Nothing with him ever seems final. An enemy that won't die, is no longer just an enemy but a monster that forges into our memory an everlasting fear. Even if we manage to kill him off, I don't think I can forget the feeling of his presence and the way it has haunted Iris.

The pain from my throbbing wound fades pulling me out of my thoughts. "Finally!" I exhale and stand with one last helping support from the tree. It was the final bit of healing that I needed to get myself up and run. My legs start slowly and pick up in a run with all I have left in me, which isn't much. I am tired to my very core. Sheer willpower is the only thing keeping me going right now. The way my body is worn and battered from the fight is preventing my muscles from properly taking in the oxygen they need to function properly. I can sleep for three days if I were to stop, which is why I plan to knock out after I see what's wrong with my Beta.

My eyes tunnel a bit with my body working double-time to make it home, zipping through trees and jumping the freezing river. I continue until my home comes into view and the sweet relief is almost too good, making me falter in my step.

I dust myself off and link to my mother that I'm close and run up to the back door barely able to breathe with my how much my muscles are on fire. She hands me a clean set of clothes and motions to follow her to our small infirmary. I toss on the shirt as I walk into the room and find Demetrius unconscious alongside Alex in the bed adjacent.

"What happened?" I question walking over to them both with wobbly knees and stiffening calves. A painful combo and a sure sign that it is about to cramp up. My mother slides a chair under me as my weight proves too much for my legs to handle at the moment. The plight must be clear as day on my face as I seek relief. "They look perfectly fine," I whisper to myself. Their IV and monitors recording their stable state agrees with my assessment.

"Well, I examined them both and all I could see was a lodged bullet that Demetrius' body eventually expelled, but other than that, they don't have anything wrong. However, I must inform you that the bullet is a match with Alex's rifle." Dr. Michael shows me the bullet in a small clear bag.

"This doesn't add up." Martha mumbles.

"So why is Alex knocked out as well?" I huff unable to believe that Alex would shoot his own mate. Even if he doesn't know they are mates, with the way they have been all over each other, it doesn't add up.

"Well, we can't get answers until they wake up" Dr. Michael sighs and we slump our shoulders in wait.

***

Two days have gone by and neither seem to want to wake up. Their vitals continue stable, and their bond seems to still be intact. Their heart rate drops when we move them apart from one another and stabilize when we put them back together. The doctor finds it peculiar since he doesn't know about the bond, but I don't want to be the one to reveal they are mates unless I think it's necessary. It baffles me that Alex has not been able to identify my Beta as his mate but that is their problem to deal with.

I leave them in my mother's care while I return to my room. My legs have not fully recovered and although my wounds are healed externally, on this inside, Dr. Michael says I'm healing slowly. His only guess is that I need to be closer to my mate to help facilitate the healing. I need her warmth and care to wash over me. I agree that it may very well be the case because I yearn for her in a way that I hadn't before. You would think that by him making that assessment that he would come to the realization about Alex and my Beta.

The stress of them not waking up is getting to me which could also be hindering my healing abilities.

I call Iris over and collapse in her arms the moment she shows up at my door. Her scent is enough to numb my pain and give me back my strength. Whether that is our bond working or not, I don't care. It is the reprieve I seek.

We spend a few days with each other in my room in and out of sleep, in attempt to strengthen our bond and erase the horrible events of what happened with Liber. Aside from my injuries, she is in shock and how could she not be. With so much going on, her mind is still trying to make sense of everything. And that's aside from the mental exhaustion of wielding so much power in a short amount of time.

We return to her pack house making sure to call a therapist to start sessions with Iris. It is the best I can do for her to help her heal. Our bond alone is not enough to mend a wounded mind. Unfortunately, when we get there, we find Cassius is not awake yet either. In an effort to do everything possible, Atlas calls Dr. Michael and asks for him to accompany him and Cassius to the hospital. I want to go as well but Atlas is refusing everyone. Instead, he asks Robert and Luna Melody to sub in for him while he is at the hospital.

***

It is now a week later, and nothing explains my Beta and Alex not waking up. Their vitals are constantly checked, and nothing is out of the ordinary. A few times Alex's heart rate spiked but it was due to the doctor not repositioning them together again. At this point, I tell Dr. Michael about them being mates to see if that provides any clues to their conditions. He thinks that the bond can be what's keeping them under, so from here on out it's a waiting game.

I sigh wondering when everything became so hectic. At least Cassius is awake from the coma as of two days ago. Although, he is acting unusual saying something about figuring it out. Dr. Michael says, the trauma forced Cassius to remain unconscious as a self-defense mechanism. Atlas, who is a sobbing mess, is by his side trying to make sense of the fragmented conversation Cassius claims he had with the previous shamans in his dream. While I am glad that he is awake, it seems to have affected him slightly. Cassius has a bit of amnesia due to the trauma of being buried alive and he is now in a constant state of anger. Now all he does is distract himself with books and spells.

"Cass, I brought you some of mom's chicken." I knock on the open door to Cassius' room. He is finally home today after his discharge from the hospital. Cassius puts down a book he is reading and covers it with his blanket.

"I'd love some." He smiles up at me.

"Do you still not remember anything from when you were buried?" I ask as I pass him the food.

"No." The word sounds dry and rid of any lightness from a second ago.

"Need anything else?" I change the subject, but the mood is already ruined due to my question earlier.

"I'm fine," Cassius answers stiffly with a scowl brewing on his face.

"Okay, eat up then." I turn around getting his message loud and clear that he doesn't want to be bothered when the sound of a plate hitting the nightstand makes me flinch.

I turn to find him reading again and a mess of chicken and rice against the wall and floor.

"I don't know what is going on with you but that doesn't mean you have to be an asshole." I scoff and leave the room shaking my head at the tantrum.

I feel like we have been fighting nonstop for a while now and the precursor to it all is Cassius' biological father. Sometimes I wonder if any of this would be happening if Honovi had never showed up. Atlas walks by me with some water, completely ignoring my presence and unaware of the mess he is about to encounter. There is a long road ahead for those two. I sigh and make my way downstairs to Iris to say goodnight.

***

The sun warms my face waking me gently from my sleep. I give a good stretch under the sheets with my arms and groan at the cracks my bones make. I'd say it's from sleeping in a weird position, but I know that's a lie. My bones crack more than a glow stick. Yawning, I make my way to the bathroom. Sleep escapes me every chance it gets and last night is no different. At best, I got three hours of sleep.

With cold water, I freshen up my face and rinse my mouth before grabbing the toothpaste. It reminds me that I have yet to get her some things for the bathroom here that she can use. I make a mental note to stop at the store later and finish up.

Iris is still sleeping in the bed and stirs at the creak the floor makes when I reach the door. Mid-step

I freeze and wait for her to settle before I leave and close the door to head to the kitchen for some coffee. Cassius is at the table furiously reading a book already drinking a freshly brewed pot. By furiously I mean that he is giving his book a mean mug and aggressively turning the pages.

"Morning Cass. Nice to see you up this early." I smile.

"Never slept." He replies and takes a sip of what could be his tenth cup if that's the case.

"Is that Liber's spell book?" Taking a seat across from him after serving myself a cup, I get a better look, and it is indeed the spell book Jesika had found.

"I need to learn as much as I can. I won't let that man toy with me any longer." Cassius mutters between his teeth something about being buried twice without so much as looking up.

"You mean, toy with us, right?" I lift a brow, and Cassius slowly breaks away from the book and looks up at me with narrowing eyes.

"Right, us." He corrects himself and then continues reading.

"Luna Cassius, don't forget that we were all wounded by him. It's not your job to defeat him alone, nor is it Iris'. We work together or we fall divided." I leave him there to think on his own and sit in the living room by the window with my mug.

Just outside is Atlas keeping Uncle Robert company who is mourning the death of his son in soft cries on the porch. I find it odd that Atlas isn't on

Cassius like he was in the hospital, but I can only assume it's because of the book. He probably pushed Atlas away, so he is redirecting his attention elsewhere.

Atlas hugs his uncle and enters the house where he greets me with a tired smile. The bags under his eyes suggest he is struggling with the same condition as me. Lack of sleep. From the living room, I can hear Atlas telling his mate that he will make him some breakfast and proceeds to make clanking sounds which I can only assume is him cooking. It's reassuring that Atlas still makes his Luna food and cares for him despite the cold shoulder Cassius seems to have developed toward everyone.

I remember asking Iris about the wedding plans for Cassius and her brother. Cassius wants to have a spring wedding with lots of flowers and pastels. Iris is almost as bad as Cassius with the planning, and I know she will go crazy setting everything up. The second she hears about a spring wedding, she will be pulling connections for catering, picking patterns, and creating a guest list. She is so happy to be the maid of honor that becoming the wedding planner may seem like a given to her.

Atlas, on the other hand, wants a winter wedding but Cassius refuses to let go of the idea of a spring wedding. He wants to wait for the snow to melt and the weather to warm up so they can hold the wedding at Ryan's town up north. Ryan's home holds a lot of good memories for them both and some that I'd like to forget. The bond grew between them during their time there and flourished into what it is now. It's also where Atlas reunited with his mother. It's perfect and remote for a romantic wedding. The location is the only thing they seem to agree on.

The smell of cleaning spray distracts my thoughts, and I sneeze. Martha giggles and I give a half-hearted smile to her as she cleans up together with Maeve. The pack house isn't as crowded since some of the families left to bring Pearson and the other remains back to their hometown.

"Maeve, how is your mother?" I ask the feisty wolf.

"She is resting well. Mostly healed and is now breathing better but I am afraid she lost her left eye." Maeve sighs, shoving another plastic cup into a garbage bag she's holding.

"Jeez, I'm so sorry."

"Don't be. She wears her eye patch proudly. She said she would give another if it meant protecting her people from an elf like him." Maeve did her best impression of Luna Melody.

"Yes, that sounds very much like her." Martha chuckles.

"Indeed, and I barely know her." We all laugh lightly and go about our business. Martha leaves with the trash while Maeve starts to sweep around me. Out of habit, I lift my feet out of the way and continue sipping my coffee.

***

Waking up from the unforeseen nap in the living room, I make my way to the kitchen for something to eat. Cassius is still sitting there with a cold plate of food half eaten and a mess of papers.

"Hey, any progress?" I open the fridge and grab a soda while I lean against the counter to ponder my options.

Cassius looks at me with an annoyed scowl, "no". But then eyes my soda then the fridge and the soda again.

"Thirsty?" I chuckle.

"Yea", Cassius sighs and closes the book with a bookmark. "Sorry, just grumpy I guess." He admits and I ignore the opportunity to rub it in his face how much of a dick he is being.

"So, what have you learned so far?" I pass Cassius a soda of his own and watch him drink the can in one go and belch.

"Well, there's a spell in there that I can use to trap him. I want to combine this with another spell that will render him powerless temporarily. It's what the Shaman in my dream taught me while I was unconscious. I just can't seem to get it to work together." With a light thump, Cassius hits the table with his forehead and growls in frustration.

"Ask Jesika to come over and help you. I am sure with her magical inclination, it might work." I chuckle when Cassius shoots his head up with a light red circle on his forehead. "Like I said, you are not in this alone", I wave and leave the kitchen to order my food instead. This fight seems like it will never end and as an Alpha I feel powerless, but I have faith in Cassius, Iris, and her friend. I heave a deep breath, if I am to draw up a plan, I need a clear mind and need a full stomach to do so.

Chapter 24

Kristofer

AFTER A COLD DECEMBER NIGHT, the morning sun peeks into the room where Alex and Demetrius sleep. The rays slowly flicker between the trees, greeting with arms of light stretching through the woods. Gold and orange hues paint the remaining snow with warmth as birds sing their morning song and squirrels run up and down the trees looking for breakfast. The giant morning star sneaks into the room and silently crosses the floor. Shadows that are cast on the floor crawl up the beds and disperse into the ceiling.

I lean on the entrance door of the infirmary checking on the two sleeping and flinch when I see movement. Alex groans a bit and then blinks his eyes open. He squints at first and covers his face with his hand before his eyes adjust enough to look around. Everything must be so bright to him despite the small amount of light beginning to fill the room. Alex runs his fingers through his hair sighing at the exhaustion not realizing that I am standing here observing. He grabs his neck and groans again. His throat must be dry and itchy with how long he slept. He squints into the light and takes in his surroundings. Alex recognizes the infirmary immediately and relaxes. Maybe being in an environment that he recognizes gives him peace of mind.

I'd feel that way too if the last thing I remember is the battlefield. He pulls out the oxygen from his nose, still not noticing my presence, and freezes as something has his eyes rolling back in what looks like pleasure. *I think this is my cue to leave.*

Alex

Musk and rosewood fill my lungs, *my mate. I have a mate.* Everything inside me does somersaults. Tingles travel up my arm from my right hand which I now realize is holding on to someone. I wiggle my fingers and find resistance against the hand that is interlocked with mine. With a deep breath, I turn to the person beside me. *How?* Demetrius is asleep with an IV hooked in his other arm like me. He stirs a bit against my tugging hand. *Demetrius is my mate!* I stare at his beautiful features still trying to process this new fact. I would have given everything to make him my mate because I fell for him long before our training, way before he showed even the slightest interest in me. My mind naturally always led to him. The crush I had on Cassius is nothing to what I feel for Demetrius.

My eyes follow down his half-naked body. The pure muscles of his chest and perfectly sculpted abs make my mouth water. His enticing v-line leading to the grand prize I've felt so many times through his jeans makes my knees weak. *Damn, all of that is mine now?* I prayed every day to the goddess to not let me fall in love, but I am, and now I no longer need to feel guilt over it. *What I can't understand is why am I only smelling him now.* That one question knocks my senses into check.

I can only assume it is the medication I'm on that awakened me like this but still. This sudden burst of pheromones flooding my senses is hazing my better judgment. So, this is what it's like. I bite my lip staring at his package remembering his size from the times he pressed it against me. A small growl gathers in my throat, but I shake it off. This isn't the time to think of such lewd thoughts.

"Like what you see, pup?" A raspy voice pulls me from my thoughts, a welcomed distraction. But his question is just as stimulating.

I nod my head with a wicked smile still partially lost in my fantasy world that is now forming and overwriting my rationality. Demetrius' eyes nearly pop out of his head at my direct response. It sends giggles bubbling out of me, blushing an even tone of red from the ridiculous look on his face.

The embarrassment now that the initial onslaught of the pheromones is fading allows the hidden throbbing headache to come through. Dr. Michael comes in and Demetrius flinches his hand to let go, but I squeeze it tight. I am never letting this man go.

"Shit, that hurts." I place my hand on my head with my eyes closed and a new throbbing headache growing.

"You guys sure took your time to wake up," Dr. Michael smiles and walks around to remove my IV. "How do you feel?" He looks over at us curiously.

"Thirsty," I croak out. He nods and pours me a glass of water, which I chug.

"Do you remember anything?" Dr. Michael walks over to Demetrius removing his IV next.

"I do." Putting down the empty glass. The doctor looks back at me.

"Okay, I will call Alpha over and then we talk." He leaves the room closing the door behind him just in time for my chest to squeeze.

"Mi amor, why are you crying?" Demetrius props himself up and scoots over to me. With his strong arms, he pulls me into him, and I break down in guilt. My mind is now clear. I can see everything as it happened. The chaos, the screams, the fighting, and most of all, my almost killing Demetrius. It's my fault we are in here. *I can't believe I shot him.*

It is like something opened the floodgates and I can't stop. He strokes my back as I drench his chest in tears unworthy of his concern. "Shhh, it's okay chiquito. Let it out." His voice sings to my heart.

"I'm sorry." I squeal between cries. It hurts knowing that I shot the man I had fallen for and even more so now that I know he is my mate.

"Everyone cries. No need to apologize." Demetrius hugs me tighter.

"That's not it, Demi..." He pulls away with eyes full of confusion. "I'm sorry, I shot you. I I-" my breathing quickens as I sob into my hands trying to hide my face.

"Is that what happened? All I know is that I blacked out."

I shake my head crying even louder. Demetrius rubs my thigh in comfort, but it does little to calm me down. "I was aiming at the goblin and shifter that were trying to get the jump on you. The moment I pressed the trigger my senses hit me like a ton of bricks, and I blacked out. But before I did, I knew the shot hit you."

Demetrius wipes my nose with the blanket as snot bubbled and popped. Sometimes I wonder if he considers me disgusting since it's not the first time that he sees me ugly crying like this. There have been too many times to count because of my father, and Demetrius was always the one that listened when Cassius wasn't around.

"Then you shouldn't be sorry. It wasn't intentional." He kisses my forehead repeatedly. Each kiss is working its magic calming me down further.

"I would never shoot my own mate on purpose," I mumble only loud enough for him to hear.

"Wait, you know?! Since when?"

I nod. "I realized it when I woke up just now... wait how long have you known?" Demetrius hugs me tighter than before.

"Since your birthday." He mumbles.

"WHAT?!" I struggle against his hug, but he doesn't let go. "Why didn't you tell me? All those things I said to you. Goddess, you must think I'm stupid. Am I a joke to you? Is that it?" My voice goes up an octave. *How could he not say anything? Why would he let me go through all those emotions knowing I was his from the start?*

I take in his scent, but tears sting my eyes again. How can he be so cruel? He strokes my head holding me tight rocking us back and forth. "No llores, Alex, I'm sorry. I thought that you didn't want me or that the goddess made a mistake", he whispers. "I was scared."

I love when he talks to me in Spanish but I'm angry and that sexiness won't work on me this time. "You still could have told me." I snap at him.

"But what if I told you and you became quiet because you didn't want me? You are too polite to say no. I didn't want to be rejected. I want you, Alex Santos. I want all of you. You and your wolf Peyton. Please don't hate me because of this." *Crap he is really good.* I sit up when he finally loosens his grip and hit his arm as hard I could.

"You are not in this relationship alone, Demi. Whether you wanted a rejection or not, I deserved the chance to make that choice for myself. Intiendes? You can't take away my free will, damn it."

Nothing Stays Buried

"Si", Demetrius nods trying to pull me back into his arms but I'm fuming. I can't think straight. I push him away and go to my room. I need space. I hate people trying to control me. I hate decisions being made for me. Ever since mom died, it's been hell with my father, and I don't need another person doing the same. Not now, not ever.

I lock myself in my room. All I want is to smother myself on him but I'm so angry that my emotions are getting the best of me. How can I be so happy and angry at the same time over the same person. I cry myself to sleep, cold and alone, with nothing but the memories of the horrid battle replaying in my mind lulling me to sleep in a lullaby of horrors.

Cassius

"I'm not hungry!" I slap the spoon away from my face and out of Atlas' hand.

"You know. I am being patient because what you went through is not easy. What he did to you not once but twice would mess with anyone. But what right does that give you to invalidate everything I am trying to do for you?" Atlas shouts at me not with anger but with hurt. He has never done this, and it gets through to me in a way the burrows deep into my heart.

"I'm sorry." I genuinely plea. How could I have been so blind to how he hurts as well.

"Sorry? Do you have any idea how much our pack has been suffering not just because of everyone we lost but because they think our bond has changed. Do you think it's easy for me to attend to everyone, help mend the pieces of everyone else but myself, to then finish falling apart by your hand day in and day out. Cassius, I love you, but I am barely holding on to the last bit on sanity I have left." Atlas walks out of the room and slams the door causing the frame on the wall to fall and break.

He is right. I can't even recall how long it has been since the fight and here I am, locking myself away after being in a hospital, ignoring my duties, and swimming in wanting vengeance. And for what? Pride? Yet the entire time he is by my side handling all he can quietly as he chips away. I get out of bed and clean up the mess I made on the floor before I change my clothes and leave the room.

I'm sorry Atlas. I'll be waiting at the back porch when you are ready to talk.

I walk through the house with a warm fleece and go to the back porch to snuggle up. The sun is beginning to set, and the air grows colder with the diminishing rays. My breath forms with each sigh as a testament to the cold. Looking up at the vast navy, one by one the stars appear in the blanket of the night. *Atlas must really be mad to leave me waiting for so long*, I think to myself.

I am angry as all hell for what Liber did to me and even though I cannot remember the specifics, I hate him even more for what it is turning me into. Yet, I am the only one to blame for allowing that hatred to consume me while my mate pays the price.

"I'm here." A voice pulls me from my thoughts making me jump. "Did you not here me step out?"

"No, I didn't. Sorry." Looking at his tired expression makes me want to cry. My chest bubbles but I need to apologize properly before I cry it out.

"Well?" Atlas takes a seat next to me.

"I will give a formal apology to everyone for my lapse in duties as their Luna but first and foremost, I want to apologize to you. I can't imagine the burden you had on you when all this ended and then with me in the hospital. We lost so many, and so much more were injured. I failed you and I hate myself for it. I will do better as your Luna and your mate."

Atlas remains quiet and takes a deep breath. His silence terrifies me more than his shouting did earlier.

"Please say something." I beg with a trembling voice.

"You really think, that's what I wanted to hear right now? While I am happy that you acknowledged all this and will apologize to our pack, where is the apology for what you did as my mate?"

"What I did? What did I d-"

"YOU....." Atlas calms himself with a deep breath, "you blocked me completely from you. So much so that I actually felt our bond weakening. I was tormented thinking that you were slowly severing me as your mate and the way you were acting only further affirmed it." Atlas takes another deep breath as tears stream down his cheeks.

"What? No, I would never do that. I didn't even realize that was happening. Atlas, please believe me."

"Cassius, my heart was literally breaking into pieces. I couldn't sleep a single night. I lost my ability to feel where you are and most of all I no longer feel the usual tingles when we touch. I can barely even smell you." Atlas cries into his hands and I fall apart because he is right. I haven't smelled him in a while.

"Atlas no, please don't cry. I'm sorry. I would never leave you. I don't want to ever be apart from you. You are my world. Look at me. I was just angry and lost. I hate myself for failing and not protecting all of you. But most of all, I was scared." I grab his face dropping my blanket. "Look at me, please."

Atlas finally looks into my eyes, "I love you, Atlas Ellwood. You are my mate now and forever. I will never break our bond nor leave your side." A glow begins to emerge around us. "I am yours and you are mine. Feel me, smell me, know where I am for, I will not let you go and even in death I will stand by your side." I beg the words to leave my lips and embed in his heart. And with that I slam my lips to his.

Our pheromones burst to life and the wonderful scent of lavender and oak floods me, reminding me how wonderful Atlas smells and how calming it is. *Our bond really was weakening.* Our lip's part and I take another breath looking into his eyes. Atlas' pupils dilate wide, and he takes in a deep breath as well. Watching the relief pour over his face fills me up inside with so much love that it's hard to contain it all. I can feel him now and the immensity of his emotions. It's overwhelming but I am elated that I can feel him again.

"Please forgive me," I whisper as I place my forehead on his.

"Don't desert me nor our pack like that again. Mate or not, I cannot forgive you if you abandon us." Atlas takes another deep breath, and a soft rumble leaves his chest.

"I promise, I won't abandon any of you again." I reply firmly and Atlas grabs my face to kiss me. Never have I felt more at home than I do now on his lips.

Chapter 25

Iris

I'VE LOST COUNT OF THE days that have gone by. I know it's been more than a week, but I can't wrap my head around how much more time has passed since. The sound of the pen hitting the floor, falling off my ear makes me jump, breaking my thoughts and giving me a slight heart attack. My coworker giggles at me but continues working on her computer as she races against her clock. Lucy is a little uptight, but she is the only other person I talk to on occasion in here. If not, I'd go mad.

All the others are either too busy to make small talk or have a distaste against me and my kind, so they keep to themselves. At this point, I take it with a grain of salt and keep it moving. The day flew by as I finished up the paperwork I had piled up and through it all, I managed to acquire a new client. There is no such thing as downtime in the office and because of that it is a bit of a mess with holidays around the corner. Papers are stacked on all desks due to having our hands tied. Files are piled everywhere and the person that usually organizes everything has been out sick with the flu but for me, it's what I need. Chaos to focus my attention on.

The infighting between Alex and Demetrius is consuming the house on top of everyone being on edge waiting for Liber's next attack. The only thing that is good lately is the relationship between my brother and Luna. They finally talked it out and now they seem to be inseparable again.

I look at the time and click my teeth when I see the digital numbers change to the new hour. It's seven in the evening and I haven't had dinner, nor have I spoken to Kristofer. My desk is still riddled with paperwork that I need to finish for tomorrow's team to take to court and going home at a reasonable time, is no longer an option.

"Okay, a trip to the deli it is," I mutter as Lucy waves me off while I grab my coat and step out into the bitter cold. The wind howls its icy breath and pushes against my best efforts to walk straight but it's doing a great job in clearing my mind. Either that or I have an extreme case of brain freeze. So, either way, it's working.

"Hate the winter". The deli lights appear in the distance. Luckily, it's only a five-minute walk from the office but when it's winter, the treacherous walk on frozen toes feels like an hour's journey through the Arctic, barefoot like a hobbit.

"Good evening, Iris." The deli clerk calls out from behind the counter looking tired. The bag under his eyes tells me he still isn't sleeping well from the insomnia he developed.

"Evening, Bernie. Can I get a coffee?"

"Just a coffee?" Bernie hovers his hand over the paper cups neatly stacked by the coffee machine waiting for a response.

"No, gimme today's special too. Whatever you got." I smile and rub my hands to warm them up.

"Another late night?" He sighs. "You know hun, you shouldn't work too hard. You look thinner every time I see you." Bernie shakes his head and hands me the coffee.

I have no idea where his eyes are because I am far from thin. My thighs alone can suffocate a person and let's not mention my belly that won't tighten no matter what I do.

"C'mon Bernie. You know that the office will fall apart without me." I chuckle. He is such a sweet old man. I wouldn't come here if not for him.

"Okay, here you go, meatball sub with extra cheese and extra marinara on the side".

"Thanks. Sounds delicious. How much I owe ya?"

"$6.75 should do the trick." Bernie laughs at me, while I hop with excitement.

"Okay, have a good night, and say hi to Geraldine for me." Bernie gives me a big smile and waves me off. I step back into the freezer that is the night and make my way back to the office excited to eat the best sub in town. I sip my coffee along the way, making the walk a bit more bearable and hum with delight as it warms me up. But only a bit. It's at least warming my quivering lips and hands.

Skittering catches my ears. My eyes dart around, and I stop to look. Cars drive by and people walk to and from, all shivering in their coats but nothing seems out of the ordinary. I speed up and take out my keys to the office, fumbling them as I search for the individual key. Another swoosh and skittering catch my ears. This time, I drop my keys in fright and look around again before picking them up. The wind picks up and pushes the door open a bit before letting it slam.

The lock is broken, and I can only guess that I will not like what I find when I go inside. Someone must have been watching me. With slow careful steps, I walk with my back against the wall. My heart thumps louder than my boots can echo in the hall announcing my presence. Clanking and papers shuffling grow louder as I turn towards the open door that leads to my office. I stop, too scared to look inside.

"I know that's you, Iris."

My blood turns cold. Why is he here? Why now when I am alone? Reluctantly I turn into the office and find Liber sitting in my chair making a mess of the paperwork I had so diligently organized. Wait, what did he do with Lucy?

"Why are you here?" I ask with a shaky voice.

"To pick up my daughter from work of course." He smiles but my eyes are too busy noticing the red stain on his fingertips. "Don't worry about the human. I'm sure she will keep this secret." He snickers.

"What?" Is all I manage to ask before I notice her body on the floor by her desk and I am snuffed out cold by him with incredible speed.

***

My eyes are heavy as I struggle to wake up from the shakes and bumps of whatever I'm in. The pounding in my head puts pressure behind my eye like a jackhammer chipping away at me. Slowly I open my eyes to the dark back seat of the vehicle. I'm lying down in the backseat facing forward and driving the car is none other than...Liber. That bastard kidnapped me after killing my co-worker.

Tears sting my cheeks at the thought of my life ending this way. I haven't even lived my ever after with my mate and I am already meeting my end. With a deep breath, I give myself a mental slap. Stop thinking this way. You need to save yourself. I repeat to myself instead of resigning so quickly to my situation. I wiggle my hands to try and see how much movement I have. The tightness around them and my feet suggests that I am bound with something thick like tape, but the darkness and my blurry vision don't allow me to confirm it.

I'm stuck with no strength to break free due to whatever drug or spell I am under. I can't do a thing and the sudden soreness in my neck stiffens my posture. Did he inject me with something?

"I see you're awake." Liber never looks back. He continues driving as if having done nothing wrong and adjusts the rearview mirror. He is so confident in himself that he continues to underestimate me, but I can't blame him if only moments ago I gave up in seconds. I contemplate using my powers but being tied up puts me at a disadvantage. I still can't use the stronger spells effectively without weaving my hands. The best I can do is move objects and being in a moving vehicle limits my options.

"What do you want with me?" I try my best to ask but my words come out a slur as if drunk.

"Well, my sweet daughter. At first, I was hoping you inherited more of me than your mother. That way I can easily get you to side with me and tear those dreadful wolves from the inside out. Obviously, you grew up nothing like me. All sweet and loving with those damn wolves. I loathe those disgusting things. Nothing like how I wanted you to be, so now I look to unleash whatever potential you might have for my benefit. If I am to overthrow the elf queen in Latfri and begin my rule, then I need more power." Liber laughs. A selfish bastard to the end it seems.

"Latfri?"

"Yes, my homeland and your lineage. How do you not know about the elven race that lives in the mountains?" Liber snaps at me as if I am to know about a history of a part of me that I didn't know existed.

"So, I am just an experiment for you?" Ignoring his question, I slur my words but not as much as I did the first time around. The drugs must be wearing off.

"No, no. You're not that important..." Liber puts the car in park and turns around, "You're just a means to an end for me. A way to get rid of your kind once and for all." He smiles and winks. None of this is amusing yet he finds it appropriate to wink despite announcing the annihilation of my race. My mind swirls in a fog. Whatever he gave me is extremely strong. Bits and pieces of what happened before ending up in the car float around in hazy fragments.

I try to mind link with Kristofer to see if I'm still close enough to home for it to work. But nothing. A radio salience responds to my call and dread tries to settle in quickly. I try my brother, Atlas, next, and once again, nothing. Then Cassius and again, nothing. Either I am too far, or the drug is interfering with my ability to communicate. The backseat door opens, and Liber pulls me out by the ankles. I try to hold on to the back of the driver's seat but Liber yanks me out hard enough to make me let go and bang my head against the car door and onto the ground.

"You bastard, is this how you treat your so-called sweet daughter?" I scream at the non-expressive features of his pale face while throbbing in pain.

"Yes, it is when she doesn't listen." He replies with a matter-of-fact attitude. A slight curve on the corner of his lip shows he is enjoying this, but it quickly changes back to his cold façade. The ridiculous smirk summons the hatred stored within the very depths of me but being bound renders me helpless to do anything about it.

I look away in defiance but what I am really trying to do is catch my bearings like landmarks or anything that can be distinguishable. Nothing but trees and a strong scent of pine. PINE! It's rather curious and a relief since there's only one area just outside the city that naturally has these many pines. Liber lifts me from the ground and carries me over his shoulder. The thin figure he sports is misleading considering how muscular his back feels. He must be rather fit to be able to lift me as easily as he does. I sway from side to side as he carries me to the house like a sack of potatoes. He quickly makes his way up the driveway to an old establishment. From the little I can see when he tosses me to his other shoulder, the home is old and antique-like.

The land itself looks secluded with a large number of acres and well-manicured shrubs. My head bobs against his bottom as a set of cement steps pop into view. They lead up to the porch where I am put down to sit in pain from the pounding headache. The blood rushing to my head tugs at the urge to vomit which I ignore and take a deep breath. He did a number on me between the drugs and head trauma.

"What are you going to do to me?" I manage between the bile building in my throat.

"Well, sweety, I am going to have dinner while you wait in the room I prepared for you. You'll be a good girl and wait for dad to finish his dinner. Okay?"

Liber opens the door to the house and lifts me back up before walking up a spiral staircase. A faint scent of Sulphur and wood surrounds the home. I gag a bit, both from the smell and his annoying tone in his voice but I hold it in. I try to mind link again but it's still radio silence.

My muddled mind won't let me form a proper connection, at least I hope that's the reason why and not that I'm too far from home. Liber lays me on the bed with a grunt. I eye him up and down and stop at the broche on his jacket. It sits on his left shoulder. A spider with the body made of a jewel of some kind. *I wonder if...* He leaves the room making sure to lock the door behind him.

I need to get out! I scream the thought to myself and begin chewing the tape that is binding my hands. Had I realized it is tape, I could have attempted to chew out of it in the car. Then again, with the grogginess after waking up, I doubt I'd succeed.

With clearer mind and enough chewing on the edge of the tape, I pull my wrist apart and break free. Burn lines decorate my wrist but I don't have time to treat the wounds. There is no time to waste, and I quickly skitter my eyes across the room looking for something I can use as a weapon or at least a cutting tool for my legs. I am not flexible enough to bend and bite off the tape from my ankles so finding an object is my best bet.

I open the drawer of the nightstand next to me and rummage through it until I find a pen. "That'll do".

Quickly I start poking holes into the tape in a straight line in hopes that I can weaken its integrity to then break free. With all my strength, I pull my ankles apart to break it. A warm feeling covers me slightly at my small victory and I ready myself for my escape.

As quietly as possible, I tip toe to the window and slide it open careful not to make a sound. The cold air bites against my skin. Moments like this, I wish I wasn't half elf because I hate the cold. It sucks. Bracing myself, I scan the area for cameras or guards, but the area is clear of everything. If anything, the place may be protected by magic, but it is a risk I am willing to take.

The moon is high in the sky and the night is clear as if lighting the way for me to go home. I thank the moon goddess. The jump as a human is too high and I can easily injure myself. However, if I can get low enough out of the window and then transform, I can make the jump as a wolf.

I undress to avoid my clothes snagging on the siding of the home and climb out of the window shivering against the cold attacking my naked skin. One leg goes over the edge of the window and then the other. Holding on tight to the window ledge, I reach over to the lattice going down the side of the house. I climb halfway down before jumping off to shift in mid-air.

Nora

The cold doesn't feel as bad in wolf form. My fur fluffs out and covers me in warmth. I give my mind link one more try as I run, and Iris flips inside when it finally works.

Kris, help me.

Nora, where are you? I have been trying to reach you for hours.

Liber kidnapped Iris but we escaped. I don't know where I am. All I smell is pine, so we might be just outside the city. I huff as I run faster than I ever have before.

Keep running, I'll use the bond to find you. So glad I can finally feel you again. Are you okay? I want to cry hearing the worry in his words.

Yes. Iris was drugged but it's wearing off. Please hurry. I continue running without looking back, without hesitating or questioning the direction I am going. I need to focus and put distance between me and the house.

In the clearing, there is what seems like the edge of the property. The fence seems low enough, so I pick up speed and jump it. A bit of the pointed fence scrapes my hind leg with the jump. *Shit it's covered in silver,* but it doesn't matter. I can't stop.

I change directions and continue running. The air is cold, and I am having a hard time breathing through the pain in my leg. The adrenaline is enough to keep me going but the slicing pain with this cold is slowing me down slightly. My stamina is shot, and I am sure the drug still lingers a bit in my system. Everything is catching up to me, but I refuse to stop. There is no way I can go back to that ma-

The cemetery before me brings me to almost a full stop. Huffing uncontrollably, I scan my surroundings as I walk slowly through the turned-over plots. What if this is where he dug up the bones? The thought is unsettling, but I push the thought aside and continue running as best I can and until I find a mausoleum. Unable to push myself further, I go inside for refuge just as my muscles are giving out.

Nora, I'm close. Where are you now?

Kris! In a cemetery. Inside a mausoleum. I can't run anymore.

Okay, I'm coming.

***

The sounds of yelling and thrashing about wake me. I jump up from the cold ground not realizing I fell asleep. Ironic given I am surrounded by the dead. The ache in my leg throbs from where the fence scratched me. With my slow healing ability, it could be a bit more before I recover and with nothing to flush out the wound, the healing may delay even longer.

I walk over and peek out to see what is causing all the commotion. Iris trembles inside me but I need to be brave for her. I peek my head through the iron gate to see Liber fighting with Kristofer and Cassius while Atlas is already making his way toward me. Someone else is hiding behind a tree but I can't tell who it is. The plan. I bark and Atlas smiles with relief when he spots me. I shift back to Iris.

Iris

"I'm so glad you are safe." Atlas opens the gate and gives me a long coat to put on before he hugs me. Zeus howls pulling my attention away from Atlas. Liber is standing there with a knife huffing and puffing, not his usual demeanor. Cassius is in Shoneah form preparing an arrow and Zeus is on the ground bleeding profusely with Uncle Robert tending to him. If anything is to break my string of insanity, then this is it. Liber has taken too much from me and it needs to end.

I walk over to where Liber is and confirm what I thought. He isn't wearing his broche nor the jacket it is clipped to. His clothes look in disarray and he is missing a shoe somehow. On the ground near Zeus is the jacket with the spider jewel and I nod in satisfaction. It is definitely his medium for controlling his powers and I need to break it. Liber immediately stops laughing as I approach. I know I got this now that everyone is here.

"What is this?!" Liber screams writhing in pain. I hold my hand out commanding his blood to my will.

"Oh, you see, my sweet father. I have already tapped into the part of me inherited by you. Let me show you my potential thus far." I make his arms swing open wide and slowly twist them backward. The cracks in his shoulders echo along with his screams of anguish.

"Stop. How? How are you this strong already?" Liber screams at the top of his lungs.

"You will not take from me more than you have already." I feel my strength waning, but I have to hold it together. Too many have died and suffered at his hand.

"Atlas, grab the broche on his jacket and break it," I yell out as I hold the dark elf in pain.

"What?" Atlas runs to the jacket confused.

"That's his medium. It's what he uses to control his power. Break it." I explain.

"You think that's my medium. Foolish child." Liber tries to joke but I can see the fear in his eyes. He wants to trick me into not breaking it but I'm no fool.

"Oh! So, you wouldn't mind me breaking it then?" I smirk.

"Shoneah!" Atlas shouts and tosses the broche in the air. Shoneah turns to it and quickly draws a flame arrow and hits the spider's jeweled body, shattering it into pieces.

"Nooooooo. What have you done? That was passed down for generations." Liber's rage consumes him but with no use. He can no longer control his power as well anymore.

I nod to Shoneah in a silent agreement to do as planned and he draws another arrow. Jessica comes out from behind the tree with a book in one hand and a bag in another. She circles Liber in a mixture of some kind, possibly salt. Jesika and I cut our hands to draw blood and slam it onto the salt while she reads a passage from the book. She chants and the ring of salt turns red at the same time that Shoneah's arrow goes straight into Liber's chest.

Watching the glow of the arrow sticking out of his body gives me no sense of pleasure or sadness. I just want it all over with. I want him gone and out of our lives for good. His chest begins to burn very, very slowly with the flames of the arrow spreading over his body. The blood ring around him then engulfs in flames as well and Jesika steps back.

"He is bound to the circle. He shouldn't be able to use his magic at all now." Jesika calls out. Shoneah smiles at our handy work. But that smile quickly fades when Liber manages to put out the fire. My mind goes into a blur as my vision spins. I am too weak to do this right now. I can't hold on to Liber. He is slipping through and taking back control. Liber strikes a blade of ice my way, but Uncle Robert jumps in, taking the hit in my stead.

"No, Uncle!" I scream in tears. Atlas runs to his aid as my deafening scream blanks my mind. Shoneah runs behind me and so does Jesika to hold me up.

"Jesika, place your hand on her shoulder. Focus on sending her your power and strength. Picture it is flowing from your body to hers. I don't know if it'll work but I've had it done to me before." Shoneah closes his eyes and concentrates. I catch my breath for a bit and place my hold on Liber once more as he sends another blade of ice my way but this time it ricochets off me. I don't even feel the impact as I deflect it with a flick of my hand.

"How?" Liber screams in pain once more. Jesika returns to the salt circle and reinforces it before binding it once more in blood. The flames return and grow a mixture of blue and green this time. Proud of my best friend, I release my hold on Liber and move my attention to his ankles, twisting them backward one by one.

crack goes the left foot.

crack then goes the right.

They turn in the opposite direction of their natural disposition. Liber belts out a deafening tone looking ready to pass out with the way his eyes roll back. There's no one here to save him this time. No dead shifter or goblin to do his bidding. No one under his command. Or so I thought. One lion shifter appears from behind Liber trying to find a way into the ring of salt.

"Get them," Liber speaks between his teeth and commands the dead lion-shifter to fight. The way the shifter moves seems of his own free will. Almost as though he could think freely from Liber's command but is still willing to do his bidding anyway. The lion-shifter lunges towards me but Atlas and Kristofer are quick to interfere. They distract the shifter while I focus on Liber.

"What happened to the big bad elf that was coming for his daughter?" Shoneah taunts. Liber's face contorts in pain. None of Shoneah's words seem to register and it brings an odd warm feeling inside. Shoneah then pulls back his invisible bow and blows into the air a whisper too low for me to hear. He releases his grip but nothing happens or at least that's how it seems.

Just as Shoneah puts down his arms and replaces his hand on my shoulder, the arrow appears with a bright green flame crackling through the air and penetrates where the first one hit. Similar to his first arrow, the flames never die out but unlike the first, it burns hotter and faster, engulfing him from head to toe. The burn is hot enough that I almost step back from the heat. Walking over to Liber with my witch and shaman by my side I scoff and ask, "Before we kill you. Tell me the real reason why?"

Liber tries to laugh but the green flame that is burning off his flesh is too painful to let him succeed. He groans instead. "You really want to know?......It's because you are mine. I made you. You are the last ......l-living elf to carry the blood of my legacy." Liber screams from the pain as more flesh sloths off. It almost triggers a gag from me, but I hold it in.

"Your brother was magnificent and much purer than you, a m-mere half b-breed, but he was killed by you wretched wolves." He falls to his knees. "When I showed the capability for black magic, I swore my revenge. Never did I think that the wolf to kill my son was one of your own in one of his drunken fits." I freeze at the possibility of it having been Rick, but it would be too much of a coincidence if it were. Liber continues.

"Unfortunately, the council had different plans for me when I approached them about Paxel, so while I used them to move around freely and kill anyone who recognized me, I began my plan. Ugh, w-when I met your mother, the idea of putting my seed in her and tearing you wolves apart from the inside out, popped into my m-mind. It was an impromptu decision to impregnate her, but it worked. The stupid bit-"

I ball my fist, "Don't you dare speak ill of my mother! We are not just incubators for you to use as you please. Men like you disgust me. All this because of a wolf I don't even know. A wolf that existed before I did over an elven brother, I didn't know I had. Why am I to pay for the sin of another? You vile pig, fuck your revenge, father. Fuck you and your childish dream to rule over Latfri." I lift my arms in the air and release my fist, slamming my hands down to the ground.

The mark appears on my arm again, but this time completed like the crest from Liber's spell book. A guttural scream erupts out of Liber pulling my attention back to my father. His body slams to the floor morphing in shape and size. His skin flares up in boils and pops, melting off, oozing puss and blood. His legs spread apart until breaking at the hip and snapping until it lies directly next to his torso. Liber's screams stop as he passes out from the pain but that won't do.

"Oh no, we can't have you missing out on the fun." I pump his heart with a gesture from my hand, while unnecessary, I know the pain will jolt him awake. Shoneah tries to stop me but it's too late and I shrug him off tossing him to the side effortlessly. There's too much rage that I am blind to. The darkness that I try to ignore is out and filling me with power. Liber jolts awake screaming once more. "Ready for the grand finale?"

"Iris, please. You're my dau-...Ah! Don't do this. You bear the crest..." I step closer, no longer needing Shoneah or Jesika to lend me their strength. My skin is crawling with black veins like they did when I attacked Kristofer but this time I feel in control of it. Whatever it is, I can feel it is lending me its strength as I wield it. The surge of power helps me breathe a bit easier as I place my hand on his chest.

"I am not your daughter." I smirk and turn his body into a balloon before it explodes. Bits and pieces of what he was flies everywhere, bathing me in his dark unforgivable embodiment. I turn around drenched in blood and body parts of the nightmare I can now wake from. "Done", I whisper and collapse.

***

Kristofer

I heal from most of my wounds along the ride home although with a missing finger and a couple of badly broken toes, along with a bitten ear, I won't be fully myself again. The lion shifter was nasty, had Atlas not been there to help, we would have been done. The only thing that saved us was Liber dying. Whatever magic the lion shifter held on to died when Liber did.

Alpha Robert however is another story. I am not so confident he is going to survive. The blade of ice thrown his way almost cut clean through his side. I have no idea if it hit anything vital either and the best we can do is apply pressure and hope his healing kicks in enough to save him. The pack house is an hour's ride, providing too much time for things to go south for Alpha Robert. The only thing keeping him breathing is the constant magic that Shoneah and Jesika are pouring into Robert to assist in slowing down the bleeding and easing his pain. But with everyone exhausted, it's not enough to get Robert out of mortal danger.

A sigh escapes my lips. Iris did great out there but I for one didn't want Liber dead so soon. Her anger got the best of her and if she is to be my Luna, she needs to think with a clear mind. Not an angered one. We need to work together, to help her strengthen her mind and control her emotions because a decision made with feelings can have consequences. We should have found out more about his ultimate plan and about the council.

The house approaches in the distance. I let go of the stress on my shoulders in relief that home is in sight. Her soft breath whispers against my body as I lift her and walk towards the pack house. Now covered in dried blood, she sleeps soundly against my bare chest. She exerted so much energy doing what she did, but I am proud of her for surviving. She essentially faced her fear head-on through another kidnapping. Watching her use her powers is a terrifying sight to see. Even the way she tossed Shoneah is terrifying. Yet she is the most beautiful terrifying woman I've ever seen.

All I know is that my mate used all her strength, fought her demons, and protected her pack. Protected me. The mental power wiped her out and I realize only now that I have a Luna that can hold her own. The goddess is one crafty woman. Although Iris hated not being up to par with other wolves, now she has the means to surpass them. But I need to teach her to control that anger, should it ever cloud her better judgment in any situation it could cost her own life instead.

I carry my mate to the tub and run her some warm water. Carefully, I place her tired body down and scrub away all the blood, along with the lies and treachery it holds, the demons she conquered, and the uncertainty she carries. Satisfied, I wash her hair returning it to its dirty blonde shade. Through it all, she remains asleep in an almost coma-like state. The tub drains and I refill it with clean water. I let her body soak in the warmth and relax. My eyes never leave her face as I count how many times she whimpers. I am completely ensnared by this woman when a knock pulls me away.

"Everything okay in there?" Cassius calls through the door.

"Yeah, can you bring me towels?" Cassius hums an okay and I return my eyes to her. She is staring back at me with sleep-filled honey irises.

"Hi, beautiful", I get up from the toilet and sit on the edge of the tub. "How you feeling?"

"Very tired but I'm okay." Her voice croaks. The bathroom door creaks open, and a hand pops in with towels.

"Thank you, Cass. Can you wait there a minute?" I grab the towels and help Iris out of the tub. She wobbles a bit, but I hold her tight walking her to the door. I give her arm to Cassius, and he nods at me that he's got it.

I drain the tub once more and turn on the shower. My feet are encased by a bloody pool of water, dirt, leaves, and twigs. I scrub myself and wash my hair. Images of the battlefield filled with bones and the way Liber exploded flood my mind once more but the only thing that keeps replaying is my mate and how she went ballistic. I have never seen so much hate and anger in her before. It scares me to think such a small person holds so much inside.

Quietly I cry into the shower. Everything drains from my eyes in a river of exhaustion. I step out with my towel around my waist and head over to where I hear talking. Atlas and Martha are sitting with Iris, and she is crying in her mother's arms. "Hey Kris, want some clothes?" Atlas offers and I nod.

"Babe, are you okay?" I sit on the other side of Iris, and she switches from her mother's arms to mine. "Hey, it's okay. Talk to me." I run my fingers through her damp hair.

"She hasn't said a word," Martha rubs her daughter's back.

"Okay, give me her car keys. I'ma get us out of here." I ask and Martha goes to fetch the keys as Atlas walks in with joggers and a sweater.

"I'll keep you posted on Uncle Robert's condition. We sent him to the hospital where Dr. Michael works." Atlas pats my shoulder, and I nod. I change quickly and scoop up my mate. Martha hands me the keys and I carry Iris to her car so I can drive us to the cabin for some quiet. It isn't as messy as before since we tried cleaning it up a bit after the incident and our little impromptu alone time. I carry her inside and lay her on the bed.

"Babe, do you want hot chocolate?" Iris beams at me. I chuckle at how adorable she is in allowing herself to be herself around me.

"Extra marshmallows please." She sniffles. Even when sad she is adorable, but I won't tell her that.

"You got it." Pulling the covers I tuck her in on the sofa and get to work.

***

The sun is now setting, and I put some wood in the fireplace.

"Babe, do you want to talk about it now?" I pull Iris into my lap.

"I'm scared," she whispers.

"Of?"

"My powers, how angry I felt, everything. What if I'm a monster now? I wasn't in control back there, but neither was it the darkness, my anger was. It's like everything I've been feeling since Rick, came gushing out the second you got hurt." A tear rolls down her cheek an onto my arm.

"Well, I can tell you with certainty that you're not a monster. You have been dealing with a lot on your own. Although I am a bit worried as well, don't bottle things up. If you like, we can add it to the therapy sessions. " I stroke her leg trying my best to comfort her.

".... okay. Will you go with me?" She turns up her sweet face sporting the most heartwarming puppy eyes.

"I'll take you and wait for you but it's something you should do on your own the way you have been. There may be things you might not want me to hear, and I want you to feel free to open up." She smiles and kisses my chin. "What's that for?"

"For being amazing. For being patient. For being you...I love you, Kristofer." She smiles and I kiss her softly before pulling away just enough.

"I love you too".

She returns my kiss and lingers against my lips. A smile creeps up against mine and she giggles. "Your beard tickles." I rub my face against her prompting more giggles. "Babe?"

"Yes, Iris?"

"I'm worried about Uncle Robert." Iris snuggles her head under my chin.

"Yeah, me too."

Chapter 26

Iris

WHY IS IT SO DARK?
Iris? Cassius? Demetrius? Where is everyone?
My chest, I can't breathe.
Someone, anyone, help me!
I-I can't brea-

I wake up with sweat dripping down my face and panting for a chance at a deep breath. That nightmare I had is not mine or at least it doesn't feel like it is. It was dark and full of pain and the only thing I could do was look on from a third perspective while still reeling through the emotions. I look over at Kristofer who is whimpering and tossing in his sleep next to me. He looks the way I was feeling in the dream.

"Babe, wake up," I shake Kristofer a bit, but he doesn't respond. Instead, he whimpers louder unable to escape the grip the dream has over him. "Babe, wake UP!" I shake him harder. His eyes pop open and a tear rolls down one eye as he looks around to gather his bearings.

"Wa...was I dreaming?" He fumbles his words confused but the way his face relaxes tells me how relieved he is to be awake.

"Yes, babe. It's okay now. Are you alright?" I ask trying to sound soothing while I lift his arm and nestle himself on his chest.

"I guess. The dream was so weird though. It was dark and I couldn't see where I was going. I called out to people, but no one answered me. Then I couldn't breathe as I ran and ran. It felt like I was suffocating." He looks down at me taking in my appearance as well. It must be obvious that I also had a rough dream by the way he stares at my damp hair against my forehead, but his dream lingers on my lips.

"This is... are you sure you're remembering your dream correctly?" It's exactly what I dreamt. Is it a new power?

"Yes, why?", Kristofer shifts a bit to get a better look at me, essentially moving me so I have my head on his arm instead.

"I had the same dream, and I even knew it wasn't my own. I was like a fly on the wall, but I still felt all the emotions from it. When I woke up, I saw you having a nightmare too and tried to wake you." This is insane. I sit up on the bed brushing my hair back with my fingers. The idea of possibly discovering a new ability is bringing my anxiety up to an all-time high. Might as well get my day started.

"So, you intercepted my dream? How?" Kristofer props himself up on his elbows.

I shrug and slip on the pajama pants I had on the floor. As much as I love the pajama set, all the extra body heat has me wanting to sleep naked more often than not. Looking back at my mate, a sigh slips my lips. At this point, I can't make heads or tails of anything that happens out of the norm. I'm simply exhausted and will chalk it up to that for now. "I don't know, but let's keep this between us. I'm not sure if this is a mate bond thing or if my power is growing. Let's see if it happens again first." I turn to go shower not wanting to think about it right now.

I just want to focus on helping with the wedding, helping out Alpha Robert with his recovery, and myself.

It's been several days since Liber, and I haven't had time to process everything. Rather, I haven't given myself time. I take every distraction I can get. Suddenly, strong arms wrap around my waist.

"Where do you think you're going?" Kristofer begins kissing my neck sweetly.

"Eww, stop I was sweating, let me shower." I struggle because it feels amazing despite him being gross. The last thing I want to do right now is sex no matter how hot and bothered his touch is making me.

"I don't care, you're about to get a whole lot sweatier than this anyways." He tosses me onto the bed like a rag doll. I giggle because I am always down for business but not when I am a pool of sweat. Kristofer roams his hands all over my body and the betrayal of how responsive my body is to his touch has me mentally slapping myself. My body is more honest than I am, and it is saying yes to everything that Kristofer is doing. The only thing I can do now is cave to his caress. I am not saying no to sex with this man, ever. Especially if this is what he does to me every time.

"Well then Alpha, what did you have in mind?" I arch my back running my hand down my chest and into my pants where the heat is building and yearning for him to get working on cooling me down. A growl escapes his throat. Oh, I'm in for it. For some reason whenever I call him Alpha, it lights a fire under him that turns him into a beast. It is a switch I accidentally found and made a mental note to use whenever I want him to get a bit rough.

Kristofer crawls onto the bed and pulls off my pants in a move so quick it doesn't even register until he is lining kisses up my legs and then stops at my core. His hands move up my body like a snake stalking its prey, slowly feathering my skin. They each find my breast and latch on, kneading them simultaneously before his fingers roll my nipples between them.

I moan with ripples of electricity sparking with each touch. I look down and he stays there between my legs in pure torture with a grin suggesting that he knows exactly the kind of game he is playing. His hot breath is heavy against the thin fabric of my underwear. And it is moments like this that I truly question if he really is a virgin. His massive hands massage my breast again and his beautiful green eyes pierce through me as he works my breast to manipulate the reaction out of me that he seeks.

"Kris, don't torture me," I whisper already wet from excitement. He grins, "Then tell me, what does my queen want?"

Damn, this man and his sexy ways. "I want your tongue to please me until I cum. I want your hands to grab hold of me firmly while you find my core with your cock and fuck my brains out." I demand and squirm trying to nudge myself closer to his lips. His eyes flicker with a soft glow of arousal. Man, this is hot on so many levels. Kristofer runs his tongue against my core over my underwear. I moan at the heat and touch against the hard nub of my sex.

A finger runs the edge of the thin fabric and slips underneath it. The same finger runs all the way to the other side, hooking the fabric and pulling it up so that it wedges in the center and exposes my outer lips on either side. The pressure of how my underwear sits against my core like a thong strums a vibration through me. He pulls it up tighter causing a rush of arousal from my clit up to my stomach.

He is such a quick learner and the way he takes his time to give my body attention with no regard to his own only adds to his appeal. I sit with him at night sometimes to watch porn that I like, and he picks up everything very well. So well in fact that I find it tempting to show him a few of the riskier videos that I know I'd be willing to try with him. A shudder pulls me from my thoughts and the image of him on a leash.

Kristofer is sucking me through the underwear while tugging the fabric. Fuck this is amazing.

"Don't let your mind wander my queen. Focus on me." My Alpha mumbles between his licks but then yanks the fabric off and spreads my legs wide. He growls at the view of my wet mess and the way my thick arousal stretches from me to his finger. A smile finds his lips. It should be illegal to be able to smile like that with that face. He is too handsome for his own good. He traces my nub and then slides down my inner lip before finally going inside me.

I gasp, "Kristofer..." Shit, why did I say his full name. His eyes flare and I know I am done for. The only thing that does him in more than calling him Alpha, is using his full name. He snaps and loses all the gentleness he is showing me and with his mouth clamps onto me while another two fingers make their way inside.

My Alpha fingers me rough and hard with his long thick digits. Moans spill out of me uncontrollably between gasp and unintelligible words. It's too much. He is going so fast that the sensations are making me lose touch with reality.

Kristofer curves his fingers hitting my g-spot while his tongue moves rapidly all over me. My breathing is erratic, and my thoughts are a mess trying to keep up with the build-up. My orgasm is reaching its peak, but I fear that even that won't be enough to satiate the hunger developing inside me that makes me beg for more of his touch whenever he isn't near.

My mate continues to furiously lick and nip at me while his fingers rapidly jerk in and out of my central pleasure. "Kris, I'm almost...", I swallow the words at the tip of my tongue as I shake violently against his face. A low deep growl emanates from his throat, and he jerks his fingers faster to assist my release. I scream at the burst of pleasure compounding in my core and in turn, it pushes my orgasm over the edge.

"Babe I-" The words don't come out as he closes his lips around my clit and sucks long and hard. He releases me when I scream, and he starts slapping my clit while I spray everywhere. Once again, my release is furious and plenty. Each slap sends another wave of pleasure through me in a wave that washes over me. "Fuck," I groan under my breath waiting for my orgasm to settle.

Kristofer looks at me hungrily and pulls down his briefs. His thick member is already dripping and eager to taste the quivering drip between my legs. He slides himself right into me as he climbs on top and centers himself at my entrance. I gasp at his size as if it were the first time but it's something I still can't get used to.

"Iris...I-" Kristofer moves in slow strokes within me lost in thought.

"What's wrong?" I wrap my legs around his waist guiding his strokes deeper within me, still caught up in my last orgasm.

"I'm ready when you are. I want to mark you." Kristofer gives me puppy eyes in a way that could melt the heart of the coldest person, and I chuckle. I was ready for a while now but with everything going on, I guess we never had the right timing to talk about it.

"Take me", I lean up to kiss him and he relaxes onto my mouth. I could taste myself on his lips and I don't mind it. It's another thing I find kinky, but I will never tell him that. I like that he kisses me without thinking and it is a guilty pleasure I will keep to myself. Kristofer picks up his strokes turning into rapid thrust against me. The pleasure builds again and the wet slaps of his hips pounding against me mounts the rising need within my core. Pound after pound, he shapes me into a perfect mess.

"Kris...I love you," I whisper, and I know my release is close.

"Fuck, Iris...I love you too", Kristofer sinks his teeth into my neck in a growl. His erection, growing impossibly bigger within me and stretching me to my limit. Every wrinkle inside me is smooth against his cock. Wave after wave of what I can only assume is a euphoric high, courses through me. The initial pain of the bite barely lasts a second and immediately replaced by this wonderful roller coaster of love, desire, lust, pleasure, and everything that is good in this world.

Kristofer slams into me hard at the sound of me moaning his name repeatedly and I cum instantly. My release pulsates around his dick and unravels him in return. His member pumps a never-ending ribbon of ecstasy that fills my already full cavern. He grunts against my neck and licks the mark he just left. Finally, our mating is complete. He pulls out and gives me soft kisses on my lips.

"Thank you for being so perfect," he whispers. I smile because I am at a loss for words. He is the angel here, not me. What did I do to deserve him?

"Pleasure is all mine." I wrap my arms around his neck and kiss him with a passion all our own. He sucks my tongue in response, and I fall for this man all over again.

"Let's get you clean." He lifts me together with the bedsheets and walks me to the bathroom. I lay my head on his shoulder and close my eyes taking a deep breath. I do not regret what I just did, but sex is no longer a good enough method to keep back the darkness I am locking away in my mind. I need help to teach me how to deal with what I went through. I don't want to ruin our sex by associating it with a horrible memory. For now, I'll enjoy this moment but soon enough, I know I will break if I don't do something soon.

Chapter 27

Kristofer

ANOTHER NIGHT AND NOT an ounce of sleep. The moon is high and here I am unable to close my eyes and drift. Ever since the first nightmare, they have come consistently ever since. Interestingly, all of them begin in complete darkness but the things I say are different each time. Iris snuggles into her pillow next to me soundly and I must admit that I am slightly jealous of her right now. She just falls back asleep tired.

Poor thing wakes up every time I have a nightmare because she somehow experiences each one with me. Eventually, I told her brother and the others, but they can't make heads or tails of it either.

I toss my covers aside and gently slip out of the bed making my way to the backyard. Not a stir in sight under the calm night. I fill my lungs with a deep cold breath and bask in the clarity that it brings. The new moon is in a few days, and I can't wait to give in to Zeus so he can run free. It's also a couple of weeks until Christmas which everyone is excited for.

This will be my second holiday with Iris, and I can't wait to share it with her. It still doesn't feel real that I finally managed to find a mate. And to think, she was the girl next door this whole time. There has been a lot of crazy going on in the last month and having a moment where we celebrate each other and pay respects to the ones we lost is exactly what we need. Aside from the battle and overall stress, we also thankfully have some good that we can reflect on.

An owl hoots in the distance turning my attention to the bird in the tree and I shake my head as Robert pops up in my mind. Alpha Robert is back with his pack on his side of town and is holding a meeting to elect a new Alpha because despite surviving, he isn't mentally nor physically fit to be the Alpha of the pack. He thought long and hard after he lost his son Pearson on what he should do and concluded that stepping down would be best.

After the fight, he received too much damage to his torso and even lost a rib. He can barely breathe right because of it. That coupled with his grief, he just wants to live the rest of his days in peace and to himself. As for our pack, a few members have new pups born within this week, bringing in new members to our growing family. The Christmas tree is overflowing because of it. A lot of the presents are stuffed under the tree we set in the family room. It's barely been set up a day and it already looks to be more presents than tree. I sigh into the night watching my breath disappear with the cold.

What do my dreams mean? I wonder, hoping the silence of the night will answer me this time.

"Can't sleep either?" Alex steps out next to me bundled up in his favorite fleece. I'm so proud of this guy. He has always been the weaker wolf in our pack and for the longest time I thought it was due to his weaker constitution but maybe it was late puberty.

Lately, he has been filling out a bit more and seems more confident in himself. But even at his frailest he always holds his own. He is easily my favorite of the pups in our pack, but I'll never tell him that. Goddess knows it will only go to his head if I did. Plus, I am sure Cassius won't let me live it down for having a favorite.

"Yea. I actually had a strange dream." I cross my arms looking out to the stars hoping for a lost answer to shine through one of them.

"Oh, I love dreams. I'm good at deciphering them... most of the time. Tell me," Alex giddily replies looking like he just won a million dollars. The excitement in his eyes is adorable. Again, I'd never tell him that.

"Well, I am always in the dark but every time I dream, I say something different." Alex nods his head with a serious pensive look as I continue. "At first, I felt alone and was looking for people. Then in another, I was arguing with someone. Then in another, it sounds like a battle. But with each dream, it's getting harder to understand what's happening, like if they are fading memories".

"At first it sounds like maybe you're manifesting your anxiety of what we went through but they keep changing so what if you are foreseeing something instead? Something that is going to happen that hasn't yet?" Alex paces a bit back and forth still wrapped in his fleece.

"Hmm, interesting. Do you think Iris being able to see my dreams has something to do with it?" I turn to Alex as he stops pacing.

"What if she isn't seeing your dreams but you are seeing hers instead?" Alex clearly has a light bulb going off in his head. "You guys finally completed the bond, right? To do that you need to bite her causing you to swallow her blood. So, what if her elf blood is allowing you to see her dreams and she is the one with the ability to foresee?"

"Alex, are you smoking weed again? I thought I told you to stop that while you are under my roof." For a minute he has me going but he clearly secretly smoked one too many.

"No, I haven't touched that stuff in years, you meanie." Alex sticks out his tongue before he continues, "Iris has magic in her blood and not just any magic. The high elf clan runs through her. Her powers will begin to grow in ways we won't understand since she is the last of her kind according to Liber. All we have is..." Alex begins jumping in excitement. "The book, where's the book?"

"Shit, you're right. There might be something in that journal." I ruffle Alex's platinum hair. This kid never sticks to one hair color but this one I like. "Thanks. You really helped".

"I try". He beams happily.

"So why are you out here? What's going on between you and Demetrius? You have been avoiding him like the plague and my poor Beta is acting like a love-sick puppy left in the rain." Alex fidgets with his fleece bringing it closer to his face. All the sparkle and smiles he is giving me are slowly fading.

"He knew that I was his mate and didn't tell me. Now, I understand why he did it, but it doesn't make it okay. Do you have any idea how stupid I must have looked going on about him having a mate out there and not wanting to get serious? I was trying hard not to fall in love, and he intentionally was making it hard for me because he already knew. I feel so humiliated. I honestly already forgive him, but I also want him to feel like shit for a while. I'm out here cuz he snuck in my room just now and wouldn't leave." Alex stares out to the woods most likely not realizing that he is crying. These two are idiots for each other.

"Hey, I get you want to teach him a lesson, but I think he gets it now. I don't want my family fighting especially not with Christmas around the corner. I see how he looks at you. He is so in love and is practically dying right now. You, lil pup, deserve happiness as well. Aside from Cassius you never let anyone in and after his mate appeared, you have been alone." I rub a hand over his back in my best effort to comfort him. I knew this was going to bite Demetrius in the ass, but he deserves it for waiting too long to say something.

"Go give him a good scolding and then makeup. Si?" I smile proudly at my use of Spanish which prompts Alex to look at me confused.

"What?"

"Since when do you speak Spanish, mister?" Alex squints at me quizzically.

"You think I won't learn a word or two with you speaking Spanish to your dad or my Beta?"

Alex raises a brow and then smiles. "Yay, I have so much to teach you." He grabs me into a hug.

"Buenas noches, Kristofer", he returns inside, and I am left feeling slightly better than before. Alex has a way of making you calm and happy simply with his presence. He has such positive energy that it is almost enough to recharge anyone's battery.

I quietly go to bed and snuggle against my beautiful mate. Iris having the dream and me intercepting it never became a thought until now. What if what Alex said is true? It sounds possible enough. Her blood can have some effects giving me her abilities temporarily. Maybe as her blood runs its course through my system it prompts the dreams to start fading. I guess I'll have to talk to her in the morning. I close my eyes and wait for sleep to take over which this time doesn't take long.

"Hello, how is the pack treating you?"

"Why, very well thank you. How's the witch's brew shop?" I ask the sweet old lady.

"It's finally at a good place. It was rocky at first, but sales are good now" The old lady smiles and waves for me to follow. I walk with her into a large room full of all kinds of species. Witches, goblins, shifters, elves, vampires, and so many others I can't even name. Wait, I know this place. Is this the summit?

"Alpha, so good to see you this year" A man dressed in a black robe comes over to shake my hand.

"Hello, councilman," I greet and shake the extended hand.

"Good to see you too".

The councilman grips my hand exceedingly hard and then everything starts to spin. The lights flicker and screams echo into the room. The light goes out for a few seconds and then flickers back on. Everyone is dead. Blood stained the floor, and limbs decorated the tables and dance floor. I turn around to run and bump into the councilman.

"Leaving so soon?" He begins to laugh into a fit and everything becomes a swirl before I feel a cold blade against my throat and the warmth of my blood spilling out.

"NOOOOO", I shoot up from the bed in a cold sweat.

"AHH", Iris wakes up shouting in pain holding her throat.

We look at each other horrified. *What was that?* I think to myself. If it is Iris having these dreams, why are they all about me? But if they are not dreams and indeed premonitions then I am royally fucked.

Chapter 28

Kristofer

"WHAT THE HELL WAS THAT? I get out of bed pacing back and forth. My breathing is jagged, and sweat is beading on my face. A knock raps on my door. My shaky knees guide me over to answer it to find my mother is standing there panting with her hand to her chest.

"Son, are you okay? I heard screaming and ran here." Mother looks me over and then looks at Iris who is chugging the bottle of water she keeps on her nightstand.

"Mom, yes we're fine. We had another dream but this time it was so vivid and intense. It scared us half to death, is all." My heart pounding from the adrenaline has me wanting to sit down.

"Okay, go and wash up. We can talk over breakfast." I nod and close the door. Iris wraps her arms around my body scaring me a little. I didn't even notice she walked up to me. Her heart is beating against my back just as hard as mine. We don't say a word to each other.

Instead, we go into my bathroom and shower in fiery water. We wash ourselves in almost a zombie-like manner not wanting to speak. Neither of us looks well and it definitely shows on our faces. We dress and meet mom in the kitchen who is already almost done scrambling extra eggs. On the table sits a stack of pancakes, a plate of maple bacon, and a bowl of fruit.

Iris goes to the fridge and grabs the creamer for the coffee and whipped cream for the fruits while I start on the coffee pot and retrieve the plates. The aroma of the coffee brewing puts me a bit at ease along with the smell of food at the table. My stomach growls almost as loudly as my wolf, making us all start laughing. Leave it to my stomach to break the tension in the kitchen.

Mom and Iris sit down and begin chatting, waiting for me to bring the coffee pot over. Alex walks in with a very sad Demetrius by his side and takes a seat at the table after grabbing their own plates from the cupboard. I'm assuming he hasn't forgiven him yet.

The pot finally finishes its brew, and I carry it over to join my family. Once I give my blessing, we all dig in, moaning as the food hits our stomachs. I don't know if this is me naturally being hungry or if the nightmares are working up an appetite. Either way, the food is divine.

"So, tell me why both of you gave me a heart attack so early in the morning?" Mom looks over to me and Iris.

"Yeah, I heard that too." Alex's voice is full of worry but also full of pancakes. I chuckle at his chipmunk cheeks and begin to recount the dream while the table falls silent. The dread that I feel I am sure they feel as well. I can almost still feel the blade on my throat.

"This is no coincidence. This is more than a warning. This is a threat." My mom pushes her empty plate aside and drinks the coffee making a face as she does. She grabs the creamer and adds a splash of it before taking another sip.

"I still think you are picking up on Iris's abilities," Alex interjects and crunches on a bacon strip.

"About that, I ended up remembering that my dreams started before I marked Iris so it couldn't have been her blood affecting me". Alex looks stumped and continues to work on his eggs.

"What have you both been doing differently since the dreams started?" Demetrius finally speaks up. I honestly couldn't think of anything different. Aside from the crazy amount of sex, nothing has changed.

"Hmm I don-" Iris is cut off by the doorbell. "Were we expecting anyone?" Iris looks around the table and we all shake our heads.

"I'll get it". Mom gets up to answer the door leaving us to finish our plates.

"Good morning, Cecile", a voice full of too much excitement is chirping down the hall.

"Why is she here so early?" I look at my mate who is shrugging her shoulders unapologetically. Jesika pops into the kitchen with a bright smile and waves at us. I appreciate her energy but right now I don't have enough in me to seem hospitable.

"To what do we owe the pleasure?" I groan not realizing how harsh those words come out. Oh well, too late now.

"Oh, shut up, you grump butt. I am not here for you. Iris lumpkin, I brought you more tea. I hope they have been helping." Jesika pulls out a jug filled with a homemade tea she has been preparing for Iris. But I don't miss out on the fact that everyone else is laughing at Jesika blatantly calling me out on my attitude.

"THE TEA!" Iris jumps out of her chair.

"Damn, you like it that much?" Jesika curls her lip at Iris in a bigger smile.

"No, you moron. It's disgusting". Everyone starts laughing making Jesika blush. "What I mean is, that's what's been different." Then everyone looks at Jesika in question. Her blushing face then turns to worry.

"Jesika, what do you use for the tea?" I ask giving her a bit of my Alpha voice. Again, not intending to, maybe.

"That's a secret. I use it all the time though. There is nothing wrong with it." Jesika defensively hugs the jug of tea.

"I never said there was something wrong, but we need to know how it's made," I demand but she doesn't speak. Instead, she seems to be getting angry.

"Jess, bear, it's important. Something has been happening and we think it might have to do with the tea." Iris hugs her friend.

"Why the tea though? I drink it all the time and all it does is knock me out."

Jesika is being stubborn and it's honestly getting on my nerves. But I let Iris continue to coax her. "It's the only thing we had different. The nightmares all started the night you made it at the cabin." Iris explains pulling out of the hug.

"We? What do you mean we? The tea is only for you, no one else can drink it." Jesika panics a bit.

"What do you mean?" I stand up from the table accompanied by a wave of nausea and I black out.

***

I blink a few times, and Iris is wiping my forehead with a wet cloth.

"Hey, you gave us a good scare there, big guy." Iris places a kiss on my lips.

"What happened?" I sit up and the others file into the living room. I look around and realize I am on the couch. Demetrius must have put me here.

"You stood up in the middle of the conversation and fainted. You hit the table then floor pretty hard. It's been fifteen minutes. I am sure you have a concussion right now." Iris explains and I look over at Jesika who is biting her lip with worry.

"Explain," I command, and she flinches at my words.

"The tea is made with chamomile, allspice, blue lotus, yarrow, and..." Jesika pauses a bit, but my eyes must have shifted because she flinches again and continues. "And Iris' blood".

"What, why the hell would you put blood in tea?" I yell causing her to stumble back and hit the wall.

"It was made for her to drink and no one else. The effectiveness of the tea increases tremendously when it's mixed with the blood of the user. If you drank it, then you shouldn't have. I specifically told this to Iris that night. Who knows of the side effects that you might have since she is not human." I turn to Iris who is looking at her in shock.

"No, you didn't. I would remember something like that." Iris snaps.

"Yes, I did but that's beside the point. What the hell is happening and why is everyone ganging up on me for only trying to help?" Jesika stomps her foot clearly about to cry.

We give her a quick rundown and it then occurs to us that last night might have been different because Iris had two cups that night. One before bed and one more after we woke up and fell back asleep.

"Okay so, I just looked up the ingredients that she used and apparently the two flowers Jesika used are known for imbuing prophetic dreams and producing psychoactive meditative states. If that's the case, then the fact that it was mixed with elf blood could have amplified its properties." Alex puts away his phone and looks back at our stunned faces.

"Well then. Now that we know how the tea caused it, what do we do about the dreams?" I sit back trying to recollect the details.

"For now, I think we need to be cautious of the summit and the councilmen. Something doesn't add up." Mom rubs her temples.

"If we go by anything then it's the most current dream. You had a clear visual this time, so we take it with caution. The summit is after the new year which only gives us a few weeks."

I get up and walk out of the room needing some space to think. Why is the council involved again, and does it have anything to do with the weird interaction they had with Cassius back at Ryan's cabin? Nothing makes sense but I would not put it past them. The councilmen are sneaky, and they must have a connection with Liber. I walk out the back of the house and strip. The cold bites my skin but it does nothing to the mood I am in. Folding my clothes into my sweater, I shift. My fur fluffs out and I shake my body stretching out my legs. With my sweater in my mouth, I run to Atlas.

Zeus

The stress is already fading from Kristofer as I run towards Atlas' home. There is never a dull moment, and I truly feel for my human because he has not had a moment of peace since everything began with Honovi and Rick. Running as fast as I can, I make it halfway there when I stumble. Something is wrong. My vision blurs and my body contorts as it begins to shift back to Kristofer, painfully slow.

Kristofer

I scream lying on the floor naked as the last of the bones shift into place. I grab my clothes and walk the rest of the way sore and exhausted. It has to be the tea affecting my ability to maintain the shift.

Are you okay Zeus?

Yea, you?

I'm fine. Just, really tired. The amount of energy it takes to shift is tiring when it's back-to-back.

Let's hurry and get some rest at the pack house. Zeus suggests.

Yea.

I throw my clothes back on and hiss at the frozen ground beneath my feet. I am hoping to look at the journal with the spells to see if there is anything that I can learn from it. Yet now I think I am going to take a nap and read the journal after. By the time I arrive at the house, it is later than I'd like. I just can't catch a fucking break. My tired human feet are frozen from the cold and ache from the journey.

"Hey Atlas, mind if I borrow the elf journal or spell book, whatever it's called, and hang out in your den? Oh, and can I nap for a bit?" I give him a hug and a quick fist bump in greeting.

"It's cool. The book is in my office on my desk. Everything okay. You don't look so good. Did you run here?"

"I don't know. I just need some alone time to think and sleep, lots of sleep." I walk to Atlas' office, grab the book, and make my way to the den. I close myself in there and lie down on the chaise grateful to finally put my feet up. The shift was brutal and took a bigger toll than I initially thought. My body thanks me over and over again as I close my eyes and drift into a deep sleep before I dare read the thoughts of a dead man.

Chapter 29

Kristofer

The longer I live on this earth,
the more I realize that it needs to be cleansed.
It's disgusting.
The humans, along with other creatures live
as though all is right with the world. It's not.
It's tainted and rotten.
The scum that walks among me and my kind
are nothing but filth and disease
that deserve to be killed.
That's why I will take on that burden.
My clan and I
Will light the world on fire
and watch it burn into a rebirth.
I will sit on top claiming the throne, paving what
this earth needs in black and white.
One, to rule them all
and it starts with the wolves.

I close the book with a knot in the pit of my
stomach. I can grasp now why the councilmen took the

high elves out so many years ago and why Liber was so desperate to have an heir. They weren't right in trying to take out an entire race just to condemn one man. He was delusional in every sense of the word. His grandiose attitude was too far gone but he should have been the only one to pay. Not the only one to survive. A high elf with that kind of mindset is a danger to everyone including himself. Not that death is the answer to every threat in existence, but I am sure the council must have their reasons for Liber. Assuming their reasons were similar to ours.

However, it bothers me that Liber mentions having the help of someone powerful to aid him in his mission. Of course, this could mean a lot of people but who else would have known and supported such an egoistic plan? Are they even still alive? Did the council pl-

Knock knock

"Yea", I call out. Cassius peeks into the room and I wave for him to come in only then noticing how late it is in the day.

"Can you tell me the dream you had last night? Martha tried telling me through the link, but she wasn't too specific. Iris is also in her room sleeping so I couldn't ask her either." Cassius pulls a chair up next to me and I recount the dream for what is like the millionth time.

"Maybe this is why I reincarnated into Shoneah? Remember when Wolfie said that Shoneah only comes out when something big is going to happen? What if it wasn't my father or Iris's father? What if they were merely a precursor to something bigger?" Cassius rests his elbows on his knees in thought.

"What in the world could possibly happen then? Haven't we gone through enough?" I snap, not so much at Cassius but just at...everything. There has already been so much suffering and loss that to now think this is just the beginning is insane.

"...war", Cassius puts it simply and I nearly break my neck as I turn to him who is sitting there as serious as can be. His eyes close with his finger running through his hair turning white as it goes. I sit up watching him transform with Shoneah's tattoos spreading throughout his body without the flames present.

He looks up at me without a hint of Cassius in sight. It's odd, to be honest. Usually when Cassius transforms, he keeps control but this time it's like he has completely checked out the same way we do when we shift into our wolves.

"My wolf child is right, Alpha Kristofer." I blink a few times at the incredibly deep voice coming out of that mouth. I link with Atlas to rush down as panic sets in. "Don't be frightened, I am a friend. I mean no harm to anyone for all of you are my children."

The door rushes open, and Atlas stops, staring at the man now turning to him confused as to what the problem is. "Is everyone alright?" Atlas calls out but looks at me uncertain of how he should react.

"Yes, we are," Shoneah assures us but it's still an unsettling feeling. "Just heed my warning. War is coming and it is in your best interest to gather your allies and band as one. There is a trader among us, and Liber isn't the only one who seeks to wipe out my children." Shoneah turns back to me.

"How do you know all this?" I ask in disbelief.

"Remember, I am the end and the beginning. I am connected to all wolves, past, present, and future." Shoneah slowly fades allowing Cassius to regain control and transform back to himself.

"Whoa, I think I blacked out. What happened?" Cassius wobbles a bit, but Atlas is at his side faster than I can stand up to catch him.

"Your shaman spirit spoke to us directly. A bit bizarre to say the least but he gave us a warning." Atlas speaks softly to his mate as if he were a child. I roll my eyes wondering if I do the same to Iris.

"Yes, you do." Atlas answers without hesitation.

"Huh?" He didn't read my mind. Did he?

"It's written all over your face bud. Didn't need to hear your thoughts for that." Cassius chuckles at his mate's clear sarcasm.

"Cass, what did he mean by he is the end and the beginning?" I furrow my brows in question.

"He said that to you?" He's shocked but continues, "Literally just that. I know, for us when we hear something like that we think, of a god or goddess. However, for Shoneah it's literal. He is the first of the Shaman wolves and lives on through all of us. He reincarnates and is connected to everyone. So, he is quite literally the past present and future of wolves. It is why I can communicate freely with all wolves without having to do a blood bond." Cass shrugs his shoulders. Atlas and I just nod.

We step out of the room, and I glance at the clock on the wall, it's already dinner time. I am sure Atlas told everyone I was here, but it is time I head home and explain the bits that I have learned. This whole thing feels like I am receiving bits and pieces to a bigger puzzle but now I am seeing the bigger picture.

"Hey, mind if I take the book." I wave it at Atlas who is tossing Cassius over his shoulder as if he weren't the smaller one of the two.

"It's all yours." He waves without looking back, most likely heading to his room.

"Luna, you look like you need saving?" I call out laughing.

"Nah, maybe my butt will later but I'm good." They both erupt in laughter, and I shake my head and leave them to their business. I leave the house and stand outside in the cold wind remembering I have no shoes, and I can't safely shift. But the idea of going back inside and interrupting anything that may have started between Atlas and Cassius is out of the question.

Hey babe? You awake? I check.

Now I am, what's up? She replies and I make a mental note of how sexy she must look waking up.

Want to head back to the house? I want to talk but more importantly, I need you.

Okay, I'm coming. Are you okay? She asks and I can almost see how her brows furrow when she is concerned.

I guess. It's just a lot. All I know is, I need your lips to make me feel better.

"Well, kiss me then", Iris pops up behind me and squeezes me. I turn in her arms and give her a needy kiss. I love that she followed me here. That she slept and gave me space while still being close. A moan escapes my lips, and she pulls back a little with a wicked smile. "I guess my lips do make you feel better. How about we finish at your place?" She pulls me to her car and drives us back to my pack house.

"You know, my place is your home now too." I grab her free hand as she drives.

"And mine is yours. It made me feel good knowing that's where you ran off to. I like that you feel comfortable enough there to seek solace." She smiles her pearly whites at me. My goddess how her smile makes me melt.

"Okay seriously, unless you want to pull over, I suggest you stop being so sexy." Iris chuckles at how serious I sound and then puts on some music to kill the tension, but our bonds don't lie. I can feel she is just as aroused as I am, if not more. It's odd that one moment I am angry and then calm and then horny.

While I did tease her at first, I didn't have any real intentions of doing more than a kiss. But what I am feeling right now from her tells me she has other plans. Iris picks up her speed and gets us home surprisingly in record time and thankfully in one piece. I don't think I ever want to be in the car with her again if she drives like that. What got into her?

I step out of the car tripping over my feet as she pulls me out and towards the house. How she got to my door so quickly, I can't comprehend. Her arousal is a bit higher than it normally is and it is taking me a bit to realize that's the sweet arousal I was swimming in the car.

We pass a few wolves on the way in and they ignore my presence while solely focusing on her. One even dares to growl with need at her. The attention Iris is garnering is making my rage go primal and I growl back in my Alpha tone at anyone making eyes at her. She is mine and if she is to be their Luna, they will respect her. The wolves flinch away when I glare their way in a growl. What the hell is going on with everyone? Before making it to the stairs. Alex runs up to me covering his nose.

"What the hell Kristofer? Get her to your room, now!" I don't even notice Iris is holding my hand in a death grip with sweat beading on her face. "She is in heat, stupid" Alex's words hit me like a ton of bricks. How did I not realize that is what's happening? I pick her up and run upstairs to my room.

The second she hits my bed she uses her powers pulling me onto her. I have never felt something like that before. Definitely something I want to explore later. We crash into each other, and our pheromones entwine in the room as we mate. Being engulfed in her concentrated scent, my own rut kicks in. I can finally feel my wolf which I hadn't noticed missing since I got to Atlas' house. Zeus howls inside me.

Chapter 30

Iris

I GET IN THE CAR with my visibly troubled mate. He is trying to hide his sadness, but I can see it in his eyes and feel it in his words. Even apart, the confusion and anger flow into me in a way that almost feels like my own. Because of it, I wish I could carry the weight of being an Alpha so I can help lessen his burden. He is an amazing leader. I wish I had the mental fortitude he has. Instead, I am trying to fight my demons by ignoring them.

It fills my heart that he can run to my home when he feels troubled, but he could have also stayed with me. No, don't think that way. How many times have I run from him? I reprimand myself and sigh. This man has become everything to me. He helps me heal from my wounds inside and out. He has seen me at my worst and still loves me all the same.

Of course, mentally I'm still not all there yet but the therapy sessions will help when I resume them again. Kristofer grabs my free hand and a sudden surge, sparks within me. I'm hot. I know my heat is coming but this is intense. I never have it come on this strong before. I seriously need to throw away that damn tea.

My mind goes into a haze and my vision blurs. I need to undress. My body needs to be free from my clothes. My skin is on fire from head to toe like a fever taking over every inch of me. I slam my foot on the gas in hopes of making it home before I pass out and kill us both. I barely make it, and I drag my mate out of the car. I want to lie down with him and cure this heat that won't go away.

Everyone is staring. The glares and shifting eyes slow me down a bit. The glares and shifting eyes slow me down as the predatory looks bring me back to how Rick used to look at me. The stares are burrowing into me with lust, and it fills me with disgust. I squeeze my mate's hand because I can't cave into their stares. Only one man can undress me. One wolf has that privilege.

We almost make it to the stairs when I vaguely hear Alex running up to me. What's he saying? I try to focus but it's impossible. This arousal is eating me alive. I'm intoxicated by it, and I need my mate to cure me of this heat. I'm off my feet and then a bed appears beneath me.

"Babe, touch me", I breathe out in a whisper extending my arms. I can't see him very well, but I smell him. He looks like he is floating towards me. Weird?! His surrounding scent in the sheets and room begins to calm this fever I'm running. A growl rumbles from his throat, and I gasp as his hands rip my clothes off and replace them with his lips.

"Yes", I moan arching my back. His lips close over my right breast while he massages the other. Small sparks of pain erupt from my sensitive peaks as he twirls them with one hand and bites. He works his tongue and spreads my legs apart with his knee. I am a mess. I don't want sweet and gentle right now. I want rough and Kristofer must be picking up on it because he flips me over and slaps my ass before spreading them apart.

No more words are exchanged. No more niceties as Kristofer ravishes me completely. He replaces his tongue with his massive cock and teases my entrance before he pushes in. Over and over, he pounds into me. His length fills me up completely and suffocates me. I am a screaming moaning horny mess. By the time I regain my senses, the sun is already coming up. Kristofer then rocks his hips slowly, noticing my eyes finally focusing on his.

"Welcome back". My mate caresses my cheek moving in and out of me slowly.

"Hi", I whisper with a very hoarse voice.

"How you feeling?" Kristofer places a kiss on my nose.

"Exhausted", I chuckle but moan as his length slides back in. "So, me passing out doesn't stop you?"

"Not with you, but if you don't want me to do that, I won't".

"Hmm," I contemplate it. "I trust you."

"Mmm, okay baby. But since you're tired, I'll finish myself off." He pulls out, grabs his erection, and masturbates while looking me dead in the eyes. It is the hottest thing to witness him do. So erotic and sensual yet intimate and vulnerable. I love it. "Babe I'ma cum," he grunts. All of his warm seed spills onto my stomach and breast. He kisses my lips in satisfaction.

"Sorry, I couldn't help." I yawn as sleep takes over. "Why was my heat so intense though?" I stretch while Kristofer wipes me clean. Such a gentleman.

"Honestly, the only thing I could think of is that it's your first heat since you awakened your elf blood. What concerns me more is that I didn't even notice until Alex said something." He throws away the tissues and cuddles up beside me.

"Really?" I mumble half asleep. It's not that I don't care but man am I tired.

"The tea has been messing with my wolf, but I honestly feel a little better after having all this sex. It's like I fucked it out of my system," He chuckles into my neck.

"I'm glad" I whisper and fall asleep.

Kristofer

Listening to my mate fall asleep after such an intense session, eases my heart. I feel good knowing that she is calming down. My stamina truly isn't up to par anymore. The first thing I'm going to do tomorrow is sign up for a gym membership.

Zeus, you good bud?

Yeah, I'm mostly recovered. Still a bit weak.

Was it the tea? I ask because I am sure that's what it is.

Yes, the tea and the mating bond. Shoneah said ingesting elf blood inhibits my abilities. It's poisonous to us. I suggest no more biting.

Damn, okay. Wait you spoke to Shoneah?

Yeah, it's weird. He explained how we are all technically connected. Zeus replies and I honestly forgot that Shoneah had said that.

That's right, he did mention something of the sort. As long as you are safe. Sorry, I almost lost you buddy.

It's okay, it's not like you knew. But now we do. Zeus settles inside me, and I know he is readying to sleep. I inhale our mixed scent and fall asleep to the sound of Iris' breathing.

***

I open my eyes to the darkness of the room. There is barely any light filtering through the window as the moon is hidden by snow filled clouds releasing their flurries. I slip out of bed watching Iris groan slightly at the departure of my heat. But she quickly settles down when I slip my pillow into her arms and smile as she hugs it for comfort. The house is quiet with everyone off in dreams of their deepest desires and nothing but my soft footing filters into my ears. I tiptoe down the stairs and stop when a familiar deja vu kicks in.

"Para! Can you not? I'm still mad at you?"

"Chiquito, please forgive me already." Demetrius sounds hilarious begging; guess he is still in the doghouse by the sounds of it.

"And if I forgive you, what will you do?" The pout in Alex's voice is so clear I almost cackle.

"Anything and everything you want, mi amor."

"La ultima vez," Alex retorts and then a bit of spit-swapping commences. These damn love birds. I clear my throat and start down the rest of the stairs. This does nothing as I surprisingly find Alex the one on top, pinning down Demetrius. I continue to the kitchen and grab a bottle of water. While I am hungry, nothing grabs my attention, so I turn to the doorway of the kitchen and stop at the sight of Demetrius carrying Alex and slamming into the wall with their tongues intensely locked.

Their hands are roaming everywhere in search of skin. It makes me realize that I must seem this hungry in front of others when I am around Iris, and I can't blame them one bit. I try to pass them, but my Beta suddenly jerks off the wall and stumbles down the hall knocking over a picture frame. They giggle like idiots drunk off each other and I almost yell at them to hurry up and go to the room.

I start up the stairs at the same time another crash turns my attention back to the couple. They drop and break a vase from the hallway stand as they fumble into Alex's room slamming the door. I sigh at how quickly Alex can wrap my Beta around his finger.

I walk quietly into my room despite all the noise downstairs and slip back into the bed. As much as everything is going to shit, again, I need to truly sit back and appreciate everything that is going right. I am so in love with this fiery ball of a woman, and she gives me so much to look forward to. There's this sense of belonging that I now have that I didn't know I was missing in the first place. Let's also not forget how much of a freak she turns me into. A burst of laughter pulls me from my thoughts followed by shushing and giggles downstairs. Those two are annoying. I chuckle and kiss my mate falling asleep in her scent.

Chapter 31

Kristofer

IT'S THE NIGHT OF the full moon and something feels off. I don't know if it's because of last time but I feel like something is coming, deep down in the pit of my stomach. I try to brush it off and revel in the fact that this is my first moon run with Iris. Our wolves will be thrilled running freely together. I won't be surprised if they even get a little frisky, but I know Zeus has something in mind, then again so do I. My mom and Martha are giggling away as they step out into the night wrapped in one big blanket. They look hilarious but they have done nothing but find joy in the little things since they got back together.

I for one don't feel bothered anymore with their relationship. My mother hasn't been this happy since my father passed. And Martha brings out in her a child-like happiness that I can't possibly deny her. I love seeing her that way, however, watching my mother have a make-out session still grosses me out. Her locking tongue is not a memory I wish to remember. Even watching her kiss dad was annoying.

I turn to my mate and walk with her in our towels to stand outside in front of the pack. The moon is almost about to peek above the tree line and initiate our shift.

"Everyone, this will be the last moon run of the year. I want you all to heed my warning. Stay close to territory grounds. Do not wander alone. Link with anyone at the first sight of danger even if you are unsure and most importantly stay with your pair. So, under the guidance of the moon, enjoy your run, and may the moon goddess bless us all". Everyone salutes and bows.

The moon rises above the tree shining its light and the air changes around us on cue. I shift and so does Iris. We howl into the night and almost instantly everyone shifts as well as they howl in return.

Now run free. I link with everyone and in a burst of energy, we run.

Zeus

My mate keeps up alongside me in all her beautiful glory. Nora is simply exquisite in every sense of the word. Being able to spend time like this is something I cannot describe. It's an overwhelming feeling. We run for what feels like forever and the bliss of being able to do this with my mate is exhilarating but I have a plan.

I stop running prompting Nora to stop as well. She tilts her head at me, but I walk up to her and nudge her to follow. We huff and puff a bit as we walk under the blessing of the goddess. I lead Nora over to the cliff and have her sit. The moon is high, and the small clouds are scattered. Small stars twinkle away on the beautiful cold night. The ground is freshly blanketed in snow from the day prior giving the whole area a serene feel.

A sense of peace and stillness washes over everything with the moonlight adding an ethereal-like glow against Nora's fur. The river is moving slowly beneath us and nothing but happy howls can be heard from the surrounding wolves. It's perfect. I turn to face my mate fully.

Nora. Iris. There are no words that could express what Kristofer, and I feel. We waited twelve years, since I turned eighteen for our mate, thinking that it just wasn't in the stars for us. Then you came along and showed me what it was to fall in love. What it means to be alive. You filled a hole in my heart that I thought was permanent. You even managed to make the thirty-year-old boy inside me into a man. Sorry Kris, I couldn't help myself. Nora and Iris, it would be a great honor, if both of you accept my selfish wish of being my forever. Will both of you take my paw before the moon goddess tonight and forever be the other half that makes me and the other fool happy till eternity do us part?

Nora whimpers and walks up to me. She nuzzles her snout against mine before rubbing her face and head against me.

You foolish wolf, did you really think I would say anything other than yes? You not only stood by my side through it all, but you helped Iris, and I become stronger. Both of you gave me and Iris strength when we were at our weakest. So yes, you're stuck with us way longer than eternity can provide. We love you both.

We place our heads on one another. Hugging as best we can in wolf form. The moment is beautiful and there is nothing that could ruin it. I lick my mate in delight and howl into the moon. A newfound adrenaline fills me as I nudge her and run. Nora follows in a sprint, and we roll around in the snow. Our huge bodies tumble over one another. Time is moving so fast which Kris for one is grateful for. He has a ring waiting for Iris at home. Without Iris knowing, Kris had Jesika come while we run so she can set up the house for the engagement party and a more formal proposal.

Thirty minutes to go and I make a link with everyone to start heading back to the house. The night is perfect. As my pack gathers in the backyard they are to shift into their human form. Everyone is in on the engagement. So, they all are to rush inside to change into proper attire. I tell Iris that as Alpha I always stay behind until everyone is accounted for.

Of course, she sees nothing wrong and proudly stands next to me. The air then changes around me finally and I shift into my human form.

Kristofer

Iris shifts as well and by then the last of my pack has made it inside. I walk with her and give her a set of clothes that mom put aside for us to change into by the back door. I then grab a blindfold and hand it to Iris.

"What is this for?" she asks even though she proceeds to put it on. The trust she has in me is beautiful.

"I have a surprise for you," I whisper and proceed to dress her in the nice clothes my mother left out for her. She giggles but all it does is make me want to throw her over my shoulder and have sex in the woods. Instead, I grab her hand to lead her through the house and into the living room. Jesika did an amazing job in two hours. The floor is covered in petals and candles are lit on the table and mantle. A large bouquet of roses sits in the center of the room with a small box that I pick up and place in my pocket. I face her towards me and kneel beside the bouquet.

"Okay, remove the blindfold." Iris takes it off and gasps. She covers her mouth realizing I am on one knee.

"I know Zeus said his proposal to you and Nora, but I wanted to say one as well. I must honestly say that I never felt more alive and yet more scared than I do right now. Not because I think you will say no but because I want to make sure I do everything right by your side. I want to be perfect for you. I want to never fail to make you smile. I never want to fail in protecting your beautiful soul from blossoming further and most of all I never want to fail us and our future together.

You make me a better wolf in every way possible. You are why my wolf is now insatiable and I wouldn't have it any other way. Will you, Iris, be my mate, lover, best friend, and Luna to my pack till eternity and more?" I pull out the box and open it the show a crescent-shaped diamond ring.

"EEEEEEE," Iris squeals in such a manner that I'm sure would have been different if she knew the whole pack was watching behind her. They burst out laughing and her face turns to horror as she turns around red in the face.

I stand up chuckling bringing her attention back to me. "Is that a, yes?" I hold up the ring.

"Yes", she whispers in embarrassment. I slip on the ring and tears roll down her cheek, but I cup her face catching a few tears and bring her into a kiss.

"Thank you for coming into my life," I whisper. She sniffles and looks up to me.

"Well, someone had to teach the old dog new tricks." Everyone dies laughing a little harder than I appreciated and it's now my turn to become a few shades of red. Iris giggles and wipes her face.

"LET'S GET THE PARTY STARTED!" Alex shouts.

"TO OUR LUNA!" Demetrius shouts.

"TO OUR LUNA!" The whole house repeats and the music fades in. Everyone breaks out in dance. Drinks make their way around and everyone is having a ball. It's a night to remember.

Nothing Stays Buried

***

Waking up with my Luna in my arms is a whole new kind of feeling. My boner seems to think so as well but right now is not the time for that. I need to pee badly. I look at the time and it's close to nine, so I hop out of bed and in the shower to get myself ready to do some of my duties. I have unfortunately neglected a lot of them leaving it to my Beta but it's about time I step back into the game.

I leave a note on the stand next to my Luna and leave for the woods to train with my warriors. It has been way too long since I have had proper training which is most likely why my stamina has plummeted. There honestly isn't much need to have elite warriors with everyone under a peace treaty. But if I did not have them, this thing with Liber could have ended differently.

The only real threat we have is the hunters but now with everything we went through the past two and a half months and now the dreams, it's best we prepare. My wolves and I train hard for the next week. We push our limits and then break them over and over. It is the only way to ensure we get back to our maximum potential.

Tonight is Christmas Eve, and the pups are running around excited to stay up late so they can open presents at midnight. The adults are gathering in groups around the house drinking the coquito that Alex made and snacking by the taco bar. I hug my mate and kiss her enjoying the lingering sweet cinnamon on her lips from her drink.

"Guys it's almost midnight, gather around the tree." My mother, Cecile, calls out. Both packs are here, and the family room is overflowing with people. One by one Martha and Cecile call out names handing out the presents. The clock strikes twelve and we all yell Merry Christmas. The destruction of presents commences with the adults being slightly worse than the pups. Wrappers scatter everywhere.

"NO WAY!" A loud voice calls everyone's attention. Atlas is standing in shock holding a small box open and Cassius is a mess in tears but smiling.

"Wait. Wait. Like for real? We...I... your? Wait...really?" Atlas begins to cry and hugs Cassius as he shakes his head yes and whispers something to him.

"I AM GOING TO BE A FATHER!" Atlas yells jumping up and down with Cassius still in his arms who is now in a fit of giggles.

"Wait, how?" I call out happy but confused stopping Atlas from jumping to look at his mate so he can explain.

"Well apparently if the wolf that reincarnates into Shoneah is mated to another male then the body changes to allow the bloodline to continue. So basically, I developed a womb. Shoneah explained it to me in a dream when I started having symptoms. I thought I had a stomach bug. But after the fight with Liber when I had my mood swings and not wanting to eat, those were pregnancy symptoms." Cassius explains.

Nothing Stays Buried

With all that we have experienced, I am not that surprised. "Well, I say, congratulations to Luna Cassius!" I raise my glass and so does everyone else in cheer. We turn the house into a wrapping paper fiasco. It's fun but now is the dreadful cleanup. All of us pitch in and make our way home or to our beds after.

"Hey, wait, we missed one." Mom calls out to Iris and me.

"There's no name though".

I grab it and sniff the box. Nothing seems odd so I open it. It is a sealed black box. I shift my finger to expose a claw and break the seal. I open it slowly and am almost knocked out by the stench of rotting flesh. A rotten finger lays neatly with a ring still attached.

"What the fuck? Is that Francis' finger?" I gag at the putrid smell. Iris takes the box and looks at the ring.

"Oh my god, it's Finn! Who the hell would do this?" Iris hands me the box unable to handle the smell. I link to Atlas, and he comes running in. He grabs the box and recoils like everyone else.

"Someone has Finnie!" I exclaim.

"That's the closest you've gotten to his name." Atlas retorts.

"What the hell is going on?", he closes the box inspecting it.

"There is a message underneath."

-A traitorous wolf, a clan's undoing
You will take the blame that causes the fall.
Nothing stays buried, deaths are looming

When the truth is revealed, we've conquered all-

"What in the shit does that even mean? Is it saying Finn is the traitor?" Iris questions Atlas.

"I don't know. Maybe? But I thought he was down south visiting his cousins." We all nod thinking the same.

"Okay, lets keep this between us for now. If he were dead, they wouldn't have sent a finger wrapped up nicely. Let everyone enjoy Christmas, we have earned this much. The day after tomorrow we can deal with this with fresh sober minds." Everyone agrees.

Cecile and Martha go to bed arms interlocked. Atlas grabs his now-pregnant Luna and heads home while Alex and Demetrius are already shagging in Alex's room.

My Luna and I retire as well to enjoy a night of passionate sex. I don't want to think of anything else right now. Tonight, I am going to show her a few things I learned on my own instead. Let's just say a few toys are involved. Iris gasps at the box of toys I present her but the glint in her eye tells me I might be the one in trouble. I chuckle and kiss her soft plump lips.

"I love you, Luna Iris."

"I love you too my Alpha."

The End

Safe

Word

Lobo

By L. Concepcion

Chapter 1
Alex

"HOW DID I END UP HERE?" I huff at my tired reflection in the mirror. I thought we were happy and that my mate would never treat me like that and yet, here we stand. Demetrius isn't speaking to me and barely looks my way the few times we are in the same room. I thought we were inseparable but the way he gives me the cold shoulder tells me otherwise. What's worse is the fact that he looks more hurt than angry, and for the life of me I can't fathom why. He said he needs space. My heart holds hope that he will come to me when he is ready but the look in his eyes did something to my soul. I'm shattered and I have no idea how to mend the pieces.

The silent treatment hits too close to home and that same feeling I get when my father does the same, rushes through me like a flood. It rattles me in a way I didn't expect and I'm exhausted. The emotions weighing me down are draining everything from within me and I'm spent. It's too much and I don't like the feeling.

Demetrius blew up on me a week ago, on Christmas day. He refuses to tell me anything and says that I should know what I did wrong. But I don't. We welcomed the new year separately because of it. And while everyone else counted down, drinking and singing songs with one another, I cried. I brought in the new year crying like I used to do so many times before curled up in my blanket, in my closet, and tucked into a corner.

I drop down onto my bed, tired, lonely, and most of all, hurt. I finally got used to having my mate's warmth constantly around me but now, it's gone. I am blessed to feel something as great as someone's undivided affection, only to have it ripped away from me.

Then again, I should consider myself lucky to have experienced that warmth at all. For as long as I can remember, life is always something I must work at doing because if I didn't, I'd want to give up. I never found happiness, love, or a family and it all started when my mother left. For the longest time, I thought I had to accept things as they were because I am no one to question my father. Nothing but a hindrance.

I grab my pillow and toss it across the room along with my other pillow. It pisses me off that I must find out the hard way the truth. More than anything, I'm baffled that I never questioned my father until recently.

Even though my father told me my mother died, I later find out she is alive and happily living somewhere else. She simply doesn't want us. Well, okay, that's not true. My mother did want me at one point and my father blames me because she rejected him. I was only two years old when it happened, and I still don't understand how I am to blame.

From what he told me, my dad packed up our things to get away from my mother and we left our country, Wilderness Den, ending up here in Lunar River roaming around for a months before former Alpha Jude found us and took us in. I don't know how life would have been for me had we never found this pack after bouncing from home to home. Having Alpha Jude and then Alpha Kristofer made growing up alone less lonely.

I am surprised my father made the long journey with me being so little considering his short temper and how he treats me now. I doubt that he treated me any better when I was a pup. That's not even considering the dangers of travelling alone. We could have been attacked by rogues or starved to death. But the determination to get away from anything that reminded him of my mother must have been what kept him going.

No one takes kind to rogues roaming around with nowhere to go. And as far as anyone was concerned, that's what we were at the time. As advanced as we are with our species, rogues are usually treated as a threat to a pack. Guilty until proven innocent. Rogues almost always have evil intentions that could put a pack at great risk. So being lucky enough to meet Former Alpha Jude was the key to our survival.

I honestly don't remember any of the travels since I was so young. So, for me, my whole life started here. My father and I have our small cottage close to the pack house which comes in handy when there are guests that bring kids I can hang with. The clearest memories I can recall are around five years old with fragments here and there. However, there is one feeling I recall clearly since I was three and that is that I hate being alone with my father.

The only time happiness graced was when Cassius was found and brought into the pack. I was either six or seven and we quickly became friends. I spent so much time playing with him just to avoid my father's random mood swings in the cottage. Eventually, I developed a major crush on Cassius. It's what confirmed for me that I was indeed gay. I first had the thought when I was in school, and we had to change in the locker room for gym class. Yet another thing my dad learned to hate me for.

Unfortunately, because of my dad, I lost all my trust in all male figures with authority. At least until Atlas showed me how to trust again and so did Demetrius. *Stupid Demetrius.* I forgot I was thinking about that jerk. That stupid, annoying, gorgeous, delicious jerk. I miss him.

I toss in my bed in a silent scream, hating the cold that the lonely sheets provided. I miss his body next to me with his big arms wrapped around my waist. I need my mate and his touch to calm the storm in my heart. Being depressed and covered in self-hate is all too much of a comfortable state to stay in. It is a state of mind that I made friends with long ago and I don't want it.

Nothing in this world made me feel worse than the dread and hopelessness that knotted in my throat from the thought that my mate doesn't want me anymore. Being alone, and in my thoughts, meant being trapped within the walls I'd built around me. These walls were once meant to protect me and eventually became my prison under my father's scrutiny.

Tears pool within my ears like wells that keep my sadness hidden from the world. These familiarities of having lived in fear my whole life creep back in like licked wounds. I didn't even tell Demetrius I love him yet. I had plans to do so during the holidays until everything went to shit and I was left alone.

A sob escapes my lips as the image of him turning his back on me popped into my mind.

In a defeated huff, I drag myself back out of bed and trudge into the bathroom to fill up my tub with hot water. I am lucky enough to have one of the four bathrooms in the house in my room. My eyes skim over my body in the mirror and mock the slender arms that removed my clothes. *How does Demetrius even find someone like me attractive?* I think to myself.

Even though I have gained a good amount of weight in the last several months, I am still too skinny for my liking. I want to be more like Demetrius with muscles. Not the gangly looking thing that I am right now. My heart skips a pained beat with a warning that our bond is weakening. Whatever my mate is doing is slowly severing the bond. *Does he hate me now that much already?*

Bonds can break if both parties are at odds with each other but I'm sure that my self-hatred is playing its part. The damage might already be done and maybe it is time that I accept it. I cry as quietly as possible into the mirror with my shoulders slumped. This is a different hurt. I don't want to accept that it may be over.

My chest clenches unbelievably tight. The bond is breaking, and I can feel it slowly coming undone. I can't. I won't accept it. **DEMI, TE QUIERO. PLEASE, COME BACK TO ME**. I scream in my mind as my heart shatters into tiny pieces. Yet, those broken fragments pound harder than I ever thought possible. *No, something is wrong.*

My breathing quickens making it hard to fill my lungs. I haven't felt like this in a long time. I can barely fill my lungs, and it hurts. It feels as though they are on fire as air struggles to inflate them. A loud bang faintly makes its way to my ears right before I hit the side of the tub with my head and black out.

***

I open my eyes wincing as the throbbing pain booms through my skull. If I were ever hit by a bolder, I am positive this is how it would feel. My damn anxiety got the best of me, but it has been years since I last had an attack to this extent. Sniffling and soft whimpers fill the room around me, and I can't tell if I am hearing things or not.

I groan in my attempt to move because the slight movement made the pounding worsen, sending a wave of nausea to catch right at the base of my throat. But I swallow the bile as another tear slides from my eyes from the way my heart hurts more than any physical wound.

"Chiquito!" The deep beautiful voice I love so much is calling out to me. But I'm scared to see him. I'm scared he is going to check if I'm okay and disappear again. I can't bear to watch him leave twice.

A finger wipes my tears before the bed sinks in with what I could assume is his weight. His strong body spoons into me and his arms wrap around me in a comfort so sweet that I cry harder.

I never deserved a man like him but after I having a taste, how can I let go? Am I not allowed to be happy? I turn into his arms and sob uncontrollably. His warmth. I miss his warmth so much that the chills ripple through my skin as he hugs me tighter bringing me the relief I crave. So many scenarios race through my mind. They all shout at me and scold me. Scenarios of pain, reasons for his cold shoulder, rejection, all of it just swirling in circles as I cry. **Why? Why?** My heart goes off in another round of panicked beats. The irregular beating of my cruel thoughts thumping and thus begins another attack.

"Chiquito, please breathe. Calm down for me." Demetrius strokes my wet hair. I only now realize I have dry clothes on. He must have changed my shirtless body. But why is my hair wet? "Shh, I'm here now", my mate continues to soothe me, intensifying his scent so I can find comfort in it. *My goddess, his scent is everything.* Musk and Rosewood hug every inch of my soul.

After long agonizing minutes of ragged breathing, I manage to finally calm down enough to think. **PLEASE STOP HATING ME. DON'T REJECT ME. I'M SO STUPID. I KNEW I'D NEVER BE LOVED**. My mind continues to attack me, continues to repeat the words I heard so often as a child. My own thoughts betray me just like everyone else. Over and over, I was reminded how useless I was. My father makes sure I know that I am never wanted and can never be loved. Maybe he is right.

"Whoa, Alex. What is going on in that pretty little head of yours?" Demetrius pulls away a bit to look at my snot-ridden face. I squeeze my eyes tighter because if I look at him, I'd break.

"I I-Demetrius. Please tell me what I did wrong," I know I sound like a hot mess but how can I not? He is the only man I have ever fallen this deeply in love with. He's my mate, my other half. The very soul reason why I'd fly to the moon and back. The only reason I can stand tall. He is my strength.

"Chiquito breathe, please don't scare me like that again." Demetrius hugs me, bringing me back into his chest. "Your thoughts are screaming at me. And I don't like what I'm hearing. Alex, you did nothing wrong. I see that now. I'm so sorry. I was so angry that I never sat down to talk to you about it. I just assumed everything, all on my own. I didn't mean for you to hurt like this." I push him away confused, this time looking at him straight in the eye.

"What do you mean? I don't understand." I can barely see him through my blurry vision, but I blink away my tears a few times. Demetrius wipes my nose with his shirt with a half-broken smile and sighs.

"What I mean is, listening to your thoughts, it's obvious you don't want to break our bond and leave me.

You weren't planning on running away." Demetrius tears up. *Is this what he thought?*

"When did I ever say that's what I wanted!?" My voice cracks like a prepubescent teen.

"Hugo came to me on Christmas and gave me an envelope with a bunch of documents. I asked him what they were, but he simply said to decide for myself and left." Demetrius pauses to wipe his tears. "When I opened it, there were papers with you opening new bank accounts and a lease to a new apartment. Your passport and other things were in there too. It all pointed to you leaving. But why did you have those things if you weren't?" Demetrius closes his eyes as if to fight more tears from coming out. He hurt from the thought of me leaving him.

"Wait, my father gave you that?" Demetrius nods still with his eyes closed unable to speak as his lip quivers. "That son a bitch. Yes, what you found there is right but not for the reasons you think. I also decided to stay a long time ago and canceled the lease because of you." I sigh and dig my face back into his chest. I inhale his scent allowing his pheromones to calm me down. Hints of relief invade my senses, but pain still lingers. "I'm not ready to tell you my story but before I realized you were my mate; I had every intention of leaving after the new year." I nuzzle further into his chest, making sure our bodies touch from head to toe.

"But, not anymore, right?" My mate asks with a sadness dripping in his voice. He is hurting as much as me.

"No Demi, not anymore", I whisper back.

"Did you mean what you said earlier?" Demetrius whispers with his face buried in my hair.

"What did I say?"

"That you still liked me. When I heard that and I felt your emotions through what was left of the bond, I ran as fast as I could. I was happy and scared because I thought something had happened. I thought I lost you for good. When I got closer to your room, I felt this wave of nausea and I heard you hit your head." Demetrius squeezes me a bit making my tension fade.

"Yes, te quiero with all my heart." I look up and kiss his trembling chin.

"Me too, chiquito," his shaky voice replies. He is ready to cry again but does everything possible not to do so. Such a big guy with such big emotions. I snuggle my face into his neck to take in his scent. Sleep then kicks in and all my adrenaline fades as quickly as it came. Relaxed in his arms I let go of my pain and dream of our future.

Authors Other Works

Lunar River Series

The Silver Lining
Nothing Stays Buried
*Safe Word Lobo

Stand Alone Works

Color Me Sugar